THE
Survival
LIST

The SURVIVAL List

COURTNEY SHEINMEL

KATHERINE TEGEN BOOKS
An Imprint of HarperCollins Publishers

Katherine Tegen Books is an imprint of HarperCollins Publishers.

The Survival List
Copyright © 2019 by HarperCollins Publishers
All rights reserved. Printed in the United States of America.
No part of this book may be used or reproduced in any manner whatsoever
without written permission except in the case of brief quotations embodied in
critical articles and reviews. For information address HarperCollins Children's
Books, a division of HarperCollins Publishers, 195 Broadway, New York, NY
10007.
www.epicreads.com

Library of Congress Contol Number: 2019934619
ISBN 978-0-06-265500-4

Typography by Torborg Davern
19 20 21 22 23   PC/LSCH   10 9 8 7 6 5 4 3 2 1
❖
First Edition

For Diane Buda & her sisters,
in loving memory

The deeper that sorrow carves into your being,
the more joy you can contain.

—*THE PROPHET*, KAHLIL GIBRAN

EVERY STORY WORTH TELLING BEGINS LIKE THIS: I WOKE up thinking my life was the same as it always had been, and then it wasn't.

For some people, the change comes in the form of bad news: a car accident, or an illness diagnosed, or a secret revealed. For others—for the lucky ones—it's a good-news kind of change: a winning lottery ticket, a large inheritance, the news that the Home Shopping Network just bought a million units of your latest invention, and you're set for life. Not that good news necessarily means more money, but those are the first examples to spring to mind.

My point is, that's how this story begins, too: I woke up thinking my life was the same as it always had been. And then it wasn't.

My sister died.

She died by suicide, and she didn't leave a note to explain why. Just a list, written on a sheet torn from a spiral notebook, folded over five times, tucked into the front pocket of her jeans.

I woke up thinking my life was the same as it always had been, and then it wasn't, and I didn't know why. But the list was where I'd start.

chapter one

WE CALLED MY SISTER TALLEY, WHICH WAS SHORT FOR Natalie.

Natalie Belle Weber. That was her full name.

The Natalie part was for our maternal great-grandmother, Nellie, who died before either of us was even a thought in our parents' heads. The Belle part was because our mother's maiden name was Bellstein.

Weber was her last name because it's Dad's last name, and we live in a patriarchal society where kids automatically get their dads' last names, which Talley told me is completely sexist, and I agree with her. Mothers are the ones who have to squeeze their kids out. Shouldn't *their* names be the ones that get passed on? At the very least, they should get to draw straws to settle it.

But that's not a subject I'm going to take on just now.

I want to talk about Talley. Talley, herself. She was . . . well, she was everything. She was a ray of sunshine. She was a beam of moonlight. She was lightness and darkness and all that comes in between. Talley was small, smaller than I am, which is just a smidge over five feet tall. I've always been the smallest in my grade. In elementary school there were all sorts of nicknames I hated: Shorty Spice, Small Fry, El Shrimpo. I used to stand on my toes a lot, trying to be at least as tall as the next shortest person.

Talley was a smidge *under* five feet. But she never stood on her toes. It's like she didn't realize she was so tiny. I don't think anyone else noticed, either, because she was MIGHTY. I used all caps there on purpose.

Maybe you think that I sound like a typical younger sister, idolizing Talley the way I did. But I wasn't the only one who looked at Talley like that. I watched how other people reacted to her, too—friends and strangers alike. They were as enthralled with her as I was. When Talley walked into a room, people noticed her. They woke up. It reminded me of Plato's *Allegory of the Cave*. We read it in school sophomore year, but Talley told me about it long before then.

Talley was always telling me things like that—things she thought were interesting or important. Sometimes she'd make up puzzles for me to figure out, or she'd make me play the Imagine If game, which is what I called it when she tried to teach me perspective by telling me stories about people who had it way worse than I did. Like if I complained about how long a bad cold was lingering, she'd tell me about a book a father had written about his daughter who'd been sick—really sick, for way more than a week or two,

4

and they didn't know if she'd *ever* get better. Or if I was having a meltdown over the internet acting wonky when my research paper on industrialization after the Civil War was due the next morning, she'd tell me how long Puerto Rico had been without power after Hurricane Maria, and wasn't I so lucky that my biggest problem was a wonky internet.

The Plato story was about perspective, too. Here's how it went: a prisoner lived in a cave, and all he'd ever seen were shadows of things, not the things themselves, so he thought that's all there was to the world. One day he was freed from his shackles. He turned around and saw all the actual things—dwellings and statues and people and animals, along with the fire that had cast the shadows of them. Then he got out of the cave, and there was more to see. It went on and on.

Why did this remind me of Talley? (I mean, aside from the obvious reason that she was the one to tell me about it in the first place.) Because that's what it was like to be around her. She helped people see beyond their own limited perspectives. She made things appear bigger and brighter than they were before.

Don't think my sister was oblivious to her own charm, because she wasn't. She never danced like no one was watching. She danced like *everyone* was. It was like she went through life pretending she was the star of a show: The Talley Show. As if you'd bought a ticket to see her, and she didn't want to disappoint.

Often, she let me be part of the act. "Sloane, today we're going to go to McDonald's, and you have to order in a British accent." "Will you be in a parade with me, Sloaners?" "I just decided to be a model and I need someone to take my head shots!"

Even for all her doom-and-gloom Imagine If stories, I'd never met anyone who could enjoy life more than my sister could. She could get positively giddy about things, and it was catching. I'd find myself practically breathless, saying, "Sure, Talley!" "Of course, Talley!" "Let me help you, Talley!"

As we grew up, we grew apart in some ways. There was the geographical apartness. Talley was five years older, and she'd graduated high school. She moved out even though she didn't go to college. And while she was living back home the last month of her life, she was still gone for the bulk of my high school years.

And then there was the emotional apartness, the kind that you can't measure in physical distance, which means it's hard to measure at all. While it's happening, it's so gradual, you don't even realize it. But then you look back, and you can point to times when you felt closer than you did at the end.

The end. My sister's life had an *end*.

I didn't see it coming. It was my fault. I was so, so unforgivably careless.

The day it happened, Thursday, I stayed late at school for orchestra practice. I play the flute. My best friend, Juno, watched us rehearse, which was not something she usually did. But her boyfriend, Cooper, had just officially broken up with her. A couple weeks earlier, he'd said he needed to take a break, because he had so much school stuff and track stuff on his plate. "Let's try not texting or talking for two weeks," he said. He also told her not to read too much into it, the way she usually did.

Juno tried not to read too much into it, but over those fourteen days, every other sentence out of her mouth was something that had to do with Cooper. I did my best to distract her, and made plans to do things she'd loved to do well before Cooper was in her life. Watching cheesy eighties movies in her basement, mining local thrift stores for secondhand treasures, taking aimless drives in her beloved car, that sort of thing. Still, she was always bringing Cooper into whatever activity we were doing. Cooper loved *Ferris Bueller's Day Off*. That shirt would look perfect on Cooper. She'd once driven down this same road with Cooper.

"I think you should focus on the things about him that were sucky," I said. "Like how he wasn't ever that nice to you . . . and how he's kind of shaped like SpongeBob SquarePants."

"Remember what Ms. Gomez told us in third grade," Juno said. "Don't yuck my yum. Just because he's not your type doesn't mean he's not mine."

"I'm sorry."

"Making fun of him isn't going to stop me from loving him."

"I just hate that you're so sad, Ju, and I think talking about him all the time is making you even sadder. Maybe we could put a limit on it. You can talk about Cooper for a half hour a day, and for the rest of the time, we'll talk about non-Cooper things. It'll train your brain to not obsess about him all the time. It'll be hard at first—Talley says it takes sixty-six days to form a habit. But you'll get there."

"In sixty-six days, we'll be back together again," she said. "Before then, even."

"See, you can do it. You don't even have to make it that far."

"I'll try," she said.

We still had a heck of a lot of Cooper convos. As soon as the two weeks were up, like to the second, Juno texted him to check in. He wrote back that he wanted to make the break an official breakup.

Juno, understandably, didn't want to be alone. After orchestra practice wrapped up, our friend Soraya, who plays cello, said we should go out for pizza. I looked at Juno, who nodded faintly. "Or anything else you want to eat," I said.

"Oh yeah, you pick," Soraya told Juno. "We could go to that salad place."

"Sloane hates salads," Juno said.

"I'd eat one for you," I assured her.

"You'd eat a *salad* for me?" She sounded like she might cry.

"Of course," I said. Really I'd just eat the cherry tomatoes and the shredded cheese that came on top, and leave the lettuce behind. But I wouldn't mind.

Juno blinked back the tears and shook her head. "It's okay. I'm not really hungry."

"You're giving Cooper too much power over your life," I said. "You've got to eat."

"If you guys want pizza, that's fine," Juno said.

We went to Trepiccione's, because our friend Brody's brother Mack worked there and, as long as his boss wasn't around, he always let us order beer. It wasn't a huge draw for me, since I hate beer. Soraya's girlfriend, Rachel, had joined us and she ordered a pitcher.

When she started to pour me a cup, I shook my head. "No, thanks."

"Juno?" Rachel asked.

"Can't," she said. "I'm the designated driver."

"You know, Sloane," Soraya said, "you'd make the perfect designated driver if you actually drove."

"Yeah, I know." I felt especially bad about it since Juno was heartbroken and could probably use a drink. But I hadn't taken my driver's test yet, so all I had was a permit. In the state of Minnesota, you can't drive with a permit unless the person in the front passenger seat is herself a licensed driver and at least twenty-one. It was a relief that my friends were all under twenty-one, because I wouldn't have done it anyway. "I really hate the taste of beer," I told Soraya.

"Yeah, me too," she said. "But I drink it anyway."

"That sounds like a metaphor for high school," I said, glancing over at Juno. Coming up with metaphors was a joke between us. She said I used them more than the average person, and she was always trying to come up with her own—the more ridiculous, the better. As for me, I think it had something to do with writing and looking for connections between things. I planned to be a writer when I grew up.

Actually, my English teacher, Dr. Lee, would argue that I was a writer *already*: all you need to do to be a writer is write, she often says. She also says being a writer doesn't mean you think writing is easy; it means you're willing to do it even when it's hard.

I love writing. I've loved it for as long as I can remember. It wasn't until fifth or sixth grade that I realized that creative writing wasn't everyone's favorite part of school, and that was such a shock to me. Sure, I understood that people like different things. Some people are Team Chocolate, and some are Team Vanilla. Some people like creamy peanut butter, and some people prefer crunchy. (Which is ridiculous.) But how could they prefer math worksheets, or memorizing where the oceans are, over using words to create new things? That's the best part of writing, in my opinion. Everyone gets ideas all day long. They pop up out of nowhere, and most of the time we let them go. But when you write, you get to keep your ideas and build on them. You get to make something where there was nothing. It's like magic.

It turned out that Juno dreaded when we got creative writing assignments in school. As soon as we were old enough to pick the kinds of classes we wanted to take, she swore she'd never take another writing class again. What can I say? She also likes crunchy peanut butter. But she was still amused by a good metaphor.

Except not this time. She didn't even smile.

"You know in the movies when they say, 'We'll take a break, and then if we miss each other enough, we'll meet at such-and-such time, and if we both show up, we'll know we're meant to be together'?" Juno asked.

The three of us nodded.

She went on, "It always works out in the movies. The couple realizes how much they've missed each other, which means they love each other, and they recommit in a major way and live happily ever after. I guess they don't make movies about when the guy decides he doesn't want to be with you, and he doesn't show up."

"You guys had a designated meeting place?" Rachel asked.

"No. But if we had, Cooper wouldn't have come, and that's why there'll never be a movie about me."

"Sure there will be," Soraya said. "You're just in the middle of your movie right now, when it seems like all hope is lost because the guy didn't show up. You'll get a new boyfriend before the end, a much better boyfriend, and you guys will fall madly in love with each other in a way that you never knew was possible. Boom. End of movie."

"I don't want a new boyfriend. I just want *Cooper.*"

"You won't want him by the end of the movie," I said.

"I *will* still want him," she insisted. "I'd rather have a bad time with Cooper than a good time with anyone else."

"Oh, Juno." I stroked her ponytail, and my hand caught the magnet part of her cochlear implant that was snapped to her head behind her right ear. Juno had had spinal meningitis when she was a year old and almost died. The high fevers destroyed her hearing.

As soon as she was well enough, Juno had surgery to get the cochlear implants. There are little microphones that sit right on top of each of her ears, and then pieces that snap onto magnets implanted under the skin. As long as she's wearing them, she can hear nearly as well as everyone else. But at night, when she takes them off, she can't hear a thing. She has special alarms to wake her up every morning—one under her pillow that vibrates, and another that flashes light. Plus her mom comes in to check that she's up, just in case.

Juno snapped the magnet back onto her head, a swift, automatic movement, like she wasn't even thinking about it. She slumped against me. I knew she was legitimately in pain, but there was a part of me that felt jealous. I was the only person at our table who'd never been in love, and I wondered when it would happen for me. I didn't say anything out loud though. I just squeezed Juno closer to me.

These were the things that were happening, and what I was thinking and feeling. I was living my last-ever normal moments before my life was completely upended. You don't ever get to know when you're living your last normal moments; if you did, they wouldn't be normal at all.

So even though Talley had already made her decision and done what she'd done, I remained unaware. All the while, a few miles away, my dad was getting home from work, the same time he always did. He would've pulled up into the right side of our double-wide driveway, walked up the steps, and wiped his shoes on the mat, regardless of whether they needed wiping. My dad is nothing if not a creature of habit, which is how I know that he walked into the kitchen first, put his briefcase on the counter, and grabbed a glass from the cabinet above the sink. He would've pulled open the freezer and grabbed a couple cubes of ice—he's the only member of our family who actually likes ice in his drinks—then added water from the tap and continued down the hall, toward the bathroom that is equidistant between Talley's bedroom and mine (we measured once, using our feet as measuring sticks).

That's where he found her.

Talley, still breathing, but faintly. She was on the floor, and the empty pill bottles were by the sink. My dad called 911. The attendants didn't let him in the ambulance with her, so he drove, and as he did, my dad, Garrett J. Weber, the calmest, most play-by-the-rules person I've ever known in my life, could not make himself obey the traffic laws. He was pulled over by a member of the Golden Valley police force, no doubt a well-meaning offi-cer who thought Dad was one of those people who speeds behind ambulances just to get to their destinations faster. By the time he reached the hospital, there was a team working on Talley.

Dad called me from the waiting room. My phone buzzed at the precise moment that there was a lull in the conversation I was having with my friends. It was maybe a five-second window of relative silence. If Dad hadn't called right then, maybe I wouldn't have heard it. Juno was still leaning against me, and she shifted as I reached for my phone.

I look back on those seconds—unzipping my bag, glancing at the caller ID, then pressing the phone to my ear, "Hi, Dad"—those seconds were the last seconds that I was one kind of person. Then my dad told me where he was and why, and I was a different kind of person. Before becoming after, just like that.

Juno drove me to the hospital, and she was right behind me as I banged through the doors of the emergency room. I ran to the front desk screaming, "My sister! My sister!"

Someone led us to the waiting room. Dad was pacing back and forth. I sat on a well-worn blue chair; its arms were wooden. I remember that because my palms were sweating profusely, and I was making a slippery mess of things. I rubbed my hands down the length of my thighs, drying them on my jeans, and leaned forward. Juno put a hand on my back. How quickly the comforter became the comfortee. I felt the heat from her hand, and it felt good until it felt like too much. I was too hot. I stood up, paced with Dad for a bit, then sat down again.

It was fifteen minutes, or maybe twenty, or thirty, or a few hours. It felt endless. Finally a doctor came in to talk to us. She told us her name, but it didn't register. She told Dad to sit down, which I took as a sign to spring up from my seat, like a kangaroo who'd been cattle-prodded.

You know when you just know something? Even before you really know it, you *know* it?

I knew my sister was dead. I *knew* it.

Dr. No-Name wouldn't have asked Dad to sit down if Talley was okay. I ran into a corner of the room. I was looking for somewhere to hide. I would've gone under a chair if that would've helped, even though I was seventeen years old, and seventeen-year-old high school juniors don't hide under chairs. They don't press their hands to their ears to keep from hearing the words. But if I didn't hear what the doctor was going to say, it was like anything was still possible. Talley could still be okay.

"Sloane," Dad said sharply, and I dropped my hands to my sides. My eyes darted from Dad to Juno and, finally, to the doctor herself.

"We did everything we could," the doctor said. "We used all our capabilities. But we couldn't save her."

The words were spoken and I heard them. There was no going

back. Talley was gone. She'd been alive hours earlier. Her heart had been beating, and her lungs had been pumping, and blood had coursed through her veins. She'd scratched her itches and rubbed her eyes and gone to the bathroom. But now, everything had stopped.

It's so weird. One moment, you're a living, breathing person in the world; and the next, you're not.

Talley was not.

Natalie Belle Weber, age twenty-two, had been declared dead, in the same hospital where our mother had died fifteen years earlier. Fade to black, roll the credits, leave the theater.

The Talley Show was over.

chapter two

THE MONTH BEFORE SHE DIED, TALLEY LOST HER
hostessing job at Bianca's in downtown Minneapolis. Without
her paycheck, Talley couldn't make her portion of the rent for the
apartment she shared with two roommates, so she moved back in
with Dad and me.

"It'll only be for a little while," she'd said the first night at
dinner.

"Maybe this is a sign that you should give college a shot," Dad
said.

"Oh, Garrett," Talley said, using his first name, as she tended
to do just to get under his skin. "You don't even believe in signs."

He didn't. But he believed in Talley. Her IQ score was 162,
which is, apparently, astronomically high as IQ scores go. When
she was in middle school and high school, Talley was always getting

into the local newspaper with her different scholastic achievements, and Dad saved the articles to clip to her applications when the time came. With her smarts, she could get a scholarship to Harvard or Yale or wherever in the world she wanted to go, he said.

Dad himself hadn't gone to college. His parents both died when he was in twelfth grade. He was away on a class trip, there was a fire, and when he got home, he was an orphan. I think it's hard for everyone to process that their parents may have complicated pasts; for me, the story about what happened in my dad's family was especially hard to connect to the guy I knew—the one who was super strict about bedtimes and who organized his sock drawer by color—because it was just so tragic. Dad couch-surfed at friends' houses till he graduated from high school, and then he went to work. He got married on the young side, had Talley and me, and there was never time to take a break and go back to school. By then he'd worked his way up to being the head of the IT department at a law firm, and he had enough savings, he'd assured Talley and me (especially Talley), to supplement whatever tuition our college scholarships didn't cover.

But when Talley was a senior in high school, she announced she wasn't planning to go to college. She didn't think she needed to spend four more years learning by someone else's rules. Some of the smartest, most successful people in the country never graduated from college, she told Dad. She even made him a list: talk show host Ellen Degeneres, *Vogue* editor in chief Anna Wintour, media moguls Ted Turner and David Geffen, and the guys who revolutionized the computer world, Bill Gates and Steve Jobs. "Henry

Ford didn't even make it past sixth grade," Talley said, trailing down the hall after Dad with her list in hand. "And John Steinbeck, who you yourself have called the greatest American novelist of all time? He was a college dropout, too. He started out at Stanford, but he never finished."

"Do you know how many people would kill to be in your position?" Dad had said. "The world is your oyster, and you're throwing it all away."

(*Kill to be in your position.* I bet he'll never use that phrase again.)

With Talley home again, Dad was back to lobbying her about college. She could start by taking classes somewhere local, he said, and apply to transfer somewhere better after she got her sea legs. It wouldn't be hard; after all, she had that genius IQ.

I knew Talley'd be successful, no matter what she decided. She was always picking up random textbooks and teaching herself things that piqued her interest—anything from developmental psychology to quantum physics. Things would work out for her, I was sure. In the meantime, I was happy to have her back home.

Though, admittedly, Talley wasn't being her sunniest self. But that was normal, right? Wasn't losing a job worthy of a dark mood? When I was little, Talley would sometimes get down in the dumps and take a few "mental-health days" and stay in bed for a little while. She always bounced back—usually she'd emerge from the cocoon of covers with a project, like donating her hair to Locks of Love. Well, donating *our* hair to Locks of Love—because somehow she always managed to rope me into whatever she was doing, along with all her friends. We got into the local paper that time. There was a picture of us holding our disembodied ponytails. Talley front and center, and the rest of us positioned around her like backup singers.

I thought Talley's latest period of sadness was something like her other sad periods. Though it was more like a mental-health *month* this time around. I made a few suggestions for people she could help, and causes she could get involved in. My suggestions didn't click for her. To be honest, I knew they wouldn't. That was never how it worked with Talley. It needed to be her idea. It was self-motivation or no motivation, and she was deep in the no-motivation zone. She rarely even changed out of her pajamas. Dad was bugging her about it, nagging her, really. But I was still able to rationalize it: *Well, it's not like she has anywhere she has to be anyway.* I missed all the signs.

I missed her last phone call, too. She called me that morning, the morning of the day she died. I'd spoken to her before I'd left the house. I thought she'd been sleeping, but when I walked past her room as I headed out to school, she called to me, and I peeked in her doorway. It was dark in there, and there was the smell of something ripening. She hadn't showered in three or four days. She probably hadn't changed her sheets in all the time she'd been home.

"Hey, Tal. I gotta go," I said. "Juno will be here any second."

"It's already a shit-slammer of a day," she said, and she patted the space on the bed next to her. "Stay home with me."

"I can't, Tal."

She twisted over and picked up her iPhone from the bedside table. "You know what I just read? There are these refugee kids in Sweden, and when they found out their families were being deported back to their home countries, they stopped speaking, they stopped eating, they stopped moving completely, like they were in comas. As far as doctors could tell, their brains were totally healthy. But they knew the world wasn't safe for them, and they lost the will to live. Isn't that the worst thing you've ever heard?"

"It's pretty bad," I said.

"The doctors came up with a name for it," she said. "*Uppgiven-hetssyndrom*. The English translation is resignation syndrome, but if you look at how it's spelled, you'd think it would translate to up-given syndrome, or give-up syndrome. Here, look."

She held the phone out toward me, but I didn't step closer. "I've got to go," I said.

"I really wish you wouldn't."

"Imagine if you were one of those refugee kids," I said. "You'd be having a way shit-slammier day than you are now."

"I know that," she said.

"Are you going to do something for them?"

"What could I possibly do for them? Every time I try and help people, I end up not actually making any kind of difference. Maybe it's better not to try at all."

"That's not true," I said. "You make a difference a lot of the time. But you can't do it from bed. Get up. Call an immigration organization and go volunteer. Or stay home and look through those course catalogs Dad brought home. There's a whole stack of them on his desk."

"Later," Talley said. She burrowed back into bed. I gave a little wave and started to walk off. "Wait, Sloaners."

"What?"

"Please stay home with me."

"I have a quiz, and orchestra practice, and Cooper broke up with Juno."

"You should go be with her, then," Talley said. "She needs you. It's been tough for her."

"Cooper sucks. Juno doesn't see it that way yet, but she's better off without him."

"I meant her hearing impairment and all that," Talley said. Talley always had empathy for people who'd been through hardships, just like in the books and articles she read.

"I think she's more upset about the Cooper stuff right now, to be honest," I said. "I'll see you later, okay?"

"Bye," Talley said, and I left her.

I left her.

Juno picked me up. We were barely on the road when my phone rang. I saw it was Talley calling. Was she going to tell me more about the Swedish refugee kids, or some other tragedy she'd read about? Or was she going to change her mind about Juno needing me, and ask me to turn around and come home?

I pressed the button to mute the call and tucked my phone back into my bag.

So when I say I missed Talley's last call, that's not actually true. I didn't miss it. I saw it. I chose not to answer. Then she died, and through the dense fog of grief in the days that followed, when I was practically delirious, I was clear-headed enough to know that my sister's death was as much my fault as it was a decision that she'd made.

After the doctor left, someone came to the waiting room to give us Talley's clothes, along with the jewelry she'd been wearing. Her effects, the man who handed them over to Dad had called them.

Here are your daughter's effects.

Then the police officer who'd been assigned to the case came to talk to us—the police were involved because suicide is a crime in the state of Minnesota. Dad told me to step out. "You don't need to be here for all of this, Sloane," he said quietly.

"I don't want to leave."

"Please, Sloane."

"No, Dad. I want to stay."

So he let me stay. We stumbled through the officer's questions together. Yes, Talley had been depressed. No, she hadn't seemed suicidal. She'd been hanging out in bed for a couple weeks, maybe more. She'd been going through a rough period, but she did that sometimes.

The officer raised his eyebrows. "Weeks?" he said.

I knew what he was thinking: If Talley had been a member of his family, living under his roof, he would've been clued in. He wouldn't have let this happen.

A wave of shame broke over me. *I'd* let this happen. I was the worst sister in the entire world.

It was an open-and-shut case. No sign of foul play. The officer wrote something on his pad, then flipped it closed and put it in his pocket. He gave us his card if we had any questions. As if he could answer any of the questions we had.

It was time to say goodbye. A nurse walked us to the threshold of Talley's room, but Dad and I stepped inside on our own. It was very quiet. There weren't any machines ticking or beeping or monitoring vital signs; vitality was a thing of Talley's past.

Talley was covered up to her chin with a sheet. "She looks like she's sleeping," Dad said. Though she didn't. Talley didn't sleep flat on her back like that. She was a stomach sleeper, and she always clutched a pillow under her arm. Except the nights when I was little and I climbed into bed with her. Then she slung her arm around me.

She'd been my big sister, but in that moment I was aware of how small she was—how *measurable* her body: not quite five feet tall, not quite a hundred pounds. Those were her measurements. And yet in that tiny frame, there'd been a near-infinite number of thoughts banging around inside her.

Her body would go underground in a few days. But all those thoughts, her infinity of thoughts, what about them? How could she have them one moment, and the next, there was nothing? It made me weep. Dad was crying, too. He slumped in the corner, but I stepped closer, holding on to the side of the bed so I wouldn't fall over. I raised a shaky arm from the bed rail and lifted the sheet to find Talley's hand. Whoever had tended to my sister in death had bent her arms at the elbows, so that her hand was resting on her hip bone. I curled my fingers around hers, so cold, lifted her hand, and gasped.

"What?" Dad said.

"Nothing," I said, and I pulled the sheet back down.

But it wasn't nothing. It was a tattoo. A blue butterfly, the size of a Ping-Pong ball, on Talley's right hip bone. Just one more detail about Talley that I'd missed when she'd moved home.

Talley had explained the butterfly effect to me years ago: even the smallest act can have big consequences, like a butterfly flapping its wings on one side of the world can set off a chain of events resulting in a hurricane on the other side of the world.

Or one sister can ignore a phone call, and then the other one will end up lying prone, lifeless, on a hospital gurney.

I knew Talley was fascinated by the butterfly effect, but I was shocked that she would get a tattoo. Her boyfriend Dean had once suggested they get each other's initials, but she told him she was vehemently opposed to tattoos because during the Holocaust, the Nazis tattooed numbers onto the arms of Jewish prisoners, a way of identifying them and stripping them of their humanity—including her namesake, our great-grandmother Nellie. "Can you imagine if that happened to you?" Talley'd asked me. "Nellie had had a whole life, and friends, and things she loved to do. Then the Germans invaded Poland, and none of that mattered anymore. It only mattered that she was Jewish. The rest of it fell away, and her life became about getting out of there. Tragedies like that—atrocities, really—they rob you of everything else you are. That's why I told Dean no to the tattoo."

After she and Dean broke up, I'd thought it was a good thing she'd been so principled, because why would she want her ex-boyfriend's initials inked on her body for the rest of her life?

The rest of her life.

I thought it would be longer than this.

From his corner, I could feel my father gathering himself to tell me it was time to leave. But I wasn't ready. I'd never be ready. As long as we were in that hospital room, there were still three of us. But when we walked out, we'd only be two.

"Sloane," Dad said. "They're going to need this room soon."

"So what?" I said.

"I'd rather us leave on our own than have someone come in and make us leave," Dad said. "Wouldn't you?"

I understood what he was saying: leaving now, of our own volition, was better than having a nurse or an orderly or whoever coming in and telling us we had to go.

I nodded.

Dad rose and walked to the bed. He bent to give my sister a kiss on her forehead. His tears fell on her cheek, and that made me cry as hard as ever. I gave Talley's hand a last squeeze under the sheet.

Goodbye, Talley's hands, I thought, and the voice in my head lifted and fell softly, sweetly, the way Talley's had when I was very young and she'd read me *Goodnight Moon* every night before bed. *Goodbye, Talley's hair and hip bone and secret butterfly tattoo.*

Goodbye, Talley.

Juno had already left, and I drove home with Dad, the plastic bag of Talley's effects in my lap. When we got home, Dad didn't ask for it back and I didn't give it to him. Instead, I went to my room and emptied it onto my bed. Talley had been wearing actual clothes, not pajamas. Her jeans were now cut up the length of each pants leg from when the emergency room staff had cut her out of her clothes. Her worn gray T-shirt was cut down the middle. Her underwear, her bra, her socks, her rings, one for almost every finger. I'd end up wearing a lot of Talley's things, but not those.

Not the things she'd died in.

Still I couldn't bring myself to take the cut-up clothes out to the curb and pile them in the trash can, on top of banana peels and burned-out lightbulbs and old bills with the account numbers blacked out in Sharpie, which Dad was obsessive about because he was afraid of identity theft.

Instead, I folded Talley's clothes like they were laundry fresh from the dryer. I smoothed the creases of her T-shirt and checked the pockets of her jeans. That's when I found the piece of notebook paper, folded so many times that it was no bigger than a pack of dental floss.

I had the weirdest feeling of surreality, like I was just an actor playing a part in a movie. Here is the scene when the girl comes back from the hospital, where her sister died from an overdose of pills.

Imagine if you discovered your sister's suicide note, I thought.

I unfolded the note and looked at what Talley had written.

chapter three

IT WASN'T A SUICIDE NOTE AT ALL. IT WAS A LIST.

Oh my God. Of course. *Of course* it was a list.

Or a game, or a puzzle.

Whatever you want to call it, it was so Talley.

Writing things out in a straightforward way just wasn't her style. Even when it was something simple like shopping for groceries, she never gave me a regular list. She gave me clues: *I'm the second most popular vegetable in the United States* (lettuce). *The older I am, the sharper I taste* (cheddar cheese).

So here was another list of clues.

There were bubble letters at the top, and seeing them was as surreal as anything. *Bubble letters.* Talley used to draw my name in bubble letters and leave little notes on my bedroom door overnight, things like "I love you" or "Dream big."

This time, Talley hadn't written my name; she'd written "TSL." Underneath the letters, in her familiar, loopy handwriting, were these words:

> *Ursus arctos californicus*
>
> *Crescent Street*
>
> *Ulysses*
>
> *Lucy and Ethel*
>
> *Grease at Mr. G's*
>
> *Bel Air midnights*
>
> *NHL photo revelations*
>
> *Sunny's eggs from the Royal Road Diner*
>
> *Sunshine Crew*
>
> *A large gentleman's sunset*
>
> *Dean's lips*
>
> *Dad and Sloane*
>
> *More pie*

I knew the second-to-last entry, of course, *Dad and Sloane*. And the one just above it, *Dean's lips*: Dean, the high school boyfriend whose initials Talley *didn't* get tattooed on her body. She and Dean broke up right before he left for college in Indiana. Talley didn't think he should go with strings attached. She'd barely mentioned him since. I didn't know she harbored any lingering feelings about his lips or any other body part.

As for the rest of the list, the items seemed completely random. But that's often how puzzles start out: they seem random, and it's a matter of figuring out what they mean. These initials, words, items, names—they meant something to Talley. They were connected in some way, but I had no idea why or how.

And so I decided to take the items on the list one by one, turning them over in my head like a bright bead or coin. Starting with the bubble letters, *TSL*. Was the *T* for Talley? The *S* for Sloane? Then who was the *L*?

Maybe the *S* wasn't for Sloane after all. *T* for Talley . . . Talley what? Talley Seeks Love? That sounded like a personal ad, which this list was decidedly not. (At least I was pretty sure it wasn't.) Talley Says . . . Talley Solves . . . Talley Slays . . . Talley Still . . .

Talley didn't still do anything.

TSL could be someone else's initials, the person for whom Talley had written this list. But if this list was meant for TSL, whoever he or she was, then how come Talley had stuck it in her pocket? Wouldn't she have mailed it? Or at least written out that name so that I—or Dad, whichever of us discovered this paper—would know who to pass it on to?

I went to check Talley's Facebook page—who had the initials TSL? But it turned out that Talley wasn't on Facebook anymore. I checked the rest of her social media accounts, and then her cell phone. Everything was wiped clean. She'd erased herself.

I had to place a hand on my chest, an effort to calm my pounding heart, before I moved on, typing *TSL* into Google search. There were nearly twenty million hits. I scrolled through the first few dozen, but nothing popped out at me. I could spend the rest of my life going through these results and still never find out what Talley meant.

At least Google was a bit more helpful when it came to the items on the list itself. First, *Ursus arctos californicus* was the scientific name for a species of the California grizzly. They could grow up to eight feet tall and weigh as much as two thousand pounds, which was, obviously, terrifying. But what was the significance to Talley? Did it have something to do with hibernation, as in Talley's mental-health days? Was it that they were known to be solitary animals? Was it that they were now extinct, like Talley herself?

It was too much. It was too heartbreaking. But I couldn't stop. Talley'd left this behind. She wanted me to do this. To stop would mean letting Talley down—*again*. So on to the next item: Crescent Street. According to Google, there were dozens, if not hundreds (maybe thousands), of Crescent Streets in the United States and beyond. How was I supposed to know which one Talley meant?

I knew that *Ulysses*, item three on the list, was a book by James Joyce. Dr. Lee had once assigned the Joyce story "The Dead" for us to read. (The *Dead*.) But I'd never read *Ulysses*. Immediately I went in search of a copy on Talley's bookshelf. Perhaps she'd hidden something within its pages. I ran my hands along the spines of books she'd touched. The most well-worn were her collection of memoirs—other people's sad stories that so often inspired Talley to volunteer, or organize a jog-a-thon, or write letters of support. *Ulysses* wasn't on her shelf. I called our local bookstore, and they said they'd hold a copy for me. In the meantime, I kept going down the list.

Lucy and Ethel were characters from *I Love Lucy*, a show from the 1950s. I resolved to watch every episode—thank goodness for

YouTube. I assumed *Grease* was the movie Talley and I had long ago watched together, and now I pledged to watch it again. But who was Mr. G? I went down the list of everyone we knew, everyone who had a *G* last name. There wasn't anyone significant. Maybe it was a first name—like code for Dad, whose first name was Garrett. He'd told Talley to cool it when she complained the movie was sexist, and the women were treated like objects. "Let Sloane enjoy it in peace," he'd said.

Of course it turned out that Talley was right, as she always was. The movie was sexist. I'd just been too young to know it back then. Maybe . . . oh, God.

Maybe *Grease* was code for a time that Talley herself had been treated like an object. *At* Mr. G's. He could've done something to her at his house—something bad enough to make her want to end her life. Oh, how I ached for my sister.

The list went on. Item six: Bel Air was a neighborhood in Los Angeles, California—so that was the second California thing on Talley's list, after the grizzly bears. I didn't know my sister had any kind of connection to California—maybe there'd been a grizzly-bear spotting in Bel Air? At midnight? Or maybe she was referencing the TV show? Back in the 1990s, there was a show called *The Fresh Prince of Bel-Air*, about a poor kid from Philadelphia being sent to live with his rich relatives. Did Talley ever watch it? Were there characters on it that meant something to her, the way Lucy and Ethel from *I Love Lucy* apparently did?

Seven: NHL photo revelations. I knew NHL stood for National Hockey League. Rachel was a fan of the Minnesota Wild. But was Talley? Maybe NHL stood for something else. I went back to Google to check out the other options. New Historic Landmark? New Hampshire Library? Normal Hearing Level? Non-Hodgkin's Lymphoma? I had absolutely no idea.

I kept moving down the list. Sunny's eggs, the Sunshine Crew, the sunset. If life was so bright and sunshiny, then why did Talley kill herself?

I'd reached the end of the list. But there was something else on the paper, a phone number. It was on the other side, and written with a different pen, a darker blue than the list itself. Maybe Talley had written it down another time, and just happened to use the same sheet of paper.

But maybe not.

Google couldn't tell me who the number belonged to, but I was able to find out that the area code was for a section of California spanning San Mateo to Santa Clara counties.

California again.

I'd never been to San Mateo or Santa Clara, or anywhere in between, and if Talley had, she'd never told me. In the past, she'd sometimes taken road trips without telling me in advance, and she'd send postcards as clues. "Guess where I am right now," she'd write. California would've been a really long road trip, and I didn't think I'd ever received a postcard from that far away. But here was this list with three California references, and this phone number written in her unmistakable handwriting, on a piece of paper that had been in her pocket on the day she died.

I called the number and it went straight to voice mail: *Hey, it's Adam. Leave a message. Beep!*

His message was so short, it was hard to assess anything about him. And how much can you really tell about a person from their voice? You can't tell age, or height, or race. Thank goodness he said his name. At least I got to know that.

"Hi. Adam? My name is Sloane. You don't know me but . . . but my sister . . ."

My sister—what? My sister died? My sister killed herself?

"I found a piece of paper of hers with your number on it, and I think you must've known her. Talley—Talley Weber? I'd really appreciate it if you could call me back."

I left my phone number, thanked him, and ended the call. I refolded Talley's list, five times, and put it in my own jeans pocket. I put her folded clothing on the top shelf of my closet, and I closed the door.

chapter four

"TODAY IS A DAY OF SADNESS AND MOURNING," RABBI
Bernstein intoned. "Our dear Talley is gone, at the tender age of
twenty-two. She left us with heartbreak. She left us with frustration.
She left us all yearning for more time with her. And she left us with
over two decades of memories. That's why we are all here today—
to remember Talley. She was the cherished daughter of Garrett and
the late Dana Weber, and the adoring sister of Sloane, who you'll
hear from in a few minutes."

I was at my sister's memorial service. It was a Monday. Talley
had been declared dead eighty-seven hours earlier. Eighty-seven
hours and seventeen minutes. Which was just eight hours and
forty-three minutes shy of exactly four days.

If you'd told me four days ago that this is where I'd be, sitting in the front pew of the Beth Shalom Synagogue, staring at my

sister's coffin—*my sister's coffin*—I wouldn't have believed you.

If you'd told me four days ago, I would've done things so differently, and there wouldn't be a reason for me to be here now.

It had been Rabbi Bernstein's suggestion that I speak at the service, and tell the other mourners things about my sister's life that perhaps they hadn't ever known. At first when he said it, I'd thought, *Okay, I can do that.*

But when Rabbi Bernstein left and I sat down to write what would arguably be the most important thing I'd ever written in my life, I had total writer's block. Dr. Lee often said that there's no such thing as writer's block: "There's always something to say," she'd told our class. "You might not know exactly how to say it, but you can certainly start by saying it badly. Too many stories don't get written because their writers get stuck on how best to tell them. But a story doesn't have value to others while it's cooped up inside you. It only has value if you write it down. My advice is to give yourself permission to write a completely vomitous first draft. I'll bet there'll be some diamonds buried in there, and when you revise, you can keep an eye out for what sparkles. But you won't have anything to work with till you get that first draft down."

There were so many things about Talley swirling in my head, I didn't know where to start. She was so obsessed with dolphins that she probably knew more facts about them than your average marine biologist. She won the spelling award every single year she was in elementary school. She could convert Fahrenheit to Celsius in her head, and vice versa. She saved up a year's worth of allowance to buy me an American Girl doll for my sixth birthday. She'd go to the mall with the express purpose of giving compliments to strangers: "I love your hair" or "That sweater looks great on you." I wanted to be like her. I tried to be. But I never was, not entirely. I'd never be as good as Talley. Writing about her wasn't like writing a story. She couldn't be confined to the page. That was the problem.

Before it was my turn to speak, Tess Nyland got up. Tess had been on the Golden Valley High cheerleading squad with Talley. She read from Kahlil Gibran's *The Prophet*, a book I'd found on Talley's shelf when I'd gone looking for *Ulysses*. Tess read from a section that Talley had underlined: "The deeper that sorrow carves into your being, the more joy you can contain."

My sorrow over losing Talley had excavated me down to the core. There was no way all the carved-out spaces would ever be filled with joy. I was only seventeen years old. Presumably I had a lot of life ahead of me. But how could I ever have another day of pure joy, without Talley in the world?

Tess finished and it was my turn. I stood and walked to the podium, feeling the lump in my throat, too big to swallow, and the squeeze of shoes that were too tight on me—they were Talley's shoes. The speech I'd written was folded in my palm. I clutched it and gazed out at the audience. Every face looked blurred, except for one. Our across-the-street neighbor, Sara Gettering, sitting about a dozen rows back. She was short and rail-thin. Her gray hair was perpetually pulled back into a severe bun, and her glasses made her eyes look enlarged to twice the usual size. We'd always called her by her first and last name. Like "Sara Gettering said you were playing ball in the front yard and you almost hit her car" or

"Sara Gettering says we're not allowed to draw hopscotch on the sidewalk." I wondered why Sara Gettering was the one in crystal-clear focus; maybe because it was shocking that she, of all people, had come to pay respects to Talley.

I began unfolding the piece of paper in my hand. The last time I'd unfolded a piece of paper, it'd been Talley's list. I was thinking about that, and I was thinking about Sara Gettering showing up for Talley's funeral, and one of the pieces of the puzzle clicked into place.

More pie.

I kept my partially folded speech in my hand, and started speaking without it. "Once when I was about nine, I told Talley I wanted to make an apple pie. I hoped she'd take me to the grocery store for ingredients. But she told me to wait in my room for a few minutes, and when she came to get me, she handed me the first clue in a scavenger hunt. I went all around our house, then our back-yard, then our front yard. The second to last clue said, 'Put words in my mouth and they'll be taken away.' That took me a while, but I finally figured out she meant the mailbox. I opened it up and there was the last clue, which was a math problem. The solution turned out to be our neighbor's address. This neighbor—I'll call her Mrs. X—she had an apple tree in her yard. You need apples to make apple pie, obviously. Mrs. X lived alone, and Talley assured me she had plenty to share. But Mrs. X was the kind of person who really scared little kids. I told Talley, 'I can't go ask her for apples.' Talley said, 'Don't ask for permission; ask for forgiveness.' She explained that was her life philosophy. That was the phrase she used: life philosophy. If you asked adults for things, she told me, they'd likely tell you no because they didn't think you could handle something on your own. So the best thing to do, she said, was just go for it. If you mess up, then you can say sorry."

My eyes were trained on Sara Gettering as I went on with the story, how we'd snuck across the street onto her property. We were only there for a couple minutes before she burst out the front door. She was waving a long wooden spatula, and I was convinced she intended to spank us with it. I let go of the apples I was holding and they fell to the ground: *thud, thud, thud, thud.* Talley began apologizing right away. "I'm sorry. I'm really sorry," she said. "Please forgive me, and please don't be mad at my sister at all. She's an innocent bystander."

"An innocent bystander?" Sara Gettering asked. "What about my poor apples?"

I looked down at the apples, bruised on the ground. "Sorry," I whispered.

Talley grabbed my hand and pulled me across the street, Sara Gettering yelling behind us all the while. We slammed into our house, and Talley leaned against the closed door, doubled over. She was laughing so hard that tears pricked the corners of her eyes. "You asked the apples for forgiveness," she said, shaking her head. "You asked APPLES for FORGIVENESS!"

"Well," I said, and I could feel my cheeks heating up to the color of overripe crab apples. "They got bruised when I dropped them, and Mrs. Gettering said so."

"Oh, Sloaners," my sister said. She took a deep breath and

stepped right up close to me. "I love you so much. We'll get you some more pie."

More pie.

There it was.

"Being Talley's sister was my best thing, my greatest adventure," I told the mourners who'd gathered at her memorial service, including Sara Gettering. "I can't believe the adventure is over. That's all I wanted to say."

chapter five

THE SERVICE ENDED, AND DAD AND I WALKED OUT FIRST. I felt like I was an actor in a movie again. I was dressed in the requisite black dress, and without looking in a mirror, I knew my mascara had run in the requisite rivulets down my cheeks. The other mourners followed behind Dad and me.

We're like funeral VIPs, I thought wryly. If Talley'd been there, I would've whispered it to her.

If a tree falls in a forest, and no one is there to hear it, does it make a sound?

If you think of something that you want to say to your sister, and she's not there, does it even matter that you had the thought to begin with?

The line of people snaked down the aisle of the sanctuary, everyone waiting to greet Dad and me. I knew a lot of the people, but far from all of them. Those unknowns could've been anyone—the Adam behind the voice mail, or Mr. G, who hosted a screening of *Grease*, and might have hurt my sister in some way. I tried to interview every person whose face I couldn't place. "How did you know Talley?" I asked. "What's your name?"

The answers were mostly "I work with your dad," and not anything that had to do with Talley.

"Sloane," the next mourner said. It was Dr. Lee, my English teacher. She was holding the arm of her husband, Mr. Chan, who happened to be my statistics teacher, but she dropped his arm to wrap me in a hug that lasted several seconds. When she let go, she held my shoulders at arm's length. "Oh, dear, I am so very sorry," she said. "This is so hard, isn't it?"

"Yes," I said. It came out as a whisper and I cleared my throat. "Thank you for coming. I didn't know you'd come." I nodded to Mr. Chan. "You, too," I said.

"Talley was in my geometry class," he said. "I gave the class a practically impossible proof to complete. It was meant to stump them, but Talley pulled it off. I would've loved to have seen what she would have become—she was an extraordinary girl, your sister."

Talley would've corrected him: "Woman." She was twenty-two years old, and she was not a "girl," any more than a twenty-two-year-old male is a "boy."

"Thank you," I managed.

Mr. and Mrs. Hogan approached next. They were the parents of the triplets Juno and I would be babysitting over the summer—the last three weeks of June, all July, and the first week of August.

I wondered if the Hogans worried that my sadness might hang like a cloud over Thomas, Theo, and Melanie's summer break. The kids were only eight years old, after all.

But if that's what the Hogans were thinking, they didn't show it. Mr. Hogan gave my shoulder a squeeze, and Mrs. Hogan patted my cheek. "We'll see you soon," she said, and they moved on.

My closest friends came up in pairs. First Soraya and Rachel, and then our best guy friends, Brody and Zach. And then there was Juno. Finally, Juno. It was just her, not part of a pair, because I was the other half of her pair. Juno reached for me. No, that's wrong; she didn't reach. She grabbed. I grabbed back, and we held each other really hard.

"Cooper didn't come," Juno said, talking into my hair. "He really is a jerk, isn't he?"

"I don't care about Cooper," I said.

"Me either," she said. "I only care about you." She tightened her grip around me.

Behind Juno's head, I spotted Dean. Dean of *Dean's lips.* The one person on Talley's list whom I could identify—besides Dad and myself, that is. I shrugged myself loose from Juno and reached out.

"Hiya," Dean said, and he pulled me into a hug. When we broke apart, I took a good look at his mouth. The upper lip was bigger than the lower one, and his cupid's bow was particularly prominent. I resisted the urge to reach out and touch them, these lips Talley had touched about a thousand times and written down on her list. "You take care of yourself, kid, okay?" Dean told me.

"Don't go yet," I said. "I need to ask you something. Did you and Talley . . . did you guys ever go to California together?"

Dean shook his head. "Farthest we ever got was our road trip to Chicago, because Talley was in the mood for deep-dish pizza. Course, it's seven hours in the car. By the time we got there, we'd stuffed ourselves full of Twizzlers and Doritos. We had, like, two bites of pizza, then we spent the whole night driving home."

"Did she talk to you about it ever?" I asked.

"What? The pizza?"

"No," I said. "California."

"Oh, right. Hmm." He was quiet a few seconds, seemingly giving my question some thought. But in the end, he shook his head. "I can't remember any conversations about California, to be honest with you," he said.

"Have you heard of Crescent Street?" He shook his head. "The Royal Road Diner? The Sunshine Crew? A large gentleman's sunset?"

"No."

"What about NHL photo revelations?"

"You mean hockey?"

"Maybe?"

"I follow the Red Wings," he said.

"Were you guys in touch at all, even just by text?"

"I talked to her a few months back, for like maybe five minutes? She said she was too busy to chat. Before that, we'd gone over a year." He shook his head. "She was the most special person I've ever known. I never thought . . . I guess special has a way of hiding trouble."

I took a deep breath and nodded; yes, it did.

"I really loved her, you know?"

"I did, too."

"God, I'm so sorry, kid. I'll see you around, okay?"

Would I? Would I ever see Dean—or his lips—again, now that Talley was gone?

"See you," I said.

chapter six

THE NEXT MONDAY, ELEVEN DAYS ATD—AFTER TALLEY'S death—seven days after the funeral and burial, Dad decided it was time for him to go back to work and me to go back to school.

He came into my room that morning to tell me to hurry it up, just like always, as if the events of the past week and a half were merely the stuff of a bad dream, and now we were awake and everything was normal. On normal days, Dad worried that I wouldn't get outside before Juno pulled up, and then she'd honk and disturb the neighbors. The fact that she never had did nothing to dispel his fear. He didn't trust her. She dyed her hair a different color every week; she had multiple piercings in each ear, plus a stud in her nose. Her grandmother had died and left Juno a boatload of money. Dad thought she was spoiled and knew nothing about living in the real world; if she did, she wouldn't have so many holes in her face. "Who you hang out with is who you are," my dad was fond of saying, and I agreed with him, which is precisely why I loved being best friends with Juno.

"You ready?" he asked.

"Hang on," I told him. I was standing by my dresser. The top drawer was open and my hand was inside, fingertips grazing Talley's list. I wasn't looking at the paper, but I felt like I could feel the words with my fingers, as if Talley had inexplicably written them in braille:

> *Ursus arctos californicus*
> *Crescent Street*
> *Ulysses*
> *Lucy and Ethel*
> *Grease at Mr. G's*
> *Bel Air midnights*
> *NHL photo revelations*
> *Sunny's eggs from the Royal Road Diner*
> *Sunshine Crew*
> *A large gentleman's sunset*
> *Dean's lips*
> *Dad and Sloane*
> *More pie*

I had it all memorized, but the actual list was important to me, because it was *Talley's.* I'd planned to leave the list at home all day for safekeeping, but then I began to worry about our house catching on fire.

That wouldn't happen, right? That'd be too much tragedy.

Except I knew there was no such thing as too much tragedy: I lost my mom, and then I lost my sister. And Dad had lost not only them, but also his parents—to a house fire, no less. Still, I decided that a house fire was less likely than the list escaping my pocket while I was at school. I let my fingertips touch Talley's list one last time for good measure, then I closed the dresser drawer.

"Sloane?" Dad asked.

"Yeah. Sorry. When will you be home tonight?"

"I imagine the usual time," he said. "Six thirty. Seven. Maybe a bit later. There's a lot to catch up on."

"If it's not too late, can we drive out to Wayzata?"

"Do you know someone in Wayzata?"

"No, but there's a Crescent Street, so Talley might've known someone."

According to Google Maps, the Crescent Street in Wayzata was the closest Crescent Street to our house, out of all the Crescent Streets in the world. I knew that didn't necessarily mean it was the one from Talley's list, but it couldn't hurt to check it out. In fact, it seemed like the hurtful thing to do would be to *not* go.

"I don't follow," Dad said.

"It was on her list," I reminded him.

I'd shown the list to Dad on the night Talley had died, when we were both walking around the house like we'd returned to it in the aftermath of war. Our lives had been blown apart, and we were picking up the pieces—picking things up in our hands, examining them as if trying to figure out what they'd once been. I remember that my hands themselves felt strangely heavy that night. They still did all the things hands were supposed to do—they held things, flicked lights off and on, and swiped the tears from my face. But grief made them feel like they were somehow not mine anymore. It was as if they'd been removed and reattached. A part of my body, and yet not. When I held them out in front of me, they looked newly foreign, too. Just like everything else in our house.

Dad had looked strange and foreign to me as he squinted to read Talley's list. Then he looked back at me and said he didn't know what anything was, besides the obvious entries. I watched him refold the list carefully, deliberately, along the creases that Talley had made, before handing it back to me.

It took him a couple beats to remember the list now. "Right," he finally said.

"There's another Crescent Street in Big Lake," I told him. "But since Wayzata is closer, I figured we'd start there. If we don't find anything, we can go to Big Lake. Just to check it all out."

"You're treating this list like it's some kind of puzzle," Dad said.

"It *is* some kind of puzzle," I said. "You know how Talley loved to make puzzles for me to solve. There are thirteen clues on this list—fourteen, if you count the initials on the top. Fifteen, if you count the phone number."

Adam hadn't returned my call. Juno pointed out that lots of people never even listen to their voice mails. If Adam had seen a missed call on his caller ID and didn't know whose number it was, he might just ignore it completely. Just to be sure, I'd also sent a text:

Hi, this is Sloane Weber. I'm Talley Weber's sister. Sorry to bother you again, but I really need to get in touch. Please call or text when you get a chance. Thank you.

He hadn't replied to the text, either. But I wasn't ready to give up.

"I don't want you to spend too much time on this," Dad told me. "I know it's hard to hear, but you may never figure out what Talley meant—if she meant anything at all. She wasn't in her right mind, and part of getting through what happened is attending to things in our own lives."

"Talley being gone is a thing in my life."

"I know that," Dad said. "Don't you think I know that? When your mother died, I couldn't let the loss undo me. I was responsible for two young children."

"It must have been so hard," I said. "I'm sorry."

"You have nothing to be sorry for. You were just a little girl, and you lost her, too."

"But that's the point," I said. "I was so little that I don't even remember losing her. I'm not a little kid anymore. I don't need you to take care of me."

"No, the point is that you're old enough to feel the inertia of grief this time around. But life goes on."

"Dr. Lee would cross that line out if you put it in a story," I told him. "Life goes on—it's a total cliché."

"A cliché is a cliché because it's something that a lot of people agree on, and so it's repeated over and over again. I think we can agree that gives the phrase some merit, right?"

I shook my head. "This is different than when Mom died," I

said. "That was a car accident." Dad's eyes flinched involuntarily, as if feeling the pain of impact. "But what Talley did . . . it was a choice. And saying, 'Oh well. Life goes on'—"

"I didn't say 'Oh well,' Sloane."

"You may as well have. You just don't want to look too closely at this, but I keep wondering what I was doing at the exact moment she took those pills. Was I still in orchestra practice, or snapping my flute back into its case, or talking to Juno? Whatever it was, it wasn't important. I should've been there to stop her."

"Please don't blame yourself," Dad said.

I deserved the blame. But I didn't tell him that.

"You've got two weeks left of school. There's never a good time to have an emergency, but with your exams coming up—"

"Fine. Fine. I'll go to Wayzata without you, okay? I just thought you'd want to come with me."

"Sloane—"

"I better get outside before Juno honks," I said.

chapter seven

"WILL YOU DRIVE ME TO THE CRESCENT STREET IN Wayzata after school?" I asked Juno almost the instant I'd climbed into her car, a 2001 Mustang BULLITT that she'd bought herself for her sixteenth birthday. Juno loved old things, but it wasn't exactly a steal by the time she paid to get it up to contemporary safety standards—as required by her parents.

Juno knew all about Talley's list. Over the last week, Dad and I had been sitting shiva, which is what you do when you're Jewish and someone in the family dies. You stay home, and people come over to pay their respects. Juno came every day after school. Together, we'd watched two dozen episodes of *I Love Lucy*, and a few of *The Fresh Prince of Bel-Air* to boot. You're not supposed to watch TV during shiva, because you're not supposed to do anything that would distract from your grief. But we were watching *because* I was grieving, so I thought it was okay.

"Sure," Juno said.

"Thanks. I don't know what we're looking for. It could be a house, or a stoop, or a mailbox. I guess I can ring every bell, if it comes to that."

"Whatever it takes," Juno said. "I'll drive the getaway car."

She was looking in the rearview mirror and backing down the driveway as she spoke, which I thought of as an act of incredible coordination. I was convinced I'd never be able to do it myself without crashing into anything, which is why I barely ever practiced driving. The only reason I even had a driver's permit was because Talley insisted. She told me a story about women in Saudi Arabia who had been prohibited from driving for years. They fought for the right to drive, just like the men could. But now they had the right to drive, I'd told Talley. What did it matter whether I took my driver's test and got my license or not? So I remained Juno's passenger, which was totally fine by her. She loved driving.

I could hear music playing in the background, really softly. Usually the volume was turned way up when I got into the car, and Juno would be jamming out to her current favorite, whatever that was. She tended to fall in love with one band, and then play them in a loop for weeks on end. Unsurprisingly, she preferred the oldies. Right now Fleetwood Mac was the band on repeat. Stevie Nicks was singing—the goddess, Juno called her. Her voice was just a wisp. I knew Juno herself couldn't hear it.

But I could. This very song had been playing in Juno's car that morning, when my phone rang and I ignored the call.

My breaths were coming quickly. The thing about losing someone you love is that it's not a one-time shock. It's over and over and over again.

"Sloane?" Juno said. "You okay?"

"I'm scared to go back today. What if someone asks me something, or just, you know, looks at me, and I start crying?"

"Then you start crying. People will feel bad, and probably offer you a tissue or something."

"I'm going to be such a spectacle," I said.

"For a few days, yes. But they'll get used to having you back."

"I guess."

"I know it's hard," Juno said. "I don't like going to school on regular days. But I'm really glad you'll be there today. I hated being there without you. When you got into the car just now, I felt like . . . well, it was like that feeling you get when you're at a restaurant and you're really hungry. You're practically ready to eat your own arm. Then the food arrives at your table, and you take your first bite and it's even more delicious than you thought it could be."

"That's a good metaphor," I said. Then I added, "Thank you."

"You're welcome."

I reached out to turn up the volume on the car stereo a bit, loud enough for Juno to hear. I'd heard her mom say cochlear implants were modern-day miracles. If Juno had become deaf fifty years ago, there wouldn't have been a surgery for her to have to get her hearing back. But it wasn't perfect.

"Once in a million years, a lady like her rises," the goddess sang. It was a line from "Rhiannon," a live version. Juno pulled into the

school parking lot and slid into a spot in the back row. She always parked in back, because there was less of a chance that someone would squeeze into a neighboring spot, open a door too wide, and scratch up one of the BULLITT's precious doors.

Juno shifted into park, but she didn't cut the engine, not till the song had ended.

And he still cries out for her, don't leave me now.

chapter eight

IT WAS STRANGE THAT EVERYTHING LOOKED THE SAME.

I'd read lines like that in a hundred different books. Something enormous would happen in the story, and the narrator would be surprised by the sameness of everything around her. Such a cliché. And yet, so true. I expected school to be different, because *I* was so different, but there were the same flecked linoleum hallways, the same bluish-white walls. The odd sameness of it all made it feel unfamiliar. I felt like I'd landed from outer space and was seeing everything for the first time. There was a sign hanging in the junior hallway. Surely it'd been there all year, but I'd never noticed it before:

YOUR MISTAKES DO NOT DEFINE YOU.

Well, I thought, *sometimes they do*.

This was the last full week of classes. Next week was finals week. Kids who studied hard all the time had their noses in books, studying. Kids who barely studied were suddenly showing up to every class, paying attention, asking their friends if they could copy their notes. If anyone noticed me, they'd look away, or give me too long a look, or maybe even a hug. Then they'd move on, worrying about their own grades, their own lives.

Monday rolled into Tuesday, into Wednesday. I had four classes in the morning, then lunch, then another four classes. Juno had been right about people getting used to me, and sometimes it was easy for me to forget what had happened, too. There was, like, muscle memory of what it felt like to be in school as an ordinary person whose sister hadn't just died. Megan Hofstader made a crack about our history teacher, and I started to laugh. But then I caught myself, suddenly hyperaware of who I was and what I'd lost. In those moments of hyperawareness, nothing felt real—especially knowing that when I went home at the end of the day, I'd pass by Talley's closed bedroom door and she wouldn't be on the other side of it.

Wednesday rolled into Thursday. And then it was Friday. I'd nearly completed my first week of school, ATD. Fourth period was Dr. Lee's Advanced English Literature & Writing class. "How is everyone doing with their final stories?" Dr. Lee asked.

Dr. Lee was my only teacher not giving a final exam. Instead, we had short stories due. I'd started working on mine a few weeks back. But then Talley had died. I hadn't looked at my story since. It was still in the vomitous first-draft phase.

"I know we're not supposed to use the B-word in your class," Megan Hofstader said.

Dr. Lee gave her a quizzical look.

"Blocked," Megan said. "I mean blocked."

"Ah," Dr. Lee said. "Not the word I thought you meant, but yes—that word is prohibited in here."

"Well, at the risk of breaking a rule, I *am* blocked," Megan said. "I got to the middle of my story, but don't know if I can finish it. I can't even write badly right now."

"We can meet after class to discuss the specifics of your story," Dr. Lee said. "But speaking generally, I'll say this—writing is an act of betting on ourselves. It's saying, 'I bet this thing in my head is worthy of being in the world,' which is essentially saying, 'I bet *I* am worthy of being in the world.' When we experience the B-word, as you call it, it's usually a sign that we're worrying about our worthiness. It's the opposite of betting on ourselves. There's a famous quote by the late senator Paul Tsongas: 'No one on his deathbed ever said, I wish I'd spent more time on my business.' Personally, I've always thought that was a crock. Almost every writer I know would pull their laptops closer and type faster on their deathbeds, because on our deathbeds, suddenly, we have nothing to lose by betting on ourselves. A better expression would be: No one on his deathbed ever wished he'd spent more time worrying. So my advice to you is: Don't spend too much time worrying about your stories. Just write them, and revise, revise, revise."

She'd said the word *deathbed* four times in the space of two minutes. Each time, I felt a squeeze in my chest. Talley hadn't had a business or a deathbed. She'd had a death *floor*. Had she said any words from that floor? I'd never know. But she did leave the list in her pocket.

Remembering it, I dropped my hand to my own pocket. I'd taken Talley's list to school with me that day, and my heartbeat picked up its pace as my fingers dug to find it.

Ah. There it was.

The edges had grown fuzzy from my touching them so much, soft as velvet. When I unfolded the paper, the creases had worn thin and had teeny tears. Maybe I should have it laminated. But to laminate Talley's list would mean that I would no longer be touching exactly the thing that she had touched, and I liked thinking about how my finger could be pressing on the exact invisible trace of one of her fingerprints. It was like pressing my finger to her finger. If I laminated the paper, I wouldn't be able to do that.

When it came to the list, I felt like I was always trying to figure out what was the least bad between two shitty options: to leave it at home or to take it to school, both with their own risks; to laminate or not to laminate, both with their own shitty side effects.

I slipped a finger gently between the folds, tracing the items on the list. Thirteen items, plus the initials TSL up top, and Adam's phone number on the back. I hadn't heard back from him yet.

Adam, whoever he was, wherever he was—why hadn't he called me?

Whenever I was working on a story and working through a character's motivations, I'd picture them in my head and play out different scenarios. Adam wasn't someone I was making up, but I tried it anyway. I pictured him in my head, a faceless person getting a voice mail message, and then a text, from a stranger. What would he do next?

He'd probably try to contact Talley, but Dad had already disconnected her line. It drove me insane that he'd done it so quickly. I wanted to be able to text myself from her phone, because then her texts would still be at the top of my messages. I hated that her name was slipping down, down, down. I had to scroll so far to find her.

Besides, it was *Talley's* phone number; even if she couldn't use it, I didn't want anyone else to have it. And if Adam had tried to call or text her and say, *Hey I got a weird message from some chick saying she's your sister*, I couldn't take her phone and reply to him.

But Dad didn't think about any of that. He was too busy getting on with things.

I glanced up to check that Dr. Lee wasn't looking at me. She wasn't. She was writing something on the board. So I pulled my phone into my lap and tapped out another text to Adam: Hi, it's Sloane Weber again—Talley's sister. I'm sorry to put this in a text message, but I need to tell you that Talley died. She left a list of things along with your phone number in her pocket.

I wrote out the items on Talley's list, which made it a novel of a text. When I finished, I kept my phone in hand. It was so unlike me to send a text in a class, especially Dr. Lee's class, and to keep my phone out afterward. But I didn't care. I clutched it, willing it to vibrate with a call or text from Adam. I had little concern for Dr. Lee, or my short story, or anything other than things connected to Talley.

chapter nine

I WAS ON MY WAY TO THE CAFETERIA, STILL CLUTCHING my phone, when I was intercepted by my ex–best friend, Audrey Sheridan.

Audrey and I had been inseparable from kindergarten to the middle of fifth grade, when our drama teacher, Mr. Stuart, cast me as the title role in *Oliver!*, which Audrey considered a shocking injustice. She was the one who wanted to be an actress when she grew up, and she'd talked me into auditioning with her, figuring I'd be cast as one of the lesser orphans. She blamed me for "stealing" her role. I quit the show so she could go on as my understudy, but she still wouldn't speak to me. Luckily, Juno came to sit next to me at lunch. We didn't know each other well back then. She was the kind of friend I'd invite to my birthday party if I was having more than ten people, but not if I was having fewer. Not having Audrey around opened up room for Juno, and I realized she was much easier to be around. She didn't make up a million rules about what we had to wear each day, or how many notes we had to pass. I stopped begging Audrey to forgive me, which only made her hate me more. She hated Juno, too. I remember her confronting us once, saying we were terrible people who deserved each other. She said she never wanted to speak to either of us again.

Over the years, she mostly kept her word, only talking to me when she absolutely could not avoid it—like if a teacher forced us to work together, or once in seventh grade, when she bumped into me in the hallway, and she said, "Oops, sorry." Then she looked up and saw it was me. I think she would've taken those two words back if she could've.

But now here she was, her hand deliberately on my arm. "Wait, Sloane," she said. "I'm sorry about Talley."

"Thank you," I said.

"How are you? I mean, of course you're awful."

"I'm just on my way to—"

"I keep thinking about her," Audrey said. "Remember how she used to bring us along to cheerleading practice, and we'd sit up in the bleachers and watch her?"

"Yeah," I said. "I do."

Talley had started out on the squad when she was a freshman, which was really rare. She was the only one out of twelve girls— the youngest, the smallest, and also the best. She'd do this thing where she'd take a flying leap and basically cartwheel her way to the top. I hadn't thought about it in a long time. If Audrey hadn't brought it up, it's possible I could've gone the rest of my life without ever thinking about it again.

We live through so many experiences with the people in our lives, and some of those experiences we play like memory movies over and over again in our heads, and some just disappear, *poof*, as if they never happened. And then there are some we keep, but we forget to remember them, so it's as if they never happened, either. Every memory I had of Talley was like a small treasure buried in the recesses of my brain. I wanted to keep track of them all.

"Do you remember anything else?" I asked Audrey.

"I remember how she'd come over and talk to us on her breaks. I thought she was the coolest person. I practically wanted to *be* her. Course, I had no idea what she was going to do to herself. It's always the ones you least expect. Well, not always, but in this case, I never would've guessed it'd end like this. Then again, I hadn't seen her in years, so maybe she'd changed. Did you expect it?"

"No, I didn't."

I should have.

"Wow," Audrey said. "And you guys were so close. You'd think you would've noticed *some*thing."

"I—"

"Oh, hi, Coop."

Cooper Davies, Juno's ex, slung an arm across Audrey's shoulder. "Hiya," he said. "Hey there, Sloane."

"Hey, Cooper," I said. I was trying to think of an exit line.

Audrey kind of rested her head on his shoulder. "Wait a second, you guys aren't . . . you guys are together?"

"Yep," Audrey said.

"I guess we just went public about it," Cooper added. "You can tell Juno if you want. I know you guys tell each other everything, and it'd probably be easier, coming from you. Also, I've been wanting to tell you—I'm sorry about your sister."

"That's what I was just saying," Audrey said. "How sorry I am. And you know, Sloane, you're super brave to be here right now. I can hardly believe that you're even standing. If my sister did something like that, I wouldn't be able to make it out of my room. Not that I have a sister. I've always wanted one, as you probably remember. My parents say they broke the mold after they had me, and now my mom is going through the quote-unquote change of life." She made air quotes around the phrase. "So it's not in the cards for me. At least you got to have Talley for seventeen years. Plus you know she's in a better place." She gazed upward, presumably toward heaven, but really toward the waffle-shaped ceiling. "That's got to be some comfort, right?"

"What are you even talking about?"

"I mean—"

"Sloane," Juno said. She took a breath. "And Cooper?"

"Hi, Juno," Audrey said. "Let me just slip out of this invisibility cloak so you can see me." She gestured as if taking off a sweater or jacket.

Juno's narrowed eyes shot bullets at Audrey. "What's going on here?" she asked.

"Audrey stopped me to talk about Talley," I said. "Then Cooper came over. I didn't know about . . ." I let my voice trail off and gestured toward them.

"It just happened," Cooper said. "I was going to tell you, but then I figured you were upset about Sloane's sister. The timing wasn't right. But now Sloane's been back all week, and—"

"And what?" Juno asked. "Talley's still dead, Cooper. And you're an asshole."

"C'mon Ju, let's—" I started. But then my phone buzzed. My hand turned instantly clammy. Before I even knew what was happening, it slipped from my grip and skidded across the floor. "Shit!"

"Look what you did," Juno said—to Cooper, to Audrey, maybe to both of them. I wasn't sure. There were too many people in the hallway, and my phone had seemingly disappeared, like a lost memory.

But how could a phone, a solid object, disappear like that? My eyes went hot with pressure. I was on my hands and knees, the scuff marks of a thousand footsteps blackening my palms. Juno dropped to the floor next to me, looking; though at one point, I saw her stop and call toward Cooper and Audrey, who'd begun to walk away. "The least you can do is help," she told them. Cooper bent to the floor, and Audrey did, too. But Audrey did just barely. She was only pretending to look, and I realized Mr. Stuart had been right not to cast her all those years ago. She was a terrible actress.

Finally, a guy picked my dusty phone up from the floor and handed it over to me. "This yours, Sloane?" he asked.

I didn't know his name, but he knew mine. When something

tragic happens in your life, you become someone people know about. They learn your name; they look you up in last year's yearbook so they can see what you look like. You get to be famous, in a way—not because you did anything special, but because your life is really sad.

"Yes, it's mine," I said, grabbing the phone and forgetting to say thank you. Adam's name flashed as a missed call. I pressed to redial him and started speed walking down the hall. I didn't say goodbye to anyone—not even Juno. Behind me I could hear her berating Cooper and Audrey. I bumped through the crowd, phone pressed to my ear. It rang once, twice.

"Answer, Adam. Dammit, answer," I said.

Three rings, four.

His voice mail picked up. "Hi, it's Talley's sister, Sloane, again," I said, when the message finished. "I'm so sorry I missed you. Please call back. Please."

I walked all the way to the back stairwell and pulled open the door. Our school is a long two-story building. There's a main stairwell in the center that everyone uses. But people rarely use the back stairwell. It's out of the way, and legend has it that a dead body was found there a few decades back. Once you've seen your sister's dead body, old legends like that lose their power. I sat down on the bottom step, gripping my phone in my sweaty palms, waiting for it to ring. To cover my bases, I also sent a text:

Hi, it's Sloane Weber. I'm here now if you can call back. Or you can text—whatever is easier.

A text message popped up and for the length of a heartbeat, I was filled with relief. But it was just Juno.

Where are you?

I didn't reply. It wasn't that I was mad at her for any reason. I had no reason to be mad at her, and I knew she was going through something, too. Finding out about Cooper and Audrey like that must've been awful for her. *That* was why I wasn't replying. I couldn't deal with anyone else's awful right then.

Another text popped up. Juno again: I'm worried about you.

And then: I'm looking all over. Please answer. I need to know you're okay.

I finally wrote back: I'm in the back stairwell.

The stairwell door opened a few minutes later. Adam still hadn't called back, but Juno had found me, and the tears started. "Oh, Sloane," she said, reaching for me. "I'm so sorry you had to deal with them. Can you believe they're together?"

"They deserve each other."

"I knew you were going to say that," Juno said, her voice quivering. "And maybe it's even true. But it still makes me feel awful."

"I know. I'm sorry. I'm sorry I left you there."

"It's okay," she said. She was rubbing my back, and I wished I could go back in time and be a little kid again, lying in bed, with Talley rubbing her hand up and down, up and down, lulling me to sleep. "It's all right. It's okay."

"Adam called," I said. "I missed his call because I dropped the phone. I called back, and texted, and he's not answering. What if I never hear from him again?"

"Not possible."

"Totally possible."

"He called you," she said. "That means he'll call again. Why don't we get out of here?"

I shook my head. "I know it's creepy in here," I said. "But it feels like the only safe place. I don't want to be around anyone else."

"I could take you home if you're not feeling well," she offered.

"Cut afternoon classes?"

"Yeah, why not? Plenty of people do it all the time. I know *you* don't. But I bet you won't get in trouble for it. If you want me to stay with you, I don't think I'll get in trouble, either."

"Yeah, probably not."

"Come on," Juno said, prodding me up. "Let's go."

I stood, with effort, and took a step toward the stairwell door. And then my phone buzzed in my hand.

chapter ten

"I TOLD YOU HE'D CALL!" JUNO CRIED.

"Hello?" I said. "Adam?"

"Yep, that's me. You're Sloane?"

"I am," I said. "I'm so happy you called back. Thank you so, so much."

"No prob. It's just—hang on." He paused, then said, "Yeah, I heard you the first time, *Mother*. I said I'm taking care of it." There was a scratchy sound like he was pressing a hand over the mouthpiece. A few seconds later he said, "Sloane?"

"Yeah. Is everything okay?"

"It's fine," he said. "Other than the fact that my mother is completely irrational. But listen, I got your text. I got all of your messages, actually. I would've gotten back to you sooner, but I thought you had the wrong number. Then I read what you said about your sister and—God, I really don't know what to say. I'm really very sorry."

"Thank you."

"Was it cancer?"

"Cancer? What? No."

"I guess everyone must be asking you how she died," he said.

"It's actually the first time anyone has asked me. People around here know."

Though a few people had asked me how Talley'd done it, and I thought that was an awful question.

I told Adam without him asking: "She took a handful of pills," I said. "We don't know how she got them. But that's what happened."

"That's awful," Adam said. "I'm sorry."

"I didn't want to put that part in a text," I told him. "I didn't want to even tell you on text that she'd died, but I didn't know how else to get you to write back—especially if you were trying to get in touch with her first. That's what I would've done instead of calling back someone I'd never met before. But my dad already disconnected her line, so if you tried—"

"Hang on," he cut me off. "I have to tell you—I didn't know her. That's why I figured you had the wrong number. But after that text, it seemed wrong to leave you hanging."

"But . . . are you *sure* you didn't know her? Her real first name was Natalie. Talley was a nickname."

"I only know one Natalie, and I saw her in school yesterday," Adam said. "I'm sorry. I wish I could help you."

"But maybe," I started. "Maybe someone else at your same

phone number knew Talley. Is it, like, a house line that you share with someone else?"

"It's my cell."

"Oh, right. You got my text. Of course. How long have you had it?"

"How long have I had my cell phone?"

"How long have you had this number?"

"Oh. Well, my parents gave me my first cell for my eleventh birthday, and I've had the same number the whole time. I'm seventeen now."

So he was my age. He'd had his cell phone for six years, give or take a few months. Could the person who'd had it before him have been someone significant to Talley? Someone who she hadn't spoken to in over half a decade, so she didn't know the phone number had changed? That didn't seem right.

But then, why would she have written down Adam's number if she didn't know him? Nothing made any sense.

I don't understand the puzzle, Talley. I need another clue.

"Sloane?" Adam said.

"I'm still here," I said. I gripped Juno's hand. "I'm just trying to figure everything out. Your area code—650—that's in the San Francisco Bay Area?"

"Yep. I'm in Menlo Park."

I'd seen Menlo Park on the map I'd studied of every town within the 650 area code. It was in San Mateo County.

"You live there? You didn't get the number and move somewhere else?"

"No, I've always lived in this town. I've even always lived in the same house."

"Me too."

"Out of curiosity," Adam said. "Where is—I can't remember the area code I dialed to call you. Where do you live?"

"I'm in Golden Valley, Minnesota," I told him. "Area code 763. Have you ever been here?"

"No," he said. "Maybe your sister wrote the number down wrong."

"Yeah, but even so, she probably got the area code right. Plus there were all these California things on her list, besides your phone number, like the species name for California grizzlies, and Bel Air. That's, like, several hundred miles from you, right? I looked it up on Google Maps."

"The Bel Air in Los Angeles County is hours away. But I assumed she meant the arcade place on El Camino."

"What's El Camino?"

"It's a street. If you drive on El Camino about ten minutes south of my house, you'll hit the Bel Air Arcade. They have go-karts, mini golf, that sort of thing."

Oh! Now we were getting somewhere. "And people hang out there late, like at midnight?" I asked.

"I don't know. I never have. I actually haven't been there in years. We used to have birthday parties there when we were little, but in the middle of the day. Which is not to say that they don't have things going on late night. They totally could. I've just never heard about it."

"There's another Bel Air," I said, and I gave Juno's hand a squeeze. Poor Juno. My palms were sweating buckets, but she hadn't let go.

Meanwhile, my head was spinning. Adam might not have known Talley, but he'd just cleared up one of the mysteries of the list. So even if his number was a wrong number, it was also a right one. I never would've figured out the Bel Air thing without speaking to him. Was that why Talley'd written down his number? What if I hadn't called him, or he hadn't called me back? It was terrifying to think about how easy it would have been to miss the connection I needed to make.

"Was there anything else on the list that you knew?" I asked.

"Mr. G's—that's a karaoke place in Belmont, which is also not that far from me."

"Thanks," I said. "I'll look it up and call over there. Anything else?"

"Uh . . . what was on the list again?"

Reciting Talley's list was like reciting my own phone number, or spelling out the letters of my name. I barely needed to think about it to say it.

"No, sorry," Adam said when I'd finished. "That's all I've got."

"Well, thanks," I said. "It's—"

"Wait," he said. "Actually—maybe there's one more. This is kind of a stretch, but that street I was telling you about, El Camino—it's El Camino Real, which is Spanish for 'royal road.' Maybe Talley meant the El Camino Diner."

"Do you mean a diner on El Camino, or is that the name of it?"

"Both," Adam said. "The things you remember from kindergarten Spanish class."

"I'll call them, too," I said. "I bet you're right. Talley loved plays on words, and games like that. Thank you."

"You're welcome."

"Just one more thing—I know you said you didn't know Talley. But may I text you a picture of her, just in case? She could have told you a different name." Talley used to do that, when we were younger. If we were in the mall, and a salesperson asked her name, she'd make up weird answers, like Tempest, or Fortune, or Ambrosia. "Maybe if you just see her—"

"I know what she looks like," Adam said. "I googled her before I called you back. There wasn't much about her online. I saw the obituary, but it didn't say a cause of death, which is why I asked."

Talley's obituary had been in our local paper, the *Golden Valley Patch*: *Natalie "Talley" Weber, 22, died on Thursday. She is survived by her father, Garrett, and her sister, Sloane. Her mother, Dana, predeceased her.*

"My dad asked them not to put in the cause of death," I said.

"I found a couple pictures of her, too," Adam said. "She was really pretty. I'm sorry if that comes off as stalkerish. What I'm trying to say is, if I'd met her, I would've remembered her. I know I didn't meet her." He paused. "And you can look me up, too, if you want. That way we're even. My last name is Hadlock."

"Okay," I said.

"Adam!" I heard a call from the background.

"I know!" Adam yelled back. He didn't cover the phone, which meant he was shouting in my ear, but then he lowered his voice again, speaking to me. "I don't want to rush you, but I actually have to get going, or else it's going to be a shit-slammer of a day."

"Ok—" I started. "Wait. What did you say?"

"I said this day is going to kick my ass," he said. "You take care of yourself, Sloane, okay? Bye now."

There was a click, and I knew he'd ended the call. I lowered my phone from my ear.

"So," Juno said. "It sounded like he was helpful even if he didn't know Talley, right?"

"Yeah. But . . ."

"But what?"

"It's so weird, Ju. He just said 'shit-slammer,' which is a phrase I only ever heard Talley say. She said it that last day. The last conversation we ever had, she said it. And I've never heard anyone else say it but her."

"I've never heard anyone say it, either," Juno said. "So maybe he did know Talley?"

"Yeah," I said. "I think he did."

chapter eleven

AS SOON AS ADAM AND I HUNG UP, I CALLED THE PLACES he'd identified on the list: the El Camino Diner, the Bel Air Arcade, and Mr. G's Karaoke. Mr. G's wasn't yet open, so I tried again a couple hours later. But when I got someone on the phone, the answer was the same as the answers I'd been given at each of the other places: "No, I've never heard of your sister."

The next day was Saturday. Juno was on Eddy duty. The one and only rule that Juno's parents ever gave her was she had to watch her eight-year-old brother the first Saturday of every month. (Technically, Eddy was Juno's half brother, but no one in her family ever pointed out that distinction.) Juno's mom and stepdad, Amy and Randall, were incredibly lax about every single other thing. Their kids could eat whatever they wanted, in whatever room they wanted. No one cared if they cursed. Once Juno came home drunk and puked into Randall's open hands. The next day her parents brought her hangover cures in bed.

I'm sure my dad thought if he parented that way, I'd end up running a brothel out of our basement while freebasing cocaine, or something like that. But Juno was one of the best people I'd ever known, and Eddy was totally adorable. Even if there wasn't a rule about it, Juno would want to spend quality time with him. I never minded joining them.

But when I walked into their family room that Saturday, Juno was fuming. "I'm stuck at home while Audrey is sinking her claws deeper into Cooper," she said. "Meanwhile, where is this kid I need to spend quality time with? Oh yeah, he's too busy playing his video games to even care that I'm here, which is exactly what I told my parents would happen when I asked for the night off. And for the record, I've never, ever asked to skip a night with Eddy before. So, would a little consideration for my social life be out of line? I don't think so."

"I don't think so, either," I told her. "But it's not like you could do anything about Cooper and Audrey even if you didn't have to watch Eddy tonight."

"Ugh!" Juno said. "God, what does he see in her? What does she have that I don't have?"

"A million things," I said. "And none of them are good."

"She's like one of those female octopuses who strangle the males to death when they're mating. Did you know they sometimes do that?"

"I did not."

"I read it in one of Eddy's animal-fact books."

"The animal facts of life," I said.

"Yep."

"So Audrey has claws, *and* she's an octopus?" I asked.

"She's every awful creature you've ever heard of," Juno said. "And yet, she has Cooper and I don't. I thought . . ."

"What?"

"This is going to sound dumb. But I thought we'd be together forever."

"It's not dumb at all, Ju. It's just, maybe, a little bit unrealistic."

"But people *do* marry their high school sweethearts," Juno said. "And now it could be him and Audrey."

"Or they could break up tomorrow."

"Audrey Davies," she said. "It sounds wrong—the way both her first name and his last name end in an *e* sound. But *Juno* Davies, now that has a certain ring to it, don't you think?"

"Personally, I've always liked Juno Kirkland," I said. "You don't have to change your last name when you get married. Your husband could even take your last name. There's no law against it."

I remember when Talley told me there wasn't a law. "But why do ladies take men's names if they don't have to?" I'd asked.

"That's what they call buying into the patriarchy, my little friend," she'd said.

"I guess I'm a traditionalist at heart," Juno said. "Hey, do you think it's about these?" She knocked the heel of her hand to her ear.

"Your cochlear implants? What about them?"

"Do you think that's why Cooper didn't love me?"

"You're being ridiculous," I told her. "Just because you have a little hearing issue—"

"It's a profound hearing loss. That's not little."

"And you had surgery to fix it, so now you can hear basically the same as everyone else."

"I don't hear the same as everyone else, and it looks weird, too."

"I don't even notice them," I said.

"You *want* not to notice them," she said, "but you *do* notice them. Everyone does. And if I don't wear them, I can't hear a thing. Cooper can't, like, whisper sexy things to me in the middle of the night, and what if he really wants to? I've been thinking about this, because it's just so hard to understand. I still wear his shirts to sleep, so I can feel close to him. And that's the thing—I felt closer to him, more connected, than I ever felt to another human—I mean, not counting you, of course."

"Of course I am," I said.

"But how is it possible that I felt a connection that strong to Cooper, but he'd rather shack up with the clawed octopus? Sometimes I worry that I'll be Juno Kirkland forever."

"Talley was planning to be Talley Weber forever," I said. "She thought it was buying into the patriarchy to get married. She didn't think she'd ever do it. I guess she was right about that."

"Oh, Sloane," Juno said. "I don't want to ask you how you are all the time, because I know everyone asks you that. But I worry about you—about how you are."

"I'm awful," I admitted. "I don't understand—how does the sun keep rising every morning, now that Talley is gone? How does the world keep turning without her? How come everything happens the same as always? Doesn't the universe know how important she was?"

"Oh, my poor Sloane," Juno said.

"I don't know if I can keep doing this. It's only been sixteen days and she's already getting too far away. The other day a lightbulb in the hall went out, and my dad put in a new one. Talley will never see the light from the new bulb. She'll never be here for the new anything." Now I was crying. "Even when I'm with other people, and they're talking about something else, I want to listen, but really I'm just thinking about Talley. I can't help it. And I'm obsessed with the whole Adam shit-slammer thing."

Juno rubbed my arm. "I hate when cute guys turn out to be liars," she said.

Naturally, we'd googled Adam, so we knew what he looked like. There was a baseball team photo online, and the names of the players were listed at the bottom. Adam was kneeling in the front row, but you could tell he was tall, because his shoulders came up past those of the other kneelers. Tall with dark hair. Maybe even tall enough to be a "large gentleman."

I wiped my face. "You think he's cute?" I asked.

"Of course."

"I didn't notice."

"Oh, Sloane, that's bull," she said. "First of all, he's totally your type, with that dark-haired, lopsided-grin thing that he's got going on. And second, even if he wasn't your type, he's objectively a good-looking person. Saying you didn't notice that is the same as saying you don't notice my cochlear implants. You might not want to notice, and you might think it's not important. But you noticed it all the same. He *may* even be cuter than Cooper."

I mock-gasped.

"Look, I know that Cooper isn't everyone's type," she said. "It doesn't matter to me. I may be deaf, but love is blind."

"Ugh, Juno," I said.

"I know, I know," she said. "I set off the cheese-whiz alarm."

"Big time."

"My point is—you noticed Adam is cute."

"Fine, I noticed," I said. "But I prefer guys who aren't pathological liars."

"It's possible he wasn't lying," Juno said. "'Shit-slammer' could be an expression people use in California, or Adam and Talley could have a friend in common who says it."

"Maybe. Either way, I just need to get out there so I can do some thorough detective work, but my dad would say I need to get over it. To move on."

"We'll get you out there," Juno said.

"I mean, just calling people up on the phone isn't enough. There's no guarantee that the people who pick up are the right people. Or, even if they are, that they know Talley's name. Some people might only know her by face. I need to get out there and show everyone her picture. It's the only way. It just seems like maybe . . . I don't know. You know Talley and her puzzles. I think this is what she wanted me to do."

Juno nodded. "We'll get you there," she said again.

"It's over two thousand miles from here. It would take us about thirty hours in the car, not counting stops to sleep and pee."

"I was thinking you should fly there. School's almost over. Let's book you a ticket."

"Yeah, right."

"I'm serious," she said. "I'll put your flight on my credit card. Your hotel, too."

"Ju—"

"I know you're going to say it costs too much, but it doesn't," Juno said. "Not to me."

"Even if it wasn't too much money, I have to be at the Hogans' with you the Monday after next," I reminded her.

"I can handle the first couple days on my own," she said. "You're my best friend. You're going through the worst thing in the world right now. There's nothing I can do to change that. But I can do *this*." She paused. "I mean, if our roles were reversed right now, what would you want to do?"

"I'd want to do whatever I could to help you," I said.

"You see?" she said. "Please. Let me do this."

"I still need to tell my dad *something*," I said. "There's zero chance he'd let me go if he knew the real reason. He wouldn't even drive me to Wayzata. I'm okay with lying to him. But I want him to at least know what state I'm in."

"How about we make up a contest and say you won an all-expenses paid trip?"

"But then if he googled it and couldn't find it, he might not let me go. He's pretty thorough about things like that—about making sure things are what they say they are, and there aren't any hidden contingencies and taxes you have to pay."

"Sloane, I need to ask you something, and I need you to answer me honestly."

"Okay."

"Do you want to go to California? Like, *really*? Because if you do, then we'll find a way to make this work. But you're coming up with a lot of reasons why you can't go. If you don't want to, that's okay, too. You don't have to."

"I *do* want to go," I said. "I have to go—for Talley. I didn't know how sad she was. I wasn't looking closely enough. Dean said she was special, and special has a way of hiding trouble. But I think that's just an excuse because we didn't see what we should have seen—*I* didn't see it. I wasn't paying close enough attention, and I can't let this list go, too."

"All right, then," Juno said. "We'll find a real contest. You don't have to actually win it. You just need to convince your dad that you did." She raised up her butt to pull her phone out of her back pocket, then elbowed me. "Come on, woman. Get out your phone."

I pulled my own phone out of my pocket and went onto Google. "Win a trip to California," I typed into the search bar. *Click.* A few million results popped up, and I began to make my way through them. There was a Palm Springs getaway, but the dates were wrong; a trip to wine country, but being underage, I wasn't eligible to enter; and a Disneyland vacation, but that one was for a family of four. Actually, everything I found was for at least two people. I guess even people who are going somewhere for free don't want to go alone.

The heading for the next link was: "Stanford Wins in Closing Seconds." It was an article about a football game, not a contest, but I stared at the words for a few seconds anyway.

I remembered Talley telling Dad that the novelist John Steinbeck had been a college dropout: *He started out at Stanford, but he never finished.*

Stanford was in Palo Alto. I knew from studying maps of the Bay Area that Palo Alto was the city adjacent to Menlo Park, where Adam lived.

I had an idea and typed "Stanford Summer Writing Program" into the search box.

The fourth link from the top was an application for a week-long writing intensive offered to high school juniors and seniors. There were three different sessions, and the first one was the week after next.

Eddy pounded in the room. "Sloane!" he cried. "You're here! Neato bandito!" I braced myself for the impact as he flung himself into my arms.

"Ooof," I said. "Eddy, you're bigger every time I see you."

"Is this a good surprise?" Juno asked him.

"Duh," he said. "It's the best!" He sat down in my lap and looked at my face. "Hi, Sloaney. Are you crying? Juno, I think Sloaney is crying." He reached up and softly swiped the tear from my cheek.

I smiled so Eddy wouldn't worry. And then, for no particular reason, I started laughing. "What's going on?" Juno asked.

"There's a weeklong writing program at Stanford," I said. "It's, like, practically next door to where Adam lives. It starts a week from Monday. "I could tell my dad I applied and got in and got a scholarship—including airfare—and fly out there," I said. "I mean, if your offer still stands."

"My offer still stands."

"What are you talking about?" Eddy asked.

"Sloane got accepted into a writing program," Juno told him. "Isn't that great? Isn't Sloane our favorite writer?"

"She is!" Eddy said. He pecked me on the cheek and bounced out of my lap. "I want pizza!"

"Trepiccione's to celebrate your acceptance?" Juno asked.

"Yes, please."

chapter twelve

I GOT TO WORK RIGHT AWAY, COMPOSING AN ACCEPTANCE letter to myself from Stanford. I sent it from Juno's email account, changed the home address, and printed it out. To the untrained eye, it looked official and legit.

Juno booked a flight for me from Minneapolis to San Francisco early Saturday morning. She reserved a hotel room at the Marriott in Menlo Park. Then she handed her credit card over. "You need to show this when you check in," she said. "If you have a problem, call me and I'll vouch for you. Okay?"

"Okay," I said. I put her card in my wallet. "You are the most amazing friend I've ever had."

As if she hadn't already done enough for me, Juno said she'd take care of telling the Hogans about my sudden change of plans. But of course it was up to me to tell my dad. I was nearly shaking with anxiety when I approached him on Sunday. He was sitting at his desk in the living room.

"Hey, Dad," I said. He looked up from the book he was reading and pressed his glasses up the bridge of his nose. "I have something to tell you."

"Oh?"

"It's nothing bad. It's just . . . you know how I'd wanted to go to that writing program at Hamline in August?"

Dr. Lee was teaching a writers' workshop at Hamline University in Saint Paul at the end of the summer, and I really wanted to go. I'd talked to Dad about applying. He hadn't exactly endorsed the idea. Tuition would eat up a good chunk of the money I'd be making from babysitting the Hogans, and he wanted me to put it away for college—real college, not a week-long summer program.

I had asked Dr. Lee about applying anyway. She said Hamline wasn't considering applications from students still in high school. You had to at least be a rising college freshman to take the class, so it was a moot point anyway.

"I remember the program," Dad told me.

"Okay," I said. "So, the thing is . . . I was thinking about how I still wanted to do something like that. It turned out I'm too young for Hamline, plus that's not till August anyway, and I don't want to wait that long. I looked online to see if there was anything else, and there's a writing program at Stanford University."

"Stanford? As in California?" Dad asked.

"Yes," I said. "Someone dropped out at the last minute, so I sent in the application. I know I should've told you first. I didn't think I'd get in. But I did. Plus, I got a full scholarship. Room, board, airfare, the works. It won't cost a thing for me to go. Look, here's the acceptance letter."

I handed him the fake email and watched his pupils move quickly back and forth across the page.

"Juno said she can handle the Hogan triplets on her own for a week," I said. "It'd be good for me to go. I haven't been focused on my writing, since Talley . . ." My voice trailed off. "The change of scene is probably exactly what I need right now. What do you think?"

He lowered the letter to his lap. I held my breath. "I think this is absolutely wonderful," Dad said.

"Really?"

"Really wonderful," he said. "You're putting yourself and your future first. I know that is the hardest thing in the world to do when you're grieving. I'm proud of you."

"Thank you," I said. The relief was enormous and I leaned down to hug him. He wasn't the huggiest of fathers, and I didn't usually initiate them with him, either. It hadn't been that way with Talley. Practically every time I walked through a room, we'd reach our arms out to each other. It was so natural, the way we fit with each other, almost like we'd been two halves of the same person. Hugging my dad felt awkward, like when you're clasping your hands together and you put the wrong thumb over the other. We didn't go together quite right.

"Speaking of my future," I said, "I have finals for the next three days. I better go study."

"Yes," he agreed. "You let me know if you need any help."

"I will," I said.

I went into my room and opened my statistics textbook. For the first time since Talley had died, I was actually able to concentrate on the words and figures on the page, I think because I had the ticket to California. I'd be going there in just six days, and visiting the actual places she'd written down on her list. I could relax and attend to my schoolwork. I doubt any of my friends thought studying was relaxing, but that's how it felt to me.

chapter thirteen

JUNO AND I TOLD OUR OTHER FRIENDS THE SAME THING
I'd told my dad, and that she'd told the Hogans: I got into a Stanford
writing program at the last minute, and the change of scene would
do me good. We felt that the fewer people who knew the truth, the
better.

She dropped me off at the airport on Saturday morning. After we
hugged goodbye extra hard, I walked into the terminal and showed
the security agent my ID and plane ticket. I took off my shoes, went
through the metal detector, and put my shoes back on. I got to the
gate exceptionally early. I'd been so afraid of traffic that I'd made Juno
leave about an hour before she thought we had to, and I had nearly two
hours before the flight would even be boarding.

In the past, BTD (before Talley died), I'd people-watch in
the name of story research. It was something I used to love to

do—observe people and gather story ideas. But nothing about any-one in the airport seemed nearly as interesting or important as my own life, my own real-life story. No matter what else the other airport people might have been doing—curing cancer, or plotting a space mission to Mars—were they traveling across the country guided by the cryptic list of a dead girl? My money was on no.

Finally it was time to board. I settled into my window seat and texted Juno that all was well, despite the fact that the man next to me was taking up the whole armrest between us. I pulled *Ulysses* out of my backpack to read, but before I cracked the cover, I grabbed my phone again to text Dad and let him know I was about to take off, because isn't that what someone who *wasn't* perpetrating the biggest lie she'd ever told her father would do?

Hey Dad. On plane now. Stanford or bust!

He wrote back: Safe flight. I'm proud of you.

I felt the squeeze of guilt, but it was too late to do anything about it, and even if I could have, I wouldn't have. I knew that. The captain came over the loudspeaker to say all electronics needed to be turned off and stored for takeoff. The plane engine roared louder. I gripped the armrest as we sped down the runway, just as I always did when-ever I was on a plane. *Please, let us get to California safely*, I thought.

No one wants to die in a plane crash. But for me, it was more than that. I needed to find out the answers. I *needed* to survive.

chapter fourteen

I TUGGED MY ROLLING SUITCASE THROUGH THE SAN
Francisco International Airport, a place I'd never been before, and
now here I was, completely on my own.

Back at home, everyone knew me and knew what had happened to me. Here, no one knew anything. And I knew nothing
about them. I could make up stories about them, but I'd never get
to know their true stories. It's amazing when you think about it—
we pass by so many people in our lives, and they all have stories we
never get to know.

I looked for signs leading me to the Caltrain. Juno had told me
to take cabs and put them all on her credit card. But when I'd studied Bay Area maps, it looked like the Caltrain stopped near almost
every place I needed to go—and it was much less expensive.

I couldn't find signs for it, though, and I ended up at the airport transportation help desk. A woman behind the counter pointed me to a bus stop. I needed to take a bus to the Caltrain, and then on to Menlo Park. "Have a good trip," she said.

"Thanks," I said. "And . . . can I ask you one more thing?"

"Sure."

"Have you seen this girl—the one in the background photo?" I held my cell phone out toward her. Talley was the girl in the picture, of course. Maybe she'd needed airport help and spoken to this same woman when she'd come to California, whenever that might have been.

It sounds too coincidental to be true. But Talley, lover of puzzles and statistics, had once told me that people underestimate the probability of coincidences. They think connections are unexplained miracles, when really they're just about math. "You think it's so cool when you meet someone who has your same birthday," Talley said. "What were the chances of *that* happening? But consider how many people you actually encounter, like thousands of people in your lifetime, and there are only three hundred and sixty-five days in a year—"

"Three hundred and sixty-six in a leap year," I'd interrupted.

"Right, and *of course* you're going to run into someone with the same birthday. We always overestimate the probability of winning the lottery, and underestimate that we'll have the same birthday as someone else we know."

But the woman behind the help desk counter shook her head. "Sorry, I haven't," she said. "Can I help you with anything else?"

"No, thanks," I said.

A bus to the train . . . I knew I could just take a cab, as Juno had suggested. It'd certainly be easier, and if Juno were here, that's what she'd tell me to do, and she'd tell me to charge it to her credit card.

But what would *Talley* do?

She would've taken the bus and train combo. It was probably what she *had* done, whenever she was here. It's not like she'd had access to Juno's credit card.

Oh, c'mon, Sloaners, I could hear Talley say. *You can do this. You can do hard things. This isn't even that hard. Great-grandma Nellie came all the way to the United States from Poland. Everyone else she'd ever known ended up dying in the Holocaust. She was all by herself. She didn't speak the language when the ship arrived in New York Harbor. But somehow she got to her uncle's house in Detroit. She learned English. She got married. She raised a family. Imagine that. Imagine if you were her.*

I could barely imagine it. It was nearly unimaginable that I was even related to someone who'd done all that. Somewhere, running through my veins, was the blood of someone brave beyond measure. I speed walked to the bus stop and boarded the bus to Millbrae, which was the bus the woman at the help desk had told me to take. From there, I transferred to the southbound Caltrain. The Menlo Park stop was walking distance to the hotel, and also to El Camino Real.

I'd texted Adam a few days before to let him know that I'd be in the area, making sure to sound like I wasn't suspicious of him at all. I was simply visiting to see the things on Talley's list. It had nothing to do with the fact that I also hoped that when he met me in person, he'd finally spill whatever other information he might have about Talley.

If he'd said he didn't think it was a good idea to meet, or made up some other excuse about being too busy, I was fully prepared to show up at his doorstep. He'd told me his last name, and (thanks to Google) I had his address, too. But he'd said yes, and suggested meeting at the El Camino Real diner for lunch on Sunday. You can meet me and taste those eggs from the list at the same time, he'd written.

I wrote back: Noon?

You're on, he replied.

As the train rolled closer to Menlo Park, I decided not to wait till tomorrow to check out the diner. I'd go by myself, today, and go back again for lunch on Sunday.

It was just half a block from the Menlo Park Caltrain station to El Camino Real. I made a left and rolled my suitcase another block and a half to the diner, a square silver building in between a Target and a place called Down Dog. A little bell jangled when I walked inside, and a woman's voice called out, "Sit anywhere you like!"

I looked around. Was there a clue hidden in here somewhere that would lead me to the next clue, like a note in a mailbox? But where would it be? The diner had a few other customers—three people at the counter, where a woman (the one who'd shouted out to me) was pouring coffee, an older gray-haired man reading a newspaper at a half booth, and a couple of women who were maybe in their thirties, trying to get their kids not to eat off the floor. I decided to sit in the booth in the far corner, because it was the best place from which to see everyone else. For all I knew, it was the very same booth that Talley herself had sat in. Maybe my butt was making an imprint on the same red pleather cushion where Talley's butt had once made an imprint of its own.

Now I was obsessing about butt imprints.

I checked under the table, just in case Talley'd left a clue taped to the underside. But nothing was there. It was possible Talley'd never sat at this table; or, if she had, she might have picked the other side. I switched sides, and the gray-haired man looked up from his newspaper to watch me. The other side didn't have as good a vantage point, and maybe Talley hadn't sat there anyway, so I switched back again.

The woman who'd been pouring coffee came by. "Hiya. What can I get you today?"

Her name tag read *Anna*. Her shirt was red like the booth cushions, and she had a long, blond braid that went all the way down her back.

The place mats doubled as menus, just like at the Good Day Café back home in Golden Valley. I hadn't even had a chance to look at all the selections yet, but that didn't matter. "Sunny's eggs, please," I said.

"Did you say you want *runny* eggs, dear?" Anna asked.

I glanced down at the place mat, then back at her. "You don't have something called Sunny's eggs?"

"We have eggs sunny-side up. Is that what you want?"

"Um . . . ," I said. Could Talley have written it down wrong? Or maybe I had the wrong diner. There could be a Royal Road Diner somewhere else, and it wasn't a play on words. But where?

After the conversation with Adam, I'd been so convinced that Talley had been to the Bay Area. But what if Adam had made connections that had nothing to with what Talley'd meant, and now I'd traveled two thousand miles to a place she had never been? Juno would be out all that money—all for nothing—and I'd be stuck here.

I didn't have to be stuck. Juno could switch my ticket.

But then, my dad thought I was going to Stanford, so how would I explain that? That I'd been kicked out? The daughter of Garrett J. Weber, expelled? Yeah, right.

Anna was staring at me. "The eggs?" she asked. "Sunny-side?"

"Yes, sure," I said. And then, because one of Dad's pet peeves was when people said *sure*, when the right phrase was actually *thank you*, I added: "Thank you."

"Anything to drink?"

"Water would be great," I said.

"Coming right up."

"May I ask you something first?"

"Yes, ma'am."

My phone was in my hand. When I'd called the diner a week ago to ask about Talley, the man who'd answered hadn't known Talley, but it was entirely possible that Anna did. I pressed a button to illuminate the screen. "Have you ever seen this girl? My sister? Her name was Talley."

I wondered if I'd ever get used to saying that my sister's name *was* Talley. I hoped not.

Anna shook her head. "I haven't," she said.

"Are you sure? She died, and if she . . ."

I didn't finish my sentence, but I was thinking, *If she asked you to keep a secret, you don't have to anymore.*

"Oh, I'm so sorry to hear that," Anna said. "What a terrible thing. I'll tell you something, though—you look a little familiar. You been in here before?"

"No," I said. "I'm from Minnesota. It's my first time here."

"I figured you were traveling, with all those bags."

"I just landed a little while ago. I came straight here from the airport because my sister—I think she knew this place. People used to say Talley and I looked alike, so maybe . . . I mean, you're sure you haven't seen her? That's maybe why I look familiar?"

"Nah," Anna said. "I can't put my finger on it, but I know I've seen a face like your face before. Let me think on it, and in the meantime, I'll get those eggs. White or wheat toast?"

"White," I said. I felt deflated as she walked away. It was stupid and unrealistic, but I'd honestly thought I'd walk into this diner, show off Talley's picture, and the person would say, "Of course! I'm so glad you're here, because I have a lot to tell you!"

Dr. Lee had once told our class that most worthwhile endeavors are harder than you expect them to be. She'd meant it about writing, but apparently it was also true about tracking down the meaning of the items on my sister's list. I crossed the aisle to the gray-haired man. He reluctantly lowered his paper to glance at my phone when I asked. "No, don't know her," he said.

There were a few other people in the restaurant, but I knew in my heart that they wouldn't know who Talley was, either, and I wasn't ready for additional disappointment. Plus, Anna was already back with my eggs. How come diner food always comes out so much faster than food anywhere else?

"Here you go, dear. Sunny-side eggs," she said brightly. "One might say they look like the sunshine with the bright-yellow circle in the center. Perhaps that's what your sister meant."

I knew it wasn't. Talley and I had long ago agreed that sunny-side-up eggs looked like breasts, but obviously I kept that to myself. "Thanks," I told Anna.

"Oh, dear. I still need to get you some water."

"And I need a refill on my coffee," the gray-haired man said.

"Actually, may I have a Coke with no ice?" I asked.

"Yes, ma—" she started, but then she stopped and slapped her palms together. "I knew you reminded me of someone! I have another customer who orders her Coke with no ice, too."

"You mean my sister?" I asked Anna hopefully. Talley was a no-ice-in-her-soda person as well.

"No. As I said, I don't remember ever seeing her. Unless that was an old picture that you showed me. The woman I'm thinking of is a bit older."

I shook my head; it was a recent photo of Talley—the most recent one I had of her, taken in early December. Talley wasn't looking directly at the camera, and she was laughing at something. I couldn't remember what.

But had she really been happy in that photo? Now every good memory I had of Talley was tinged with suspicion: Was it real? Had I missed that she'd been in despair all along?

"Of course *I* think she's still a young woman," Anna went on about her customer. "She's forty-ish, maybe a year or two older. I'm sure that seems old to you, but I must have twenty-five years on Elise."

"Elise?" I said. "Her name is Elise?"

"Yes, ma'am."

"What's her last name?" I asked.

"Oh, I don't know. We're more of a first-name-basis kind of place. I'm Anna." She tapped her name tag. "And you are?"

"Sloane," I said. "Can you tell me anything else about Elise?"

"Well, you already know her preferred drink," Anna said. "She works next door at the yoga studio."

"Downward Dog?"

"Down Dog," she said. "Comes in most every day for lunch and a Coke—no ice. But I haven't seen her in a bit. I wonder what happened to her—"

"Maybe she thought it took too long to get a cup of coffee," the gray-haired man said.

"Oh, right," Anna said. "Sorry. I'll be right back. I'll get your Coke, too. And try those eggs. If they're too cold now, I'll bring you some new ones. Okay, Sloane?"

"Mm-hmm," I said.

But I didn't want eggs—not the ones on my plate or any others. My mind was racing. My stomach was doing somersaults. I only knew one Elise, and I didn't even know her. I just knew *of* her.

I didn't want to get my hopes up and think that it was the

same Elise, my mother's sister, my aunt, because I knew it probably wasn't. A woman named Elise who happened to look a bit like me, who was around the right age. Chalk it up to Talley's birthday example: coincidence is much more likely than you'd think. It probably wasn't her. . . .

I pulled Google up on my phone. She could've gotten married and changed her last name by now, caving to our patriarchal society. Or she could've moved away, and then whatever her last name was, it wouldn't matter.

I typed in her name and pressed search. A few seconds later, there she was. Elise Bellstein, in Redwood City, California.

124 Crescent Street. Redwood City, California.

CRESCENT STREET.

Oh. My. God.

Please, oh please. Let her still live here. Don't let her have moved away.

Her home number was listed, and I clicked the number and pressed my phone to my ear.

"Hello?"

"Elise Bellstein?" I asked.

"Yes?" a woman replied.

"Sorry," I said. "Wrong number."

I don't know why I did that. My hands were shaking as I lowered the phone from my ear. Anna arrived with my Coke. "You all right, dear?"

"I'm fine," I said.

I didn't feel fine at all. I felt . . . How did I feel? I didn't know.

There were so many feelings swirling inside me, I couldn't even begin to name them.

My phone started to ring, and the number that popped up on the screen was the number I'd just dialed.

Elise Bellstein was calling me back.

"Hello?" I said.

"Sloane," came the voice. "Sloane, is that you?"

"Yes," I said. "It's me."

chapter fifteen

LONG AGO, TALLEY HAD TOLD ME DAD AND AUNT ELISE
had had a falling-out. Aunt Elise blamed Dad for Mom's accident,
Talley said. It didn't make sense, since it was an *accident*. Unless
Aunt Elise blamed Dad for the fact that Mom was in Minnesota to
begin with—wrong place, wrong time. I took Dad's side. He was
our remaining parent; he was the grown-up; he was in charge. If
he wasn't speaking to our aunt, then Talley and I weren't, either.

Except, apparently, Talley *was* speaking to her, and I couldn't
shake my anger about it. *How could you have kept our aunt from me,
Talley?*

Obviously Talley wasn't there to defend herself. I had no way
to release my anger—no person to fight with. So the anger just
swirled around in my brain in the cab ride to Aunt Elise's house,
getting bigger and bigger. Big and raging enough to make my head

fly off my neck. I fixated on that image—my neck torn, and blood and fire, and my face spinning into the sky, leaving a trail of black smoke behind.

"Miss," the cabdriver said. "We're here now."

I hadn't bothered with the train this time, because I wanted to get to Crescent Street as soon as possible. But I paid in cash. Even in my incredibly distracted state, I was trying not to use Juno's credit card until I had to.

I walked up the little stone path to Aunt Elise's front door. She lived on the left side of a rose-colored townhouse with scalloped roof tiles. My anger was waning, and in its place was a feeling of cold dread. This was not going to be a happy reunion. *Here I am, your long-lost niece. And by the way, the only reason I'm here is because your other niece is dead.* I hadn't told Aunt Elise over the phone, but in person there'd be no avoiding it.

I put down my bag, wiped my palms on my jeans, and rang the bell. It took so long for Aunt Elise to open the door that I considered dragging my bag back out to the curb to check the street sign, but then the door swung open, and there she was.

We stared at each other, Aunt Elise and I. I searched her face for the things in her that Anna had seen in me. The slope of her nose, maybe. Her straight eyebrows. She had brown eyes, and mine were green. There was something there, the familiar look of someone you know; but if I'd just passed her on the street, I wouldn't have recognized her.

Aunt Elise bridged the gap between us and enveloped me in a hug. It was a little awkward because another thing about her was that she was on crutches. The bottom of her right leg was in a complicated-looking brace.

"My God," she said. "I haven't seen you since you were two years old. Whenever I picture you, you're the little girl in the red dress you wore on your birthday. I keep those photos in an album right on the coffee table, so I can reach them whenever I want. And I do—often."

She teetered a little bit. "Are you all right?" I asked.

"Oh, that's a loaded question, isn't it?" she said. "Come inside. It's easier for me if we can sit down and talk, if you don't mind."

"I don't mind," I said, and followed her as she hobbled to the living room, making small talk about her crutches. "It seems so silly now, but when I was a little kid, I thought crutches were the coolest. I envied the girls who broke their legs, because they'd get a cast with all our signatures and a gym pass, plus they got a pair of these things. I never knew how they dig into your armpits. I'm getting armpit blisters! That is probably not anything you need to know about me."

In my old life, BTD, I might've pulled out my phone and made some notes about armpit blisters, because that would've been a good detail for a story—maybe. But at that moment I was taking in the details of Aunt Elise's house. The whole downstairs was carpeted in a light gray, the kind of color that goes with everything. There was a floor-to-ceiling wall of bookshelves behind a red-and-white-striped couch. The coffee table matched the wood of the shelves.

I held Aunt Elise's crutches for her as she lowered herself onto the couch. "Ooof," she said. "I always forget this isn't easy any-more."

"What happened?"

"A friend sent me flowers for my birthday. After they'd died, I was putting the vase back on top of the fridge." She waved a hand in the direction of the kitchen, and I glanced over, but while I could see into the kitchen a little bit, the fridge itself was blocked by a wall. "I'd climbed up onto the counter to put it up there, and then instead of climbing down, like any sane person would, I jumped down. Compound fracture of my right tibia. I needed surgery, traction, the whole nine yards."

"I'm so sorry."

"It doesn't matter. I'm so happy to see you; just looking at you makes this injury feel like nothing. There's so much I want to talk to you about. I don't even know where to begin."

But I knew where we had to begin. "I have something to tell you," I said. "And it's the worst thing in the world." Aunt Elise moved a hand toward mine. Her crutches slid to the floor, but nei-ther one of us moved to pick them up. "Talley's dead. She died—by suicide."

I'd read that that was how you were supposed to say it. Not: *She committed suicide.* But: *She died by it.* The word *committed* makes it sound like a crime, something Talley did willfully, which was why we'd been met by a member of the Golden Valley police force at the hospital. But, in reality, someone who dies by suicide is probably someone suffering from a mental illness. It's a medical condition, a potentially fatal one. No one would choose to be sick, so it's not willful. You wouldn't say someone "committed" cancer. You'd say they died from it.

I understood that. As a writer, I agreed with the importance of choosing the right words. But no matter how I said it, it still broke my heart.

"I know, sweetheart," Aunt Elise told me. "I know." She began to cry, and I did, too. It went on for a while, both of us weeping. Aunt Elise kept her hand on mine the whole time. I was wiping at my face with my free hand, and she was wiping at her face with her free hand. If my face looked anything like hers, then I was a wet, mottled mess. Finally, we were slowing down. From my end, I wasn't any less sad. I was just so tired. You can't cry that hard forever. You have to cry, and gather your strength a bit, and then you can cry again.

I sniffed, and the sound was louder than I'd thought it would be. Aunt Elise said, "Let me get you a tissue. I need one, too."

"I'll get them," I said. "Just tell me where."

"You can just grab some toilet paper from the powder room. It's closer—the door to the left of the stairs."

The wallpaper in Aunt Elise's powder room had little butterflies all over it, like Talley's tattoo; though these butterflies were lilac, not blue. I undid the roll of toilet paper from the holder and brought it out to the living room. Aunt Elise tore off a piece and blew her nose. She was a soft blower. When Talley blew her nose, she made a great big honking sound. She was so little and so pretty, it was an unexpectedly loud sound, and she was impressively unselfconscious about it. Oh, to move through life the way Talley had.

Meanwhile, I was alive and she was dead. It didn't make any sense.

Aunt Elise crumpled the used toilet paper inside another clean sheet of toilet paper, and left it on the coffee table.

"Were you in touch with Talley the whole time?" I asked.

"Just the last six months, really. She called me right before the new year."

"And then—did she send you a note? How did you know what happened?"

"Your father called me," Aunt Elise said.

"You were in touch with my whole family except me?"

I knew it shouldn't have mattered, given everything else. But it did matter. It was a feeling like when you walk into a crowd of people and they all go silent. You don't know the joke, but you know the joke is on you.

"I wasn't in touch with your father," Aunt Elise said. "But he thought I should know. He called on a Friday."

"She died on a Thursday," I said. "Three weeks and two days ago."

Aunt Elise nodded. "He said the funeral was on Monday, in case I wanted to be there and say goodbye. I'd just had surgery. I was still in the hospital, and the doctor said there was absolutely no way I could travel. I wish I'd been there—not just for Talley, but for you, too. I knew I was practically a stranger to you. But still, I thought maybe you'd need me to hold you up."

What I'd really needed was Talley. Every time I'd ever gone through anything, she'd been there. And now I was going through the worst thing, and I needed her more than ever. It's the catch-22 of losing the most important person you've ever known: they're not there to help you through it. "You could've at least called," I told Aunt Elise, and I couldn't keep the anger out of my voice. "Or you could've asked Dad if you could speak to me after he called you."

"I *did* ask him," she said. "He thought it would upset you too much, which made sense to me at the time."

"You guys worried that if I spoke to you I'd get upset?" I asked, incredulously. "Nothing was going to make me more upset than I already was. 'Upset' isn't even the right word. I use that word when I get a bad grade, or if I'm not invited to a party. But what I was feeling—what I still feel—there aren't any words."

"There aren't any words," Aunt Elise repeated.

"It hurts so much. It's so big. And the worst part of it is, it's got to be nothing compared to the kind of pain that Talley was in, and I didn't even know it. That's what . . ."

"That's what *what*?" my aunt asked.

I was going to say, *That's what kills me.* "Nothing," I said.

"I'm sorry I wasn't there for you," Aunt Elise said. "I should've been. I told myself I'd call you after a little bit of time passed. Maybe after the summer, when you weren't mourning so freshly. But, then, I know from experience that mourning always feels fresh. Even when years have passed, sometimes I'll be perusing the Häagen-Dazs section in the supermarket, and I'll see Dana's—your mom's—favorite flavor, and I'll start to reach for it, like I should have it in the house for her, and then it'll hit me that she's gone. I've left the supermarket empty-handed more than once, because I was missing her so much, I couldn't possibly wait on the checkout line like I was a regular person."

It occurred to me for the first time: Aunt Elise and I were both younger sisters who'd lost our older sisters. How had I not realized that till just now?

"I'm not doing a very good job of comforting you," Aunt Elise said. "I should tell you it gets easier. And it does, sort of. It starts to feel normal."

I wasn't sure if normal sounded better, or just like a different version of unbearable.

"What flavor ice cream was my mom's favorite?" I asked.

"Mocha chip." She paused, took a deep breath, and let it out again. "My God, look at you. You're so beautiful."

"Anna at the diner thought that I looked like you."

"That may be the best compliment of my life."

If Anna had thought that Aunt Elise looked like Talley, that would've been a real compliment. Talley was so beautiful. We had similar features, but I was the ordinary version and she was the extraordinary one.

"How did Talley know where to find you?" I asked. "I thought you lived in Virginia." That was where Mom had grown up and gone to college, and where she and Dad had met. When Dad's job transferred him to Minnesota, she moved with him.

"It's not hard to find someone, if you want to find them," Aunt Elise said. "Your dad found me when he needed to tell me about Talley. Though now that I think about it, he called my cell phone number, which hasn't changed from back when Dana was alive. Talley said she'd been googling me every so often for years, so she'd always known where I was. She said she was going through a hard time and she needed to get away."

"She lost her job at Bianca's," I said. "But that must've been *after* she called you, because that was just a couple months ago, and she moved back home."

"Actually, she quit."

"No, she didn't," I said. "They fired her."

But who would've fired Talley? She was the most charming and capable person in the world.

"She told me she quit," Aunt Elise said. Her voice was soft and gentle. "Because of Dean."

"Dean?" I said. "That doesn't make any sense. Talley broke up with him her senior year of high school. They were going their separate ways, and she didn't think they should do that with strings attached. That's what she told me."

"She told me that, too," Aunt Elise said. "But she also told me that Dean got into another very serious relationship right after that, with a girl he met in college, and he called Talley to tell her they got engaged—"

"Wait a second," I said. "I just saw him at her funeral. He's *married*?"

"I don't know if it happened yet," Aunt Elise said. "Or if they broke it off. But the news of it really hurt your sister. There was Dean, a college graduate, and soon-to-be married. She felt like he'd gotten ahead of her, like she was losing some sort of race."

"But there was still time for her to do all of those things," I said. "Dad kept telling her that—I told her, too."

"And so did I," Aunt Elise said. "But for Talley, who'd always been effortlessly ahead of her friends, it was a shock to her system. She didn't know how to handle it. I think that in the back of her mind, she'd thought that she could have Dean again if she wanted. Now that door was closed. It wasn't exactly that she wanted him back. She just wanted the chance to have him back. And she worried that made her a bad person."

"Talley a bad person? Impossible."

"She asked me if she could come out here," Aunt Elise said. "Of course I said yes. Talley said she didn't want you and your dad to know. She was over eighteen, legally an adult, and your father and I . . . let's just say we have a complicated history of communication."

"I know that. How long was she here?"

"A couple months."

Months.

"At first she stayed close to home," Aunt Elise said. "I took a few days off from work to be with her. But she started venturing out. I had her meet with my therapist a couple times. She seemed to be doing better when she was out here. She got to know my neighbors, the Garfields. They're an older couple and they don't get around as easily as they used to. They asked Talley if she'd mind picking up their prescriptions from the pharmacy one day, and after that, she started borrowing their car in exchange for various errands. It was good for them; it seemed good for her. I didn't expect her to stay forever, of course. But she made the decision to leave very abruptly. She didn't even say goodbye. I came home to a note from her that she had left for the airport. She had a flight home to Minnesota that night. I called her immediately, and I was able to catch her before she got on the plane. I didn't know what had happened. All she'd say was she was just ready to go home."

"That's so Talley. Once she made a decision about something, that was it. She wanted to put it into action as soon as possible."

"I didn't know anything was wrong. If I had, I would've called your father. I thought it had actually been good for her, being here. I didn't know she was going to hurt herself. I'm so sorry."

I pictured Talley in her bed, asking me to stay home and play hooky with her for the day. I'd played that movie in my head a hundred times, a thousand times. If only I could wish my way to a different ending.

"Do you know who Adam Hadlock is?"

Aunt Elise shook her head.

"His number was on a list Talley left behind," I said. I pulled it out of my bag and handed it over.

"Talley used to go on these drives," Aunt Elise said. "She'd be gone all day, sometimes all night. I thought maybe she'd met someone. I hoped she had."

"Adam swore he didn't know Talley, but then he used an expression I'd heard her use—shit-slammer."

"I've never heard that one before," Aunt Elise said. "It's a good expression, though. Even if you've never heard it before, you know exactly what it means."

"Yeah, it's good," I agreed.

"I see Dean made her list."

I nodded. "I just don't understand," I said. "Why did Talley come out here without telling me? We were so close. And you were . . . practically a stranger."

"Sometimes it's easier to confide in people who are practically strangers," Aunt Elise said. "I think that's why, among other reasons."

"What other reasons?"

Aunt Elise shook her head. "I'm sorry, sweetheart. My brain is so foggy right now. I took a painkiller right before you called, and I need to lie down."

"Oh, I didn't mean to impose. I can head to the Marriott now."

"Save your money. Stay here instead."

"I couldn't," I said. "With your leg—the last thing you need is a houseguest."

"Actually, that's probably the thing I need most. You could really help me out. I have to take a cab every time I need to pick up some food, or go to the doctor."

"I don't drive," I told her, embarrassed. "I can't really help with that."

"Oh, that's okay," she said quickly. "You don't need to. Your company would make me so happy." She paused. "As long as you want to—and if it's okay with your father."

"I'll call him while you sleep," I said.

"There's a little guest room up there with its own bathroom and a pullout couch, if you want some privacy for the call." She lay back against a throw pillow. "I'm going to dream that it all works out."

"Talley used to tell me to do that. If I was worried about something and couldn't sleep, she'd tell me to think about it working out just the way I wanted it to, that way I could dream about the solution."

"Your mom used to tell me the same thing," Aunt Elise said, and then she closed her eyes and she was asleep.

chapter sixteen

"GOOD NEWS," I TOLD MY AUNT. "DAD SAID IT'S FINE FOR me to stay here."

"Oh," she said, pressing a hand against her chest. "That is *great* news. Tell him I said thank you."

"I will," I told her.

Of course I'd do nothing of the sort. I hadn't called my father at all, though I had texted to tell him that I was settling into things at Stanford. The campus is beautiful, I wrote to him, because I could tell from photos on the internet that it was.

Dad replied: Give me some deets, as the kids these days say. Name of dorm? Name of roommate?

A quick internet search of buildings at Stanford provided a dorm name: Branner Hall. And as for the roommate, I plucked a name out of thin air, the way I did when I was writing a story, and made up a person who suddenly seemed real to me. Isabella Lopez, I wrote. She's from Spain, and she's six feet tall. I took the top bunk because if she were sitting up there her head would scrape the ceiling.

With "deets" like that, he'd never suspect I was anywhere but where I claimed to be.

The next morning, I texted Adam to let him know that we didn't need to go to the diner after all, since I'd already been there.

The instant I sent the text, I regretted it. A diner is the perfect place for a picky eater like me. So I sent another text: But if you want to go there, that's fine with me!

My phone pinged with his reply: Let's shake things up then. If ur only in town for a week, I'm not gonna make u eat diner food 2x.

I offered to take the Caltrain and meet him wherever he wanted to go. (*Please, don't say sushi*, I thought to myself. *And no Indian food, or seafood. And also, not one of those places that only serves salad. Why, oh why, did I have to say anything about not going to the diner?*)

Adam said it'd be no problem to pick me up, and after a little back-and-forth with me saying he didn't have to do that, and him saying it really was no problem, I sent along Aunt Elise's address. As I got ready to go, I could hear a voice in my head, telling me to wear a cute top with my jeans, maybe a V-neck to show (a tasteful amount of) cleavage. *And how about some blush?* the voice said.

I was used to hearing Talley's voice in my head, but this wasn't Talley. It was me. My own voice.

But I hadn't come all this way to flirt with Adam. I put on the plainest shirt I'd brought—a crewneck (no V). I didn't put on any makeup, and I pulled my hair into a ponytail. I was going for the look of a girl who didn't care about anything beyond information gathering.

I waited outside on the front steps. Adam pulled up in a bright-blue car. I stood and he got out of the front seat. He *was* cute—cuter than his picture. Tall with a mop of curly dark hair, dark eyebrows thick as caterpillars, and exceptionally light eyes. Inwardly, I reminded myself that none of that mattered.

He loped toward me. "Hey, I'm Adam," he said. "Obviously."

"I'm Sloane," I said. "Thanks for coming to pick me up."

"Ah, no biggie," he said. "You did me a favor, actually. My parents are on me about my summer job—about the fact that I don't have one. This morning they told me they'd made the executive decision that I'll be working at my mother's office starting tomorrow. Unbeknownst to them, I've made the executive decision not to show up."

"What does your mom do?" I asked.

"She's a lawyer—and not the noble kind doing pro bono work," he said.

"My dad works in a law firm, too. Not as a lawyer. He's the IT guy."

"But you know about law firms," he said. "So you know the struggle."

"The struggle is real," I said.

"It sure is. Ready to get going?"

"Sure. Where?"

"That depends . . . what have you eaten since you've been here?"

"Just eggs at the diner," I said. "And we ordered in pizza last night."

"Round Table pizza?"

"I think it was called Amici's. But if you want pizza, that's fine with me."

"Nah," he said. "There's a good place to eat right by the San Francisco Bay. The view is cool. Sound good?"

"Sounds good," I said.

We got into the car. Adam backed out of the driveway and made a left turn off Crescent and out of Aunt Elise's townhouse development. "Can I tell you something without you thinking I'm completely insane?" he asked.

"I don't really know the answer to that question before I hear what you have to say."

"Hmm . . . well, I'm just going to risk it and tell you. On the way over here, I stopped at a red light, and I happened to glance at the car next to me. Get this—the driver was bandaged from head to toe."

"You could see down to his toes?"

"Okay, fine. All I saw was head to torso, but that was all bandaged. The only places that weren't were little slits for his eyes, nose, and mouth. It was one of those times when you're pissed to be alone, because no one is witnessing it with you. So how can you be sure you're really seeing what you're seeing?"

"You could've been hallucinating," I said.

"You better hope I wasn't. A hallucinating driver doesn't sound like the safest choice. But I swear it happened."

"Isn't that just what someone who was hallucinating would say?"

"Yeah," he said. "You're right. And get this—the guy in the passenger seat? Also a mummy. I couldn't stop staring at them. They saw me staring, and I rolled down the window—*your* window, because that's the side of the car they were on. I was hoping the driving mummy would roll down his and tell me what was going on."

"Who even knew that mummies could drive?" I said.

"Well, these were clearly not the Ancient-Egypt kind of mummies where they drain the blood and remove the internal organs," Adam said.

I sucked in my breath.

"Sorry," Adam said. "Too much information?"

"I guess I knew all that already. But I don't like to think about it too much."

"Well, anyway, this guy had a working body. His bandaged hands were on the wheel, and presumably his bandaged feet on the gas and the brake."

"So what happened? What'd he say?"

"Nothing. That's the whole story. The light changed. I didn't even notice, because I was busy staring, but the guy behind me honked, and I hit the gas. I tried to follow them, but the flow of traffic did not work out in my favor."

"Maybe they were in a fire, and they were bandaged because of the burns."

"I don't think so," Adam said. "My dad's a doctor, and he said his ER rotation was the worst, because every so often a burn victim would come in. If it was just ten or twenty percent of the body, it was bad, but not too bad. But some people were in fires that totally engulfed their whole bodies. The burns would be, like, ninety percent. You don't recover from that. You certainly don't drive with those kinds of burns."

I shifted uncomfortably in my seat, feeling a weird ache for those unknown burn victims that Adam's father had treated. Talley would no doubt play Imagine If about it, and tell me I should appreciate my unscarred, working body—and I did appreciate it. "Okay," I said to Adam. "They weren't burned. But maybe they were actors dressed up as burn victims, on their way to the set."

"If they're actors, then wouldn't they have a driver to take them to the set? And wouldn't hair and makeup and all mummification happen there?"

"It could be a low-budget film where they have to do it themselves," I said. "Or it could be some kind of Halloween thing. I know that's months away, but some people like to get a jump start on things. Like how Christmas decorations go up before Thanksgiving."

"Plausible," he said.

"Or they could be filming a video or a commercial or something that will be ready to air by Halloween."

"You're really good at coming up with different scenarios," Adam said.

"Oh, thanks," I said. "I like making up stories."

"But we'll never know the truth."

"I guess we won't."

"And if we tell anyone, they won't believe us. They'll think we were both hallucinating. So this is our mystery."

"Except I wasn't even there," I reminded him. "It's just *your* mystery."

"That's right. Well, like I said, it sucks to be alone in a car when you see something like that. So I'm happy to share it with you."

He glanced my way and gave me a lopsided grin. For a second, I felt a flutter in my chest, and I nearly forgot the point of my being with him. But then he turned into a large parking lot, and right there in the center of a circular driveway was the California state flag flapping in the breeze.

A white flag with the words *California Republic* printed across the bottom, and a big brown bear in the center.

Ursus arctos Californicus.

"Where are we?" I asked.

"The marina at Grizzly Cove," Adam said.

Grizzly Cove.

Grizzly.

As if the flag wasn't on-the-nose enough.

"The restaurant at the clubhouse overlooks the bay," he said. "I thought it'd be a nice place to have lunch. Okay by you?"

"The flag has the California grizzly on it," I said.

Was that why he brought me here? Because he'd been here with Talley? How could he deny that he'd known her? Was he in on her game?

"Oh, man," he said. "Your sister's list, right?"

"Right."

"You don't by any chance have the list with you, do you?" he asked.

"I do."

"May I see it?"

I reached for the bag at my feet and pulled the list out from between the pages of a notebook. I'd pressed it between the pages, because that seemed better than keeping it folded in my pocket, from a preservation standpoint. I hadn't laminated it yet. It was on my to-do list, but I kept putting it off, because I still wanted to be able to run my fingers over Talley's fingerprints.

Adam took the list from me. Now his fingerprints were touching Talley's. I watched his profile as he read. Once when I was little and Talley was babysitting, I wandered into the den, where Talley was playing poker with her boyfriend. Not Dean. This was pre-Dean. Her boyfriend freshman year of high school—a guy named Eric. Talley invited me to play with them, and she explained the fundamentals of the game, like how many cards I'd get, and what cards to keep, and how much each of the different-colored chips was worth. Then she said, "You don't get to see your opponents' cards, but there's a way to tell what they have. Every player has their 'tells'—things they unconsciously do that can give you a clue as to what kind of hand they have. Like when Eric thinks he has a very good hand, he stacks his chips in neat piles."

"I don't do that," Eric said. But then he glanced down at his chips and saw he'd made neat little piles, and he messed them up.

"People can tell you things without making a sound," Talley

told me. "Pay attention to the details."

But I couldn't tell a thing about Adam. He finished reading Talley's list and moved to give it back.

There was a coffee cup sitting in the holder between our two seats. Adam swept his arm toward me and knocked it over.

"Oh, the list!" I cried, grabbing it.

"Sorry, sorry, I'm so sorry," Adam said. "Shit, your pants are soaking. I think I have napkins."

I didn't care about my pants. I was holding the list above my head like I was trying to keep it from drowning. A corner of the paper had torn off when I'd grabbed it. It didn't have any writing on it, but still, where was it? Every inch of that piece of paper mattered to me, and I wondered if Adam had done it on purpose. Had he been aiming for the list instead of my left leg? If so, why? Was he mad at Talley, or was he trying to punish me?

"Here," he said, holding out a fistful of napkins. "I really am very sorry."

I put the list between the pages of my notebook again, and back in my bag. Only when it was safely out of his reach did I take the napkins and pat down my thigh.

"We don't have to stay here if you don't want to," he said. "If, you know, the flag is too upsetting."

"No," I said. "This is fine." I unbuckled my seat belt and climbed out of the car, and Adam followed my lead.

chapter seventeen

ADAM HAD THE KIND OF CAR THAT RAN ON ELECTRICITY instead of gas. I didn't realize that until he walked around to plug it into a charging station. I'd never been in an electric car before, and I was curious about it, but I didn't ask any questions. That wasn't the kind of information gathering I was here for.

"Are you starving?" Adam asked. "We could check out the boats, if you want. But if you're starving, we can eat first."

"I'm not starving," I said. The last time I'd been starving had been before Talley died.

The breeze kicked up and I folded my arms across my chest. "I really am very sorry about your pants," he said. "Are you cold?"

"I'm fine." As long as the list was fine, I was fine. But I still felt shaky from the near miss of it. Lamination was happening as soon as this lunch was over. I couldn't take any more chances.

We walked across the parking lot to a pathway that led to the docks. There were rows and rows of docks, and a couple dozen boats tied up in each row, swaying in the breeze. Had Adam done this same walk with Talley? What did she think about it?

Since she'd died, I'd tried to look at things the way she would've, tried to see things Talley's way.

"Don't you think it's weird that this place is called Grizzly Cove?" Adam said, breaking the silence that had grown between us. "Grizzlies aren't exactly aquatic animals."

In my googling of California grizzlies, I'd seen pictures of them wading into the water, spearing fish with their bare hands. "Bear hands," Talley would've said, enjoying my accidental pun. And she would've teased me, saying how else were they supposed to catch fish? With fishing rods and tackle?

"Do you want to know why?" Adam asked me.

"Sure."

"I should warn you, it's a pretty intense story."

"Duly warned," I said. "Go on."

"Okay. So. Legend has it that about a hundred years ago, a California grizzly attacked a guy named Terrance J. Tenterhook, right here on this property."

"Oh, God, really?" I asked. A chill moved up my spine. I'd already crossed my arms to the cold, but now I pulled them tighter. Maybe a walk on the dock had been a bad idea. *California grizzlies are extinct*, I reminded myself.

"Apparently Terrance thought it was possible to befriend a bear. But bears are bears, and humans are—well, to bears, humans are just lunch. Or dinner, depending on the time of day."

"God, that's awful," I said. "Why didn't they name this place after the human who was killed instead of the bear who did the killing?"

"Your guess is as good as mine," Adam said. "But it may be because I just made the story up. I wanted to make you laugh. You're not the only one who likes making up stories."

"You thought I'd laugh at a story about a guy being mauled by a bear?"

"So it was a misguided story," Adam said. "But at least Terrance J. Tenterhook still lives!"

"I should've known from the name," I said. "Tenterhook."

"Yeah. I was trying to be clever."

Adam and I had walked to the end of the dock, and I turned to head back, but he stopped me. "Wait, you can't leave before you see what we came here for."

"What'd we come here for?"

"The view of the Bay Bridge," he said. I looked where he was pointing. The bridge was far away enough that it looked like a toy bridge, like it could be a bridge in Eddy's Lego collection.

"The Bay Bridge goes to Oakland," Adam told me. "And the Golden Gate goes to Marin County—to wine country. It gets all the attention, but you get more bang for your buck on the Bay Bridge. It cost more to build and it's much longer, but the tolls are the same amount." He paused, then added, "And that's a real story, not a bullshit story. We did a bridge project in fourth grade. It's funny—I remember so much more of what I learned in elementary school than what I learned last year."

"Our brains are more plastic the younger we are," I said. "It makes it easier to take on new information."

"And how do you know that? Did you do a fourth grade project on brains?"

"No. Talley told me," I said.

We turned to walk back the length of the dock. Adam bent down and pulled on the rope that was mooring one of the boats. The name *Cara's Joy* was written on the back ledge (the "stern," Adam said it was called). When he'd pulled the boat close enough, he stepped onto it. "Are you allowed to do that?" I asked.

"I know the owners," he said.

"Who's Cara?"

He shrugged. "When you buy a used boat, you keep the name that it comes with, otherwise it's bad luck. Though I gotta tell you, I think this particular family is beyond whatever help they can get from obeying some stupid boat-naming superstition."

"What happened to them?"

"That's a long story," Adam said. I understood that was code for: *I'm not going to tell you.* I didn't press the point, because it didn't have anything to do with Talley. "Wanna come aboard?" he asked.

Cara's Joy was swaying back and forth in the water, a little closer to the dock, then a little farther away. A little closer, and then much farther away. If I didn't time my step right, I'd end up in the water.

I shook my head.

"Don't be afraid," Adam said.

"I'm not," I told him. "I'm just getting hungry."

"All right, then." He hopped off the boat. "Let's go eat."

chapter eighteen

UNLIKE THE EL CAMINO DINER, THE RESTAURANT AT the Grizzly Cove marina did not have a sign up front saying, *Please Seat Yourself.* The hostess had stepped away from the desk to seat another party. I could see her at the far end of the room, holding a pair of menus like a briefcase under her arm.

Adam didn't wait for her to return. Instead he started walking toward a window table. He gave a little shoulder bump to a waiter at the far end of the room wearing a name tag that said *Marco.*

"Hey, man!" Marco said. "Back so soon?"

"My friend Sloane is visiting from Minnesota," Adam said, nodding toward me.

Marco extended a hand. "Well, hey. Any friend of Adam's—"

"Is someone you're immediately suspicious of," Adam finished.

"Ah, man. You said it. I didn't." He turned back to me. "It's nice to meet you, Sloane. What brings you here?

"My sister was here," I said. "I wonder if you ever met her—Talley Weber?"

Marco shook his head. "I don't know anyone by that name."

"Her real name is Natalie," I said "I'll show you her picture."

I flashed my cell phone toward Marco, and he shook his head. "Sorry," he said. "You guys sit wherever you want."

Adam said it was up to me. I picked a table by the window, where we could see the Bay Bridge. Marco brought over the menus. The offerings were very seafood heavy. I ran my finger down the line of items. There was a chicken-and-seafood paella; I wondered if I could order it without the seafood part. And without the rice. And without anything besides chicken, including spices. Probably not.

There were a number of side dishes that looked all right—I could order a side of french fries, and a side of mashed potatoes, though Adam would probably think I was weird. (Did it matter to me if he thought I was weird? Not necessarily, but would he be more likely to divulge information if he thought I was a perfectly normal girl? Maybe.)

At the bottom of the second page, there was a kids' menu. *Food for the Skippers-in-Training (10 and under)*, it said.

When Marco came back to take our order, I asked if I could order the grilled cheese. I've tried ordering off kids' menus before, and sometimes it's no problem. But sometimes restaurants are really strict about it.

"Sloane is actually ten years old," Adam told Marco. "She just looks old for her age. She's pretty self-conscious about it. Don't tell her I told you."

"I won't," Marco said. "Grilled cheese it is."

"Sorry to be high maintenance," I said.

"Grilled cheese does not count as high maintenance. You have no idea some of the high-maintenance requests I've had to fill." He turned to Adam. "And you, sir? Any high-maintenance requests?"

Adam rolled his eyes. "Today I'll stick to the menu. Fish tacos."

Marco made a note on his pad. "Your wish is my command."

After Marco walked away, Adam turned back to me. "So. Tell me something interesting about yourself, Sloane Weber."

"Something interesting?"

"Yeah, we're here, and I don't really know that much about you."

"Oh, I don't know," I said. The only thing about me that I considered at all interesting was that I was Talley's sister. "I can't think of anything to say."

"I'll make this easy on you—I'll ask the questions, and all you have to do is answer. First question: What's your middle name?"

"Marian," I said. "And yours?"

"Oh no. I'm the interviewer right now."

"But I'll get a turn, right?"

"Sure. You'll get a turn. So . . . you said you like making up stories."

"I do . . . I mean, I used to."

"Do you write them down?"

"Yes."

"What kinds of stories are your specialty?"

"Realistic fiction, mostly," I said.

"Like, if aliens invaded, here's a story about how it would go?"

"I said realistic."

"So you don't believe in aliens? Out of the entire universe, you think our planet is the only one with intelligent life?"

"No, that's not what I said. But as far as we know, we've never encountered them here on earth."

"As soon as aliens land, I guess the category changes from sci-fi to realistic."

"I never thought of it that way before."

"Good thing you met me," he said. "Now back to the interview. Any pets?"

"Nope."

"Nope as in never, or nope as in not right now?"

"Both," I said. "Although, actually, now that I think about it—we did have pet chickens for a little while."

"Not the answer I was expecting," Adam said. "So I guess my next question is pretty obvious."

"Uh . . . what's your next question?"

"Do you live on a farm?"

"No, we have a regular house. When Talley was about thirteen years old, she found some stray chickens."

Looking back, I couldn't remember exactly where Talley'd found them, or how she got them home without Dad driving her.

"At first she hid them in the bathroom we shared," I told Adam. "They unraveled the toilet paper and made a nest behind the toilet."

"It's like they always say—you can take the chicken out of the coop, but you can't take the coop out of the chicken," Adam said.

"I guess not, because the rooster started crowing."

"As in, cock-a-doodle-doo?"

"Yep," I said. "My dad heard it and he went bananas. He told Talley she needed to rehome them pronto. But pronto took a couple weeks. Meanwhile, Talley moved them to the backyard and she named them. She named one after me. She was kind of a badass."

"You may be the first person to ever describe a chicken as a badass."

"Talley called her a badass," I said. "I was only eight years old. It was probably the first time I heard the word. But it was an apt description for this chicken. She was smaller than the others, but she'd peck her way to the front of the food bowl. Talley should've named her after herself, don't you think?"

I was hoping to catch Adam off guard, and have him say, *Oh yeah, that sounds like Talley.* And then I'd say, *Gotcha! I knew that you knew her!*

But, instead, he said, "I suspect you're more badass than you let on."

"Hardly."

"And the other chickens?" he asked. "What were their names?"

"The rooster was Philip. And the hens, let's see—she had Lola and Cassandra and . . . Shoot. I'm blanking on the last one." I shook my head. "I can't believe I can't remember the fifth chicken name." The only person to ask would've been Talley, which meant the answer was gone for good, just like she was.

Marco arrived with our food. The grilled cheese was on fancy bread—not plain white bread. But at least it wasn't too grainy. Adam took a bite of one of his fish tacos, chewed, and swallowed. "Thank goodness I didn't pick the chicken paella," he said. "I can eat this guilt-free."

"Talley also rescued stray codfish," I said.

"Really? How did she—wait. You're kidding, right?"

"I am."

"Not bad," he said. "So what happened to Sloane the chicken and her feathered friends? Did your mom step in and let Talley keep them?"

"No," I said. I paused, then added, "She died when I was really young."

"Oh, God, Sloane," Adam said. "I'm so sorry. How did she— sorry. It's none of my business."

"It was a car accident," I said. "She skidded on black ice and hit a tree."

Juno'd actually driven me to the spot where it happened just a couple weeks after Talley died. Years had passed since Mom had died, and it looked like an ordinary place on an ordinary street. There were no markings on any of the trees. I couldn't tell which tree was *the* tree. Maybe the offending tree wasn't even there anymore. Maybe the force of the car hurling into it had knocked it down, or at least damaged it badly enough that it had to be chopped down, carted away, turned into firewood. Logs from that tree could've kept other families warm on cold Minnesota nights.

"That's awful," Adam said.

"It's all right. It was a long time ago."

"That's what people say when they want to make other people feel better about something shitty."

In the silence that followed, Adam and I each took bites of our respective meals. I felt oddly guilty, because I'd made things awkward. As if it were my fault for having a dead mom.

It was only my fault that I had a dead sister.

The bite in my mouth seemed to be growing as I chewed and chewed and chewed. It was too big to swallow. I was afraid I'd have to spit it out, but instead I reached for my glass of water. I took a thin sip and somehow I was able to swallow my food down.

"Are you and your dad close?" Adam asked.

"Not really. We just don't see eye to eye these days. It's funny, Talley once told me there's a 'leap second' inserted every four years into Coordinated Universal Time. Even with different countries having different leaders, and sometimes being at war with each other, the powers that be got together and decided that. Meanwhile my dad and I, who are related, and who live in the same house, and who are missing the same person—we can't agree on what needs to be done now. My dad thinks I need to move on. And I can't. Not when there are so many unanswered questions."

"I'm sure your dad is devastated in his own way," Adam said. "I once heard my parents talking about this. There's a word if you lose a spouse. You're a widow or a widower. But for all the words there are in the English language, and there must be like a million of them—"

"Just under two hundred thousand," I interjected. "My English teacher has all twenty volumes of the *Oxford English Dictionary*."

"Fine. Not as many as I thought, but still a lot. And for all those words, there's no word in the English language for when a parent loses a child. It's like the people in charge of coming up with new words decided, 'Nope. No word can capture that.' That's what my parents said."

"Do they know someone whose child died?"

Adam shrugged. "My dad probably meets a lot of people who have lost a child, given his line of work."

Had the doctor who came to tell us Talley had died gone home to her family that night and discussed how there was no word in the English language for what Dad had become, a parent who'd lost a child? What would she have said about me?

"There's a word for losing your parents," I said. "You're an orphan. But when you lose a sibling—there isn't a word for that, either."

"That's true," he said.

"You know those chickens I was talking about?" Adam nodded. "They might still be alive. When Talley first brought them home, they had all sorts of problems, like mites between their toes. Talley soaked their feet in oil. She nursed them back to health. And now—chickens can live up to a decade, even longer sometimes. It seems weird that Talley saved them and she died, and the chickens don't even know it. I feel like I should find them and tell them what happened. Not that chickens would care, or even understand. It wouldn't have any meaning to them. It's ridiculous."

"No, it's not," Adam said. "Not if it would have some meaning for you."

"When your sister dies, you have bigger things to worry about than telling her old chickens." I shook my head, and then I started laughing. I couldn't help it. "God, that sounds like a metaphor. My friend Juno makes fun of me sometimes for all the metaphors I come up with. But this time I mean telling literal chickens!"

"You have a nice smile," Adam said. "And there's something else, too."

My cheeks had warmed. "What?" I asked.

"You're a very interesting person, Sloane Marian Weber."

Now my cheeks were blazing. I took a sip of water to cool down. "Do you have siblings?" I asked, once I'd swallowed. "You didn't answer before."

"Just me and the 'rents at home," Adam said. "Speaking of whom, you certainly don't corner the market on strained relationships with parents. They're always up in my grill. I don't hate them. But I don't like them, and I don't think they're too wild about me, either—which I guess begs the question: Why do they care so much about what I'm doing on any given day?" He sighed and shook his head. "It's so much easier when you can like the people you love."

"I never liked or loved anyone as much as I liked and loved Talley," I said. "And you've been acting like a totally nice guy all through this lunch."

"Don't tell anyone. I have a reputation to uphold."

"But I've been waiting for you to slip up and admit that you knew her."

"I told you that I didn't."

"Yeah, but . . ."

"Do you have trust issues?"

"No. But I have a dead sister, and she had your phone number."

"I don't know why she had it," Adam said.

"And you're hanging out with me, and you brought me to this place of all places—*Grizzly* Cove, with that flag waving front and center."

"If you'd asked me ahead of time if there was a flag in the parking lot, I probably would've said no. I've never even noticed it."

"And you asked to see the list, and then you nearly destroyed it."

"That was an accident. I swear."

"And," I said, "you used the term 'shit-slammer.'"

"No, I didn't."

"Yes, you did," I said. "On the phone when we first talked, you said it. That was one of Talley's terms."

I remembered how I'd asked him about it at the time:

What did you say?

I said this day is going to kick my ass.

Kick my ass was a much more common saying, and maybe it's what he'd said to begin with. I let out a sigh. Grief was turning me into an insane version of myself.

"Are you okay?" Adam asked me.

"Yeah," I said. "I think I must've heard it because I wanted you to say it—because I miss my sister, and I want answers, and wanted proof that you knew her."

"I didn't know her."

"I guess I owe you an apology. I'm normally a much nicer person. People like me."

"I like you," Adam said.

"I'm so embarrassed."

"You don't have to be," he said. "Really. Just forget about it."

When Marco came over with the check, Adam pulled out his wallet. "No, no," I said. "This is my treat."

"I can't let you pay," Adam told me.

"Why not? Because I'm a girl?"

"I want to be chivalrous. Is there something wrong with that?"

"Sorry, but yeah. It's benevolent sexism. It's fine if a guy holds open a door for a woman because he got there first, as long as the woman could be the one to hold open the door if she got there first. Then there's equality. But if the guy *always* holds open the door, like the woman is incompetent and she can't do it herself, well, that's problematic, and it's actually not benevolent at all. It contributes to the cultural view that women need men to help them."

"Whoa," Adam said. "Okay, well what if I want to treat you because coming here was my idea? It'd be rude for me to expect you to pay when you had no choice as to where we were going. Besides, all you got was a kids' meal. My tacos cost much more."

"But I was the one who accused you of lying, so maybe I owe you the difference between tacos and a grilled cheese."

"No, you don't. I told you to forget about it."

"Okay," I said. "How about if we each pay for our own meal?"

"If you insist."

"I insist."

"All right. I feel bad, though. I really was planning to take you to lunch. Is there anything else I can do for you?"

I shook my head. But then I changed my mind. "Could we go by Mr. G's and Bel Air on the way home—if they are on the way home?"

"They are now," Adam said.

chapter nineteen

ADAM SAID MR. G'S WAS CLOSEST, SO WE WENT THERE
first. It was on the corner of a fairly busy street. Years earlier I'd
pointed out to Talley that you could tell what the important streets
were by the direction of the traffic. If traffic only went in one
direction, it wasn't such an important street. But when traffic went
both ways, you could tell a lot more happened there.

It was a little-kid observation, and it didn't always hold true,
but as we drove down Laurel Street toward Mr. G's, I noted the
traffic moving in both directions and I thought, *Something important
will happen here.*

At least I hoped it would. Adam circled the block a couple times
looking for a place to park and finally pulled into a spot marked
Bank Customers Only.

Every time I did anything I wasn't supposed to do, I remembered my sister: *Don't ask for permission, ask for forgiveness.* As if I needed an excuse to remember her.

We crossed the street and walked into Mr. G's, and it was as if there'd been a sudden total eclipse of the sun. Outside it was bright, but the inside of the karaoke place was bathed in the blue-black color of nighttime.

Even in the darkness, I could tell the place was mostly empty, which wasn't a surprise. It was just past the lunchtime hour, which wasn't exactly prime karaoke time. There was a handful of customers, including one woman onstage belting out her version of the old Aretha Franklin song "Respect"—and I mean belting, as if she had an audience of a few hundred, and maybe a few thousand.

Adam and I stood there in the doorway of Mr. G's for a couple minutes, eyes adjusting to the dark, listening to her sing. She was as good as any singer I'd ever heard. As good as the goddess singing the live version of "Rhiannon" in Juno's car. I wondered if she was a regular, and if she'd been onstage when Talley had been here. If so, I was sure Talley would've been as astounded as I was.

"Respect" ended. The three or four people who were sitting in the audience clapped, and Adam and I did, too. The woman bowed, but she didn't step off the stage. Instead, a man joined her and they began to sing another song together.

A woman in a green Mr. G's T-shirt came over and welcomed Adam and me. She said there was a twenty-dollar minimum per person, but we could sing as many songs as we liked. "And sit wherever you want," she added, extending an arm toward all the empty tables.

Adam looked at me. "You pick again," he said. "That's your job. Seat picker."

"Oh, we don't have to stay," I told him, and I turned back to the woman. "We're only here because I think my sister was here. Maybe you knew her—Talley Weber?"

"No, sorry," the woman said.

"May I show you her picture?" My phone was already in my hand. I pressed the button to light up the screen and held it out. She shook her head. No, she hadn't seen Talley.

"I'm pretty sure she sang something from *Grease*, if that rings a bell."

"Sorry, it doesn't," the woman said.

"Is it possible to look up when songs from *Grease* were last sung, and who sang them?"

"We don't have the capabilities to look up such things," the woman said. "I think there'd be privacy issues anyway."

"My sister died," I said.

"Oh. Oh my."

"I'm only telling you because you were concerned about her privacy," I said. "If you knew her and she said that it was a secret she was here in California, you don't have to worry. I already know she was here, so I don't think she'd mind if you told me whatever you know—if there's anything you know."

She shook her head. "I didn't know her, but I'm truly sorry for your loss."

"Thank you."

"If you want to sing something from *Grease*, you're welcome to. I could talk to my manager about waiving the minimum."

"No, that's all right," I said. "But thanks anyway."

"Are they regulars here?" I asked, gesturing toward the couple onstage.

"Jenny and Gil? They come in every now and then."

"I'm going to ask them if they knew my sister. Then we'll get going."

But Jenny and Gil didn't know Talley, or so they said. Adam and I headed out. I could tell he felt bad that the visit had been a bust, because he was talking up Bel Air, saying he just had a feeling about it. He'd always been lucky at the arcade as a kid—he was the master of Skee-Ball and had earned so many tickets that he'd once won an enormous stuffed tiger. It was as big, practically, as an actual tiger, and it was suspended high above the booth, with a sign around its neck that said you needed ten thousand tickets to take it home with you. Most kids earned however many tickets they earned in a day—fifty tickets, maybe a hundred, and they made do with the lesser prizes. Fuzzy keychains, Slinkies, Chinese finger traps. That sort of thing. They didn't have the patience to collect tickets, visit after visit, and wait till they had enough for something really special. But Adam believed in delayed gratification and he kept his eye on the prize. Plus he was just so exceptionally good at Skee-Ball.

"It's still in my room," Adam said. "I did a big stuffed animal clean-out when I was in like sixth grade. I made my mom give everything away—except the tiger. I couldn't get rid of my crowning achievement!"

"Of course not."

"Look there," Adam said.

"Where."

"Out the window, to the right. See the turrets?"

"Yeah."

"That's Bel Air."

He made a turn and we went through the castle gates and over a (fake) drawbridge. The moat was just grass—or rather, patches of grass. Bel Air, on the whole, looked like it'd seen better days. The castle was a bit run-down looking, and there was paint peeling off the corner tower. "When was the last time you were here?" I asked.

"I'm pretty sure it was Roddy Vega's birthday party in seventh grade," Adam said. "They have go-karts in the back, and you know, when you don't have a license, that's about as cool as it gets."

"I guess."

"It's kind of sad, though, to come back to places you loved when you were a kid, and seeing it the way your parents must've seen it back then. And wait till you see inside—it's even worse."

The lobby was a giant warehouse-like room with dozens of video games, pinball machines, and of course the Skee-Ball machines running the length of the back wall. I saw the prize booth with various knickknacks offered in exchange for tickets, and the giant stuffed animals suspended from above (though not a tiger).

I asked the guy behind the counter if he'd known Talley. He said he hadn't. There were a few other Bel Air staff members working the floor—you could tell who they were because of their striped referee shirts. It was the same answer every time, and the same answer when Adam and I went out back to the area with the go-karts and the miniature golf course. "And how late are you open?" I asked.

I'd asked already, back when I'd called Bel Air from the stairwell at school. "We're open eleven a.m. to eight p.m., Monday through Thursday," a guy named Harris told me. "Friday and Saturday till ten, and Sunday we close at seven."

"Never till midnight?" I asked.

"Those have been the hours for as long as I've worked here," he said.

"How long have you worked here?"

"Nearly three years."

"In all of your time here, have there been any late-night parties or anything like that?"

"Like birthday parties?"

"Sure, or any other kind of party that went really late. Like maybe someone rented the place out and invited people to stay till midnight?"

"How large is your party?" Harris asked.

"Oh, it's a hypothetical party, not a real party," I said. "If I had enough people to rent the whole place out, could I?"

"I'm sure you could, but it's not really my department. Let me introduce you to my manager. Yo, Melinda—" Harris called out.

A woman in the company striped shirt and ripped jeans walked over, and my mind flicked to my father, who was (not surprisingly) staunchly anti–ripped jeans. He'd made an actual rule about it— not only would he not buy them for Talley and me, but also even if we were spending our own money, we were not allowed to come home with clothes that had purposeful rips in them. He didn't care if all our friends were wearing them, and it was the height of fashion. To him it was offensive. "When I was in college, my jeans were ripped and patched because I didn't have a choice—because I couldn't afford anything else," he told Talley and me. It was about as close as he ever got to talking about all the loss he'd experienced, and how life was harder for him, after his parents died. Talley and I obeyed the no-rips rule.

But now, of course, a pair of Talley's jeans *did* have rips in them. The jeans that were cut off her body in the hospital, and were now at the top of my closet, with the rest of her "effects."

"What can I help you with?" Melinda asked.

I asked her the same questions I'd asked Harris. Melinda said Bel Air wasn't ever open at midnight, and if anyone had ever tried to sneak in, there were alarms and security cameras, but those things hadn't been tripped up in a long time—the last time was a fraternity prank. A couple of kids tried to scale the castle walls in the middle of the night, but it was two years ago, and they were guys. One of them broke his leg. The management at Bel Air felt that was punishment enough and didn't press charges.

I showed Talley's picture to Melinda, just to be as thorough as I possibly could, though I didn't expect her to recognize Talley—and she didn't.

Adam and I walked back out to his car. "I don't have to be anywhere for a while," he said. "Actually, I don't have to be any-where till tomorrow morning, when I'm going to my mom's office against my will. So you just say the word—anywhere you want to go, we'll go there."

It was a kind offer, but I was done for the day. "Thanks," I said. "But can you just drop me at my aunt's house."

"Sure thing."

chapter twenty

I GOT HOME AND TOLD AUNT ELISE ABOUT WHAT I'D learned in my travels around the Bay Area with Adam, which of course wasn't much of anything. "I thought the list was one of Talley's puzzles, and that all I needed to do was get out here and the answers would be waiting for me. But I haven't been able to figure anything out."

"You figured out the getting-out-here part," Aunt Elise said. "And the diner, not to mention Crescent Street. I'm particularly grateful for that."

"I'm grateful, too," I told her.

And it was true—I was grateful to have my aunt back in my life. But sometimes, even when you're looking right at someone for whom you are technically grateful, there is too much sadness to actually feel the gratitude. It was like Rabbi Bernstein saying that in our time of mourning, we should be grateful that we got to have Talley in our lives. I *was* grateful to have had Talley, but that wasn't what I was feeling at her funeral.

In the rock-paper-scissors of feelings, sadness covers gratitude.

"Do you mind if I go upstairs and lie down for a few minutes?" I asked Aunt Elise.

"Not at all," she said. "I was going to do the same thing down here."

I helped her get settled on the couch, propping her leg up on a special foam pillow, and I brought over a glass of water. Then I went upstairs to my little room and softly closed the door.

This was the room Talley had stayed in, and I knew that even though time had passed, and Aunt Elise had probably vacuumed in here, dusted the shelves, and stripped her sheets off the pullout couch (before she'd broken her leg), molecules of Talley remained. In physics class last fall, we'd learned about something called Caesar's last breath. Back in Ancient Rome, Julius Caesar exhaled his last breath and died. That last breath contained sextillions of molecules, and within a few years, those molecules traveled around the planet. Now in each breath that we inhale, we are taking in approximately one molecule of Caesar's last breath. It sounds unbelievable, but it's completely true. And it's not just Caesar's molecules—we're also inhaling molecules from the exhales of *every being who ever lived on the planet.* Your favorite musician: you're inhaling her breath. Your sworn enemy: you're inhaling his breath. The *Brontosauruses* and dodo birds and the California grizzly bears: you're inhaling their breaths, too.

I inhaled a long breath—I inhaled Talley and everyone else in the whole wide world—probably more of Talley than all the others, because she'd been here, in this room. She'd slept here. I held that breath in the back of my throat for a few seconds, not wanting to exhale and let her go. Dust motes were dancing in the beam of light coming through the window. When I was little, long before I took physics, Talley had told me about molecules. "They make up everything in the universe," she'd said. "And they're invisible to the naked eye." A few days later, we were sitting in the den. The blinds were drawn shut, but there were bands of light coming through, and in them I could see the illuminated dust motes.

"Talley!" I'd cried. "I can see the molecules with my naked eyes! I CAN SEE MOLECULES WITH MY NAKED EYES!"

"Oh, Sloaners," Talley had said.

"What?" I'd asked.

"Nothing."

She didn't set me straight, and now I wondered: How many other things had Talley just let me go on believing?

chapter twenty-one

WHILE I'D BEEN OUT WITH ADAM, ONE OF AUNT ELISE'S
neighbors had made a grocery run for her, and the kitchen was now
well-stocked. I told Aunt Elise I was happy to cook for us. I'm not a
gourmet chef or anything, but I can make simple things, like pasta,
or chicken cutlets. Aunt Elise sat on a stool by the kitchen island
and told me where to find everything—the baking sheet for the
oven, the silverware, the plates. Her plates had tiny butterflies on
them, like the wallpaper in the powder room, and the tattoo on
Talley's hip bone. "Did you know Talley had a butterfly tattoo?"
I asked.

"No, I didn't."

"I saw it that last night at the hospital when we were . . . when
we were saying goodbye."

Aunt Elise closed her eyes a beat longer than a blink and nodded.

"Talley was into the butterfly effect. You know what that is, right?" Aunt Elise nodded. "I figured that was why she got it. But maybe it was something about *your* butterflies."

"When Dana and I were younger, our mother told us this story about kids in the Holocaust. My grandmother—your great-grandmother—was a survivor."

"I know. Talley actually talked about it a lot. When she was a kid, she used to write Hitler's name on the bottoms of her shoes, so she stepped on him as she walked. The ink wore off, and she wrote it again and again."

"Oh, my mother would've been so proud of that act of rebellion," Aunt Elise. "I can picture her telling her friends what a little spitfire her granddaughter was, and maybe even writing 'Hitler' on the bottoms of her own moccasins, too. She always wore Minnetonka moccasins because they were so comfortable." She paused. "I haven't thought about those moccasins in a really long time."

I ran a finger along the edges of a tiny butterfly on one of Aunt Elise's plates. "What was the story your mother told you?"

"Oh, right. She'd heard that when the war ended and the American troops liberated the concentration camps, they found images of butterflies that children had scratched onto the walls. I don't think they had pencils, so they'd scratched with sticks, or maybe their own fingernails."

I felt a chill rise up my back from the phantom sound of the children scratching pictures of butterflies into the walls of the barracks using their fingernails.

"The kids were gone so there was no one to explain why they'd done it," Aunt Elise said. "Either they were sent to the gas chamber, or shot, or they starved to death. The Americans called a grief expert to come examine the drawings, and her theory was that the kids had known they were trapped, and they'd known they were dying. They comforted themselves thinking their souls would become something like butterflies, light and free. Of course no one knows for sure if that's why they drew what they did, but Dana started her butterfly collection after that."

"Wait," I said. "My mother collected butterflies?" It was a revelation for a split second, but as the words left my mouth, I realized that it actually wasn't surprising at all. I'd grown up in a house filled with random little butterfly knickknacks. They'd always been there, and when something is always there, you don't necessarily realize its significance—the trivet that we put out on the dining room table when the casserole dish was straight out of the oven, the bookends on the wall unit in the living room, the light-switch cover in the downstairs half bathroom, that sort of thing.

Why hadn't I thought of them when I'd seen Talley's tattoo? Maybe because I was so used to seeing them. Or maybe because Talley'd never seemed particularly interested in them. We'd never talked about them the way she talked about the butterfly effect.

"Did you tell Talley the Holocaust butterfly story when she was here?"

"No, I don't think so."

"She had to have known it, though," I said. "Mom must've told her. Talley was already seven when Mom died, which is on the young side for that kind of conversation, but not too young.

It's gotta be why she got the tattoo. She never would've gotten one otherwise."

"Sometimes people surprise you," Aunt Elise said. "I once dated this guy who was the most uptight person I'd ever met in my life."

"Not more than my dad," I said.

"Oh, this guy makes your dad look like the most laid-back guy on the planet, so imagine my shock when he took off his shirt and there was a tattoo of a tiger stretching across his chest."

"Yeah, but Talley was staunchly opposed to tattoos," I said. "Dean wanted her to get one years ago. She refused because Jewish people had been forced to get tattoos during the Holocaust. But the tattoo on her hip was a butterfly, so it makes total sense."

"How so?"

"Whenever I was having a hard time about something, Talley would remind me that other people had it so much worse. It could be so annoying, because when I was upset, all I wanted was for her to agree that in that moment, my life sucked, too. But she was right, the way she always was. I mean, can you imagine how lucky those butterfly kids would've felt to have suddenly woken up and had my life—or Talley's life? It makes it sort of ironic that she died the way she did, because her life wasn't as hard as those kids' lives."

"I have a couple things to say about this," Aunt Elise said. "Number one, having perspective is nice, and it's certainly something to strive for, but hardship is relative, and everyone has bad days. It's not a contest to see who is having the hardest life."

"I know," I said.

"And number two, depression isn't about whether you have a hard life or an easy one. It's an illness, and illness comes with pain. People who are suicidally depressed, like Talley was, are in a tremendous amount of pain, and they don't see an end to it. They don't necessarily want to die, but they think that dying is the only way out of suffering."

"I know all that," I said. "I've spent so much time in front of my computer, reading every single thing I could possibly find out about it. But Talley was also someone who was always talking about perspective, and it's hard to match that up with . . . with the decision that she made. Because even if she was sick, it was a decision."

"Sloane—"

"No, really." I could feel myself losing my grip. No matter what Aunt Elise said, nothing changed the fact that Talley made a decision. A series of decisions: she picked up the bottle, she put pills on her tongue, she swallowed them down. They were all volitional acts. "I don't understand how she could do that to me. She *left* me. Didn't I mean enough to her? Didn't she love me?"

"Oh, honey," Aunt Elise said. "She loved you so much. She loved you beyond measure. But sometimes people who are considering suicide think the people they love would be better off without them."

"I just can't believe that Talley thought that," I said. "She was so smart. Her IQ was in the 99.999-whatever percentile. She was brilliant. She was beautiful—"

"People don't always suffer on the outside," Aunt Elise said.

"Those who are hurting really deeply often look exactly like those who aren't. You can't tell what's happening inside just by looking at someone."

"I know," I said. "When I got here, to California, and I was walking through the airport, I was thinking about how normal I must look on the outside, and how nobody passing by me knew anything about what had happened to me. I'm sure bad things had happened to some of them, too, but I couldn't tell. Everyone has so much inside them. Everyone has hardships we can't see."

"Yes," Aunt Elise said. "And no matter how smart she was, or how beautiful she looked on the outside, Talley had hardships, too."

"The last time I saw her, when she was on that hospital gurney, I couldn't believe how small she looked," I said. "But she'd been that small all along. She'd held so much inside her one small body. All her thoughts, and everything she read about in books, or online, or whatever. All these survival stories. She never forgot anything. She loved trying to help and be part of making things better. But not everything gets better. Not everyone survives. Like those kids in the Holocaust. That's why Talley got that tattoo. It's a piece of the puzzle she left behind, just like those kids left behind those butterfly drawings. And that's why—" My voice broke.

"Sloane, it's okay," Aunt Elise said.

"It's not," I said. "And Talley knew it. That's why she didn't survive herself. Because bad things kept happening to other people, and it was too much for her. She just couldn't take it."

Aunt Elise hobbled off her stool. The crutches clacked to the floor, but she steadied herself with the countertop.

"Talley was so busy caring about everyone else," I said. "It must have felt so lonely. I should've shown her I cared as much as she did. But I didn't. I was too busy caring about the wrong things and having fun with my friends."

"You're supposed to have fun with your friends."

"No, I'm not—not when there's so much suffering, and especially not when mys sister was among the sufferers."

Aunt Elise had reached my side of the kitchen island. She kept one hand on the countertop, but she draped her other arm around me. I didn't deserve to be hugged; I hadn't hugged Talley when she'd needed me. Not even a hug goodbye. I'd paused in her doorway, and then I'd left her. But Aunt Elise was holding so tight, after a while I couldn't help but lean into her, and then I couldn't tell if she was holding me up as I cried, or if I was holding her up as she stood on her one good leg.

"I should've stayed home with her that day," I said, but I said it so softly, I didn't think Aunt Elise could hear me. My voice was muffled by my own tears.

The timer dinged, but neither one of us moved for what felt like a very long while. When I finally let go, I made sure Aunt Elise had steadied herself back against the counter, and I brought around her crutches. She hobbled to the table. I took the chicken out of the oven. But it had burned, and neither of us was much in the mood for dinner anymore.

chapter twenty-two

AUNT ELISE AND I LAID LOW ON MONDAY. SHE TAUGHT ME some yoga moves. Given her leg situation, she had a modified yoga program. She could sit in a chair and do upper-body work. I followed along, rolling my shoulders, bending from side to side, stretching my back. "Now close your eyes," Aunt Elise said. "Pay attention to your breath. Inhale through your nose. That's it. Exhale slowly through your mouth . . . good. Inhale again, slowly. You can lengthen the inhale by counting to three in your head. Now exhale to the count of three. One. Two. Three. Good."

Later on, I called Juno to see how her first day at the Hogans' was going. We'd texted a little bit before then. Juno had written that all's swell, but when she picked up the phone, it sounded like she was in the middle of a zoo, or maybe the aftermath of an explosion.

"Is everything okay?" I asked.

"Totally under control. Don't you worry," she said. In the background, someone was making siren noises, and someone else screamed.

"You sure about that 'under control' thing?"

"Ha, ha," she said. "The things I do for you. I'm only in this mess because you said you'd be here with me."

"Sorry about that," I said.

"I'm sorry about that stupid guilt trip I just pulled," she said. "It's only five more days."

"Four and a half," I said.

"The good news is these kids totally distract me from thinking too much about Cooper. Although I still think about him, and what he and Audrey may be doing together right about now . . ."

"Ugh, Juno. Don't even go there."

"I can't help it. I was just thinking that—" She cut herself off. "Oh, God."

"What?"

"Something crashed," she said. She started panting and I could tell she was racing back to the other room. "I shouldn't have left them alone. But they're eight years old. They should be able to stay alive without me for five minutes."

In the background, the kids started screaming. Screaming never bodes very well. Then again, if you're screaming, you're definitely alive.

"What's going on in here?" I heard Juno ask, and then there was the chatter of all three kids answering at the same time.

In the harshest voice I'd ever heard her use, Juno said, "That's enough! No killing! Are you listening to me? Everyone be quiet and listen. No killing is a rule in this house!"

There were mumbles, and I imagined the kids reluctantly assenting to the no-killing rule.

"I'll tell you something else," Juno went on. "I am on the phone with Sloane—"

"HI, SLOANE!"

"No, don't say hi yet," Juno said. "Sloane just heard you through the phone trying to kill each other."

"I wasn't—"

Juno cut off whatever kid was talking (it was one of the boys—either Thomas or Theo). "I'm going to set a timer for five minutes. If you can be quiet and sit with your craft books for that long, then you can say hi to her. Sloane, you still there?"

"I'm still here. I'm amazed that you're actually setting rules. I thought your family didn't believe in them."

"We believe in implicit rules," she explained. "My mom never had to tell me not to defenestrate Eddy."

"Way to use an SAT word in a sentence," I said.

"Yeah, well, that's what was just happening here. The boys were trying to shove Melanie out the window. We're on the ground floor, but still."

"You probably shouldn't leave them alone again," I said.

"Oh, I'm not. I'm standing window guard while they're crafting. They can talk to you in . . . oh, four minutes and twelve seconds. If you don't mind."

"I don't mind."

"Good, because this is the first time they've been quiet all day—because I dangled the reward of talking to you. They love you so much. They can't wait till you're back."

"Maybe I should come back early," I said.

"Really? I can't tell if you're kidding or not."

"I'm not kidding," I said. "At least I don't think I am. I don't want to hurt my aunt's feelings. Then again, it's hard to have a houseguest when you're not feeling like yourself, so maybe she actually wants me to leave, she's just too polite to say so."

"I doubt that she wants you to leave," Juno said.

"Yeah, me too," I admitted. "It's just so hard. I realized something about Talley last night, and I've been trying to figure out what it means."

"Has it been five minutes?" came a shout.

"It's been three minutes and four seconds," Juno said. "But if you start fighting again, I reset the clock. Sorry, Sloane. You were saying?"

"I think the list was . . . oh, I don't know what it was. But it got me out here, and I met my aunt, and where the rest of it is concerned, I just feel like there's nothing left for me to do in California, and it's making me miss Talley even more. I want to come home. My dad will be disappointed in me for leaving Stanford, but I'm not even at Stanford, so that shouldn't be the deciding factor."

"You give the word and I'll switch your ticket," Juno said.

"Is it expensive to switch a ticket?"

"Oh, Sloane, you know I don't care about that. Maybe I'll even upgrade you to first class on the way home."

"No!" I said. "Promise me you won't do that."

"What was that? I can't hear you."

"Juno, please. I mean it. That would make me insanely uncomfortable."

"All right," she said. "No first class. But even if it costs something to switch the ticket, don't worry about it. I checked my credit card statement online this morning, and you haven't spent anything."

"I've only been here three days."

"People can spend a lot of money in three days. I thought the purpose of this trip was to indulge yourself."

"You know that wasn't the purpose."

"I know. I just want to make things as easy on you as possible, even if you don't let me upgrade you to first class. Maybe business . . ."

"Not a chance," I said. "But I am going to think about coming home early, if that's okay."

"Of course it's okay."

"Thanks, Ju. I'll call you back in a bit."

"It's been more than five minutes!" one of the boys called. "I watched the clock!"

"Oh, sorry, kiddo. Sloane can't talk right now," Juno said.

"Sure I can," I told her. "Put them on."

chapter twenty-three

FOR THE NEXT FEW HOURS, I WEIGHED THE PROS AND cons of staying versus leaving, finally resolving to go home. I'd call Juno after dinner and ask her to switch my ticket to tomorrow, Tuesday, which meant I'd be able to babysit with her on Wednesday. She could handle one more day without me, and I'd deal with Dad when I got home.

But I couldn't just show up at home. What if I startled him so badly that he had a heart attack? (These are the things you have to think about when you only have one parent left and no more sister.) I'd call him before I walked in the door, maybe on my way home from the airport, and tell him it was just too hard. I'd been too homesick. And if he was disappointed, so be it. I was disappointed in him, too.

There was the matter of Aunt Elise, though. We'd just found

each other. Plus she had a broken leg, and I'd been helping her out. But she'd been alone this whole time, not counting the past three days, and she had neighbors who were willing to help. Did it really matter if I left Tuesday or waited till Sunday? She was going to be alone again either way, and at least she was on the mend.

Besides, the important thing was we'd reconnected. We were back in touch, and we wouldn't let ourselves get out of touch ever again. Talley had done that.

So I made my peace with the fact that I was cutting my visit short, but I still kept putting off telling Aunt Elise. I thought I'd tell her while she sat by the kitchen island as I cooked dinner. Then I thought I'd tell her during dinner. Then I thought I'd tell her when the dishes were cleared and we were sitting together on the couch.

"Great dinner, Sloane," she said.

I'd made pasta with butter and parmesan, along with a side of broccoli for Aunt Elise. (Personally I was not a huge broccoli fan. I didn't even know how to cook it, but Aunt Elise had walked me through the steps.) "It was nothing," I said.

"It was something," she said. "It's been such a gift to have you here."

Uh-oh.

"I wish I had cake to offer you for dessert," she went on. "That is, if you still love it."

"I do."

"I figured," she said. "'Cake' was your first word."

"I didn't know that," I said.

"It must've been your mom's influence," Aunt Elise said. "She had very specific feelings about birthday cake. She thought it shouldn't only be for birthdays, and she thought there should be a rose on every piece, so that every piece was the best piece."

"Oh, wow," I said. "That rose thing used to stress me out so much at other people's birthday parties. The parent would bring out the cake. The roses would only be on the corners, and kids would start to shout out claiming them. I never shouted fast enough, so I never got a rose—one time I missed getting a rose at my *own* birthday party."

"It wouldn't have happened under your mother's watch," Aunt Elise said with a smile. But then her smile fell. I knew we were both missing my mother at that moment—I was missing what might've been, and Aunt Elise was missing the real sister she knew, which of course brought me back to Talley. I was missing her most of all.

"Talley said that all these years, your dad hasn't ever really dated," Aunt Elise said.

"Here and there, but nothing serious," I said. "When I was little, Talley said it was because he was damaged. I thought she meant his finger."

"His finger?"

"His left pinky got slammed in a car door when he was five," I said. "The top half was sliced off."

"Oh, right," Aunt Elise said. "I remember your mom once told me she loved to hold his hand and find that little imperfection. She found it soothing."

"I found it terrifying," I said. "Fingers aren't supposed to come off, and I wondered where the missing part was. Did they throw it away, or did they keep it? Was it in a glass jar in a lab somewhere—and did it get its own jar, or did it share a jar with other people's missing fingers? Was there a finger-obsessed doctor somewhere who collected and performed experiments on them? And was it *just* fingers, or was he into toes, too?"

Aunt Elise shook her head, laughing.

"Mostly, I worried that something bad would happen to my pinky finger, too. Or to even more of my fingers. Sometimes I'd have to ball my hands into fists and feel for them, to make sure they were still intact. And when they were, I'd think: *I love you, my fingers. I'm so glad you're here.*"

"With that imagination, no wonder you're a writer. It's very impressive."

"Oh, I don't know about that," I said. "But thank you."

"Have you talked to your dad much since you've been out here?"

"Not really. We've texted a little bit."

He'd written to see how the first day of classes had gone. I wrote back: Great! Teacher is almost as good as Dr. Lee. Learning a lot!

"Well, you'll be back to Minnesota soon enough—too soon, if you ask me. But I know you must have a lot to get back to."

"Aunt Elise, I have to tell you—" I started.

But then my phone buzzed. Phew. Saved by the proverbial bell. I'd take all the extra seconds I could get to avoid telling Aunt Elise my change of plans. Though I figured the text was from Juno, reminding me that I needed to decide about my plane ticket.

But it was Adam's name on the screen. I hadn't heard from him since he'd dropped me off the day before, not that I'd expected to. It had only been a day. It felt so much longer. Time bends in such strange ways. Yesterday can feel like a year ago, and a year can feel like yesterday.

"What is it, sweets?" Aunt Elise asked.

"Hang on. Adam just texted."

What r ur plans for the wk, he'd written.

Me: Heading home tmrw

I still hadn't given the official word to Juno to change my ticket, and it was getting late back in Minnesota. Juno was a night owl, but the clock was still ticking.

I'd wanted to tell Aunt Elise my revised plans first. The words were on the tip of my tongue when my phone buzzed with Adam's next text: Thought you were staying the week?

Me: Change of plans.

Adam: Well, good I caught you. Can't let you leave without trying ice cream sandwiches at Cream. Can I pick u up in 10?

Me: Yes

chapter twenty-four

I TEXTED JUNO TO TELL HER I STILL WANTED TO FLY OUT tomorrow, but I hadn't had a chance to tell my aunt yet. There were a couple different flight options online, and I wanted to ask Aunt Elise which was more convenient for her.

Me: Do you need to know now or can I meet Adam for ice cream first?

Juno: Meet him & TREAT HIM!!!!!!!!!!!!!!

Me: Planning on it—w MY money

Juno: Pls use my card. Remember, I'm monitoring you.

Adam showed up twelve minutes later, and we drove to Cream, which was in Palo Alto, on University Avenue. "Is that University, as in Stanford?" I asked.

"That it is," Adam said.

University Avenue was a happening street. There were lots

of restaurants and stores, and a couple hotels. The sidewalks were crowded with people—many of whom looked like they could be college-aged, or high school students at Stanford for a week of writing classes. We brushed past a tall girl with an olive complexion. She could've been the roommate from Spain that I'd made up for dad. What had I said her name was . . . ? Oh, Isabella Lopez.

It was nice to put a face with a name, I thought. Then I remembered that I was only putting a face with a name I'd made up. I'd done it countless times, walking through the Nicollet Mall with my friends. Juno said she could tell when my attention shifted and I started crafting stories in my head, because I'd get a fuzzy look in my eyes. I'd look at the people—the strangers—and imagine whole lives for them, and then I'd go home and write them down.

This was different. I hadn't made up the name Isabella to write a story later. I was just collecting details that I could bring back for Dad, in case he wanted any: these are the people who lived in my dorm with me, and here were the places we walked into on University Avenue.

Not that he'd care about any of those details, once I told him that I'd dropped out.

The menu at Cream gave you a choice of cookie base (I picked chocolate chip—as standard as it gets), ice cream filling (I went for vanilla), and a topping (plain chocolate chips). Adam did a waffle base, rocky road, and Nutella.

"And may I please order another one?" I said to the guy behind the counter. He had a shock of red hair underneath his Cream-issued baseball cap.

"Double-fisting?" Adam asked.

"It's for my aunt," I said. I'd decided I'd do the birthday-cake-flavor ice cream for her, for obvious reasons.

"It'll melt if you get it now."

"It's only like ten minutes to get back to her house. It may be a little mushy, but still good."

"You don't want to eat ours here first?"

"I don't think I should be out too long if it's my last night."

"I'm not talking about a late night out," Adam said. "I can eat ice cream pretty fast. What about you?"

"Yeah, but the line," I said.

As I said it, I felt the press of customers behind me, waiting for their turn.

"We can wait on it again—as long as you can stand a few extra minutes spent with me."

"Sure."

"Great." Adam grinned, and I dug into my pocket faster than he did to pay for our ice cream sandwiches.

"Aw, man!" he said.

"You snooze, you lose," I said.

"Actually, I won a free ice cream. But isn't it sexist for me to accept it?"

"You've done all the driving," I said. "So we're even."

There were only a couple tables inside Cream, and they were both taken, so we headed outside, just kind of randomly walking.

"Thank you, by the way," Adam said, tipping his ice cream sandwich toward me.

"You're very welcome. Oh, hey—do you mind if we go into that store?"

"Where? Retro Planet?"

"Yeah, I want to get something for my best friend before I go home. She loves vintage things, so . . ."

"So something from Retro Planet is perfect," Adam said. "Let's go in."

But when we walked through the door, the guy behind the counter took one look at us and our ice cream sandwiches. "No food or drink," he said. We walked back out.

"Let's sit for a couple minutes," Adam said. He pointed toward a bench that was built around the base of a tree.

"This is a redwood tree, isn't it?"

"It is. You know your trees."

"Not really. It's just when I was googling stuff about the Bay Area, there were a bunch of links about the redwoods. They're smaller in person than I expected."

"That's just because the old trees aren't here in Palo Alto. You should go to Big Sur if you want to see really big redwoods."

"Is that far from here?"

"A couple hours south," Adam said. "Maybe three. We used to go when we were kids."

"Who's we?"

"Me and other kids from school. It's a popular field trip destination because of all the trails you can explore. The redwoods have got to be like two or three hundred feet tall, and their trunks are like ten or twenty feet around. Some of the trees are a thousand years old, maybe more."

I stood up from the bench and pitched my head back, looking at the top of the redwood in front of me. My guess is it was about forty feet high. Would it still be here a thousand years from now, and how tall would it be? I stood up and walked along the perimeter of the circular bench. There were a couple dozen flyers tacked up to the other side of the tree. Talley suddenly came rushing back to me.

It was always surprising to realize she'd slipped to the back of my brain. When she was alive, I could take her for granted, and it was okay when she wasn't at the forefront of my thoughts all the time. But now that I'd lost her, holding her memory close felt like my particular responsibility.

Adam came up behind me. "Talley once told me that posting flyers is bad for the trees," I said. "Bark is a protective layer, like skin, and when you put nails or staples through it, it makes the trees vulnerable to disease."

"Well," Adam said. He'd reached forward to smooth down a crease on one of the flyers. "I suppose we could lead a protest about it, if you want. But then we'd have to make signs, and signs require paper. Wouldn't wasting paper on our protest be a little hypocritical, if our mission is to save the trees?"

"We'll use recycled paper," I said, giving him a small smile.

He smiled back. "And then we'll recycle the recycled paper. An endless cycle of environmental awareness."

"I like that. Talley would approve."

"Excellent, it's a plan." He paused. "In all seriousness, do you think we should take down the flyers that are up here now?"

"It's definitely better for the tree if we take them down. The bark can heal. But then, the people who put these up probably didn't know they were doing any harm."

"You're such a good person, Sloane Weber," Adam said.

I could feel the heat in my cheeks. I didn't want Adam to see me blushing, so I turned away to face the tree again. There was a flyer advertising piano lessons. A flyer for a student-run moving company that guaranteed safe passage for your belongings or your money back. A flyer for all your photography needs, courtesy of NHL Photography.

It took a beat for that last one to register.

"Oh my God," I said, bringing my hands to my mouth.

"What?" Adam asked.

I shook my head and pointed. He read from the flyer: "Want an expert to photograph your special day, but you don't want to break the bank? Want to learn to be an expert yourself? Text or call NHL Photography for all your (reasonably priced) camera-related needs."

The top and sides of the flyer were bordered with small photos, ostensibly taken by the experts at NHL—a bride with a ring of flowers in her hair, a little kid blowing out birthday candles, a family sitting in a field, a close-up of a man laughing. He had scruff on his face and longish hair. His eyes were covered by someone else's hands, and each finger was adorned with a different ring.

Talley's rings.

They were her hands.

I could barely contain myself. "It's Talley!" I nearly cried.

"What?"

"NHL Photography," I said. "Those are her hands! I can't believe I almost didn't come for ice cream with you! I can't believe I thought we should take our sandwiches and get right back in the car! Oh, I *knew* she didn't mean the National Hockey League. I knew it! She'd never been to a hockey game in her life!"

The flyer had tabs on the bottom with a phone number repeating, the kind where you're supposed to tear off just one. But I pulled down the whole damn thing.

"Do you want me to call for you?" Adam offered.

"Oh no," I said. "I can do it."

I pulled out my phone and dialed. The phone rang once, twice, three times, and then there was the click of a voice mail picking up. "If you're looking for Nicole, you found her. Please leave a message. If you're looking for NHL Photography, you found that, too. Please leave a message with your name, number, and your photography needs, and I'll get back to you as soon as possible."

I hadn't even thought of what I was going to say. The adrenaline was racing through my body like a brush fire, and the words came: "Hi, Nicole. My name is Sloane. I found your flyer and I wanted to talk to you about an event I'm planning. It's totally last-minute and urgent and I need a photographer. Please call me back."

I recited the digits of my phone number. Then I pressed the button to end the call.

"A last-minute event, huh?" Adam said.

"I know," I said. "Does it make me a bad person to have made that up, when I know full well I'm not going to be a paying customer?"

"I just told you what a good person you are," he said.

"I didn't know what else to say. I just wanted to make sure she'd call me back."

"I know. And plenty of people call several photographers before they hire someone for an event. Leaving a message doesn't guarantee business, you know."

I nodded. "I know," I said.

"Okay, then," he said. "Do you want to hang out here for a bit and see if you get a call back?"

"Yeah. Thanks." I still had the flyer in my hand, and my ice cream . . . where was my ice cream? "I lost my ice cream sandwich," I said. "How does someone lose something like that?"

"You dropped it," Adam said. "When you saw the flyer, you said 'Oh my God,' and you moved your hands to your mouth."

I looked down—there were the remains of my ice cream sandwich, melting into the dirt. "I don't even remember that," I said.

"I can get you another."

"No, it's okay. Let's sit."

Though it was hard to sit, feeling as jumpy as I did. Adam tried making small talk while we waited. Had he orchestrated this? The list, his phone number, my trip out here, and now coming here to this redwood tree and finding this flyer—were these pieces of a puzzle that Talley'd designed, and Adam agreed to help with? How much had she planned out, and how much had been left to chance?

The phone rang, and I nearly jumped out of my skin. But

my phone was set to vibrate, not ring. It was Adam's phone. The word *Dad* popped up on his screen. He pressed the Ignore button. A minute passed, maybe two, and his phone rang again. "Hi, I'm alive," Adam said. "You don't need to worry about me." There was a pause, and then he said, "I don't need to tell you where I am all the time. I'm not a frickin' five-year-old."

His eyes slid toward me and I looked away, as if to give him privacy. I guess if he really wanted privacy, he could've gotten up.

"I'm in Palo Alto with a friend, okay?" Adam said. "I don't know when I'll be home, but I'm not the one who . . . I'm not totally disappearing on you, okay? I'll see you when I see you."

"We can go if you need to go," I said, once he'd ended the call.

"Nah, it's fine."

"Seriously," I said. "It's not like waiting here in close proximity to where the flyer was posted will make Nicole call back any faster. It doesn't matter where I am. She has my number."

"Well, that's true," he said. "You okay?"

"I was just thinking it's not fair of me to keep this flyer. Nicole put it up to get customers, and I should put it back, even if it means piercing the bark again. But I don't want to give up this photo."

"You can take a photo of the photo," Adam said.

"Yeah, I'll do that."

I centered my phone over the picture of Talley's hands and took a picture. There, now I'd have it forever. A picture of Talley's hands. It made me wish for more pictures—of her ankles, her earlobes, her elbows. Pictures you never think about taking when someone is alive. If you did take them, it'd be accidental, and you'd delete those photos from the camera roll. But now that Talley was gone, I wanted to keep all the different parts of her close to me. I missed all of them.

I stood up and pinned the flyer back on the tree, right where I'd found it. "I'm ready to go if you are," I told Adam.

"Sure," he said. "And hey, if Nicole calls back after tomorrow and you're already gone, I can go meet her if you need me to. I'll be here."

"I'll be here, too," I said. "I'm not going home tomorrow."

chapter twenty-five

ADAM DROPPED ME OFF AT AUNT ELISE'S, WHERE THERE was nothing to do but wait. I called Juno to tell her I didn't want to change my ticket after all, and I was caught off guard when she gave me some pushback. "I feel like you can't see the forest for the trees anymore," she said. "And I get that—Talley was your sister. But—"

I cut her off. "But Ju, this tree just popped out at me. An actual redwood tree. I have to stay here for this. I don't know what else to say."

On the other end of the line, Juno was quiet, too. Silence between the two of us was a rarity. Even after seeing each other all day long in school and knowing the ins and outs of everything that had happened, we could still log hours on the phone at night. It was a surefire way to irritate my father, especially if I reached for my phone while I was with him. "Don't you and Juno ever run out of things to say?" he'd asked more than once. All I could do was shrug and tell him that's what it meant to be someone's best friend: we thought everything about the other was interesting and worth analyzing.

"I feel like you're mad at me over this, Ju," I said, breaking the silence.

"I'm not. I just miss you, that's all. I got my hopes up when you said you wanted to come home. The triplets are tough, and you're better with them than I am. I took them for a walk and we ran into Audrey."

"No way!"

"Yeah, and they like her better than me," she said. "Apparently everyone does—Cooper, and now Thomas, Theo, and Melanie, too."

"Well, what do they know?" I said. "They're eight years old. By the time they start fourth grade, they'll have seen the error of their ways."

"It's just so embarrassing to lose the popularity game to Audrey. You should've heard them shouting her name. Just hearing her name is a trigger for me. They might as well be saying Voldemort, because hers is the name that really shouldn't be spoken."

"Actually, in one of the books Dumbledore tells Harry that he shouldn't be afraid to say Voldemort's name," I told her. "He said when you make someone's name verboten, you play into your fear of them."

"I don't fear her. I hate her. I hate how she gets everything."

"She can't have me," I said.

"I know. I'm sorry I was just being a total baby about everything. Soraya says Cooper and Audrey deserve each other."

"That's what I say, too," I said.

"I know I'm supposed to think that, but—"

"Hang on. I'm getting another call." I held the phone out to glance at the number on the screen. It was a 650 area code—Adam's area code, and Aunt Elise's area code, and the area code on the flyer for NHL Photography. "Ju, I'll call you back. I gotta take this."

I clicked over. "Hello?"

"Hi, this is Nicole Lister calling from NHL Photography. I'm looking for Sloane."

"This is Sloane," I said. "Thank you so much for getting back to me."

"I hope it's not too late to call. I just picked up your message."

It was 9:47, according to the clock on the cable box. "No, not at all," I said.

"Good. You said you found a flyer?"

"Yes."

"May I ask where?" she said. "It's always good to know where the advertising is working."

"The redwood tree on the end of University Avenue in Palo Alto," I told her. And then, because Talley would've wanted me to, I added: "It's actually bad for the trees to pin things to them."

"Oh, really?"

"Yeah, bark is a protective layer, like skin. I only know because my sister told me. She's actually the reason why I'm calling."

181

"Your sister is the one having an event?"

"No, she's on your flyer. There's a picture of a guy's face close-up, except you can't see his face because someone's hands are covering it. They're my sister's hands."

"I didn't take that photo," Nicole said. "It was one of my students—and I got his permission to use it. In terms of your sister, you can't identify someone just by their hands, and you don't need to get permission to use photos of non-identifiable people. I looked it up."

"I could tell it was her from her rings," I explained.

"There isn't an event at all, is there?"

"No," I admitted. "I'm really sorry. I needed to make sure you'd call me back."

"So you could give me a problem about a photo because you think you recognize your sister's rings? Plenty of people wear rings."

"I don't want to give you a problem at all," I said.

"Okay, good," Nicole said. "And may I please give you some unsolicited advice?" She phrased it as a question, but I could tell by her tone that she was speaking rhetorically, and she was going to give the advice whether I wanted to hear it or not. "Since you were so kind as to educate me on the bark issue, I think it's only right that I should inform you that when someone is trying to run a business, it's really poor form to call them up under false pretenses and pretend to be having an event when you're not."

My cheeks were suddenly blazing. "I know," I said. "I'm sorry. It was easier to make something up on your voice mail because the truth is so awful and hard to say. My sister died."

"Oh," Nicole said. Her voice softened. "I am *so* sorry for your loss—and I'm sorry for being a jerk just now."

"You didn't know," I said. "It was totally unexpected, and she left this piece of paper—"

"A suicide note?" Nicole asked.

"No, not exactly," I said. "But you're right. That is how she died—by suicide—and she left a list of random things. It turns out that a number of them were here, in the Bay Area, even though we're from Minnesota. So that's why I'm out here—I'm trying to piece it all together. I saw the flyer, and I recognized her hands. I know a lot of people wear rings, but I *know* those were Talley's rings. She wrote 'NHL photo revelations' on her list. I've spent hours googling those words, but all I'd found were pictures of the National Hockey League."

"I should rename my business," Nicole said. "For now it's just a side deal. By day I'm a kindergarten teacher. I've only taught one group of photography students so far. 'Revelation' was an assignment I gave them."

"I don't think I knew what that word meant when I was in kindergarten."

"Oh, my photography students are adults, not kindergarteners. I told them to walk around with their cameras and take pictures without thinking too hard on it. I said the things they focus on when they look through the lens would reveal what they're interested in. I guess one of them was interested in your sister."

"Everyone was interested in Talley," I said.

"Her name was Talley?"

"Natalie," I said. "We all called her Talley."

"Listen, Sloane, I want to apologize again for how I was at the beginning of this call. It's been a long-ass day, but that's not your fault, and I took it out on you. I also want to tell you that I know how you're feeling. I hate when people say that, because personal experience is so . . . *personal*. But my dad died by suicide, too. It was exactly two years ago today. When I got your message, I wasn't in any kind of mood to talk to anyone. But I knew he'd want me to call you back. He wouldn't want me to miss an opportunity for business just because I was missing him."

"I'm sorry about your dad," I said. "And I'm sorry I didn't really have a business opportunity for you."

"That's all right. I have a feeling he'd want us to be talking right now anyway. When did your sister die?"

"Last month," I said. "Three weeks and four days ago."

"Oh, God. It just happened."

"It doesn't feel that way," I said. "It feels like I've been living without her for forever already. But I'm still not used to it. When I wake up in the morning, I always think she's still alive. So I guess my subconscious is still in denial."

"That's totally normal," Nicole said. "They say there are five stages of grief—the Kübler-Ross stages: denial, anger, bargaining, depression, and acceptance."

"I read about those online," I said. "I really can't imagine ever getting to acceptance."

"I think it's harder for people like us—people who lost someone they loved to suicide. I don't mean to minimize the pain of people who lost their loved ones in other ways. Loss is awful no matter what, but . . ."

"But at least if it's cancer you know you couldn't have done anything to change it," I filled in. "If Talley had died of cancer, I'd be heartbroken. But it wouldn't have been my fault. Or if she died like my mom—"

"Your mom died, too? I'm so sorry."

"She was in a car accident when I was really young," I said. "There was nothing I could do about it, so it feels so different. I feel really sad about it sometimes, but I don't feel guilty."

"When my dad died, I felt *so* guilty," Nicole said. "I was sure I could've stopped it. I was sure I *should've* stopped it. I would lie awake and play scenes in my head, pretending I'd said the exact right thing he'd needed to hear at the exact right time, and changed everything. But of course I hadn't. I was raging with anger at him for not getting help, and I was even angrier at myself for not knowing he needed it."

My mind flashed to Talley, the last time I saw her alive, when she was in her bed and asking me to play hooky with her for the day. "Did he say anything to you that last day?" I asked.

"No," Nicole said. "But I thought it was up to me to say something to him. Which made it all the more difficult to get to acceptance."

"I'll never get to acceptance," I said.

"I would've said that, too," Nicole said. "When I was just three weeks and four days past his death. But I don't speak in absolutes anymore. Everything can change, including your feelings about things. Today was not an easy day for me, obviously. But when my dad first died, I didn't think I'd have any more good days. Maybe I'd have a good moment or two, but no full day could be good without him in the world."

I remembered my realization at Talley's funeral. *I'll never have another day of pure joy, without Talley in the world.*

"But it turns out," Nicole went on, "that I do have good days. It doesn't mean I miss him any less, because I don't. But I have a full life with a lot of people who love me, and I love them. I can spend time with them, and laugh at jokes, and just *live*—and I don't feel like I'm betraying my father anymore. At least most of the time, I don't feel that way. Maybe that's helpful to hear."

I shrugged, then remembered Nicole couldn't see me through the phone. "You're the first person I've talked to who lost someone from suicide," I said. "Aside from people I'm related to."

"We're something of an underground. People don't understand suicide. They don't know how to react to it. I go to a support group every week, if you're interested in joining. We talk a lot about self-blame, and all the rest of it."

"I don't even live here," I said. "I'm from Minnesota."

"Oh, right. You said that."

"But there is something you can do for me, if it's not too much trouble. Can you reach out to the student who took the photo?"

"Absolutely. It may not be till tomorrow, given the time now. But I promise that as soon as I have any information, I will call or text you."

"Thank you," I said.

chapter twenty-six

I WAS GOING TO CALL JUNO BACK, BUT I REALIZED THE person I really wanted to update was Adam, and so I texted him the latest.

He wrote back immediately: I was just about to text you. Thx for the update!

Me: Hopefully I'll have another update soon.

Adam: I'm on standby

But the update didn't come that night, just as Nicole had warned it probably wouldn't. I must've fallen asleep, though I don't remember doing so. (Is it even possible to remember falling asleep? If you're awake enough to be aware that the act of falling asleep is happening, you probably wouldn't be able to do it.) But I remember waking up in the morning and reaching for my phone first thing. There weren't any messages from Nicole. But there was a good-morning text from Juno, who was two hours ahead of me, and there was an email from Dr. Lee.

It wasn't the first time I'd seen Dr. Lee's name in my inbox. During the school year, she often sent blasts out to the whole class, or if I emailed her a question about an assignment, she'd write back with the answer. But I'd never heard from her outside of school.

The subject line was: *Thinking of you.*

Dear Sloane,

As you know, I'm teaching a course at Hamline this summer. And also as you know, it is not ordinarily open to high school students. But I contacted the head of the program and explained that I had a very talented high school student in mind, and asked if an exception could be made. They said they trusted my judgment, which is to say the answer is yes.

Perhaps you are otherwise committed or no longer interested. I know a lot has changed in your life since we first discussed Hamline. Please understand that this email is not an attempt to pressure you in any way. But I wanted to pass along a couple more things.

First, in my experience, writing is the roadmap through the darkest times. When I force my characters to face hardship and craft ways for them to navigate their way out of it, I'm really figuring out how to navigate my way out of my own hardship. I wanted to give you a space in my classroom for that, should you want it.

And second, while I don't presume to be the person you need at this difficult time, I wanted to let you know that I'm here nonetheless if you need someone to talk to, or someone to simply listen.

With love,
Mary Lee

I stared at the last couple lines for at least two full minutes. She'd used her first name. Above that there were the words *with love.*

Dr. Lee had written an email to me, "with love," to tell me she'd gone out of her way to bend the rules to accommodate me. Any other time in my life I would've been absolutely giddy. Now it didn't matter.

I closed the email, put my phone down, and went to the bathroom to brush my teeth. But just knowing the email was there was making me feel twitchy. Dr. Lee had made a point to say she didn't want to make me feel pressured, but I did feel pressure. As long as it was in my inbox, I felt like there was an obligation I was skipping out on. So I picked my phone up again and deleted the email. There. Now there was nothing left to respond to.

chapter twenty-seven

I SENT NICOLE A TEXT AROUND TEN O'CLOCK IN THE morning: Just wanted to see if there's any update.

I waited for her to reply.

And waited.

And waited.

It was so frustrating that there wasn't anything for me to do. Aunt Elise's friend Frances picked her up to take her to the doctor, and I stayed back and cleaned the house. I changed the sheets on the beds, dusted the bookshelves and the tables. My fingers lingered on the brown leather photo album on the coffee table, the one Aunt Elise had told me about when I'd arrived.

Whenever I picture you, you're the little girl in the red dress you wore on your birthday.

I flipped through a few pages before I found the red-dress

pictures. There was white trim on the collar and on the edges of the capped sleeves. Talley was next to me, in a white blouse and a red skirt that was clearly made by the same company as my dress. Mom was in a few of the photos. In one of them, I was on her lap.

She must've picked out Talley's and my clothes. Matching outfits weren't anything Dad would've thought to buy us.

And there was Dad, looking like he did now, but less gray, and less . . . I don't know. Less something else.

I flipped the album closed and put it back on the table.

It was hours before I got a text from Nicole. Finally, nearly twenty-four hours after our first phone call. My phone buzzed: It's Nicole from NHL. Can you chat?

Of course I could chat. If I were undergoing dental surgery, I'd still find a way to chat. I pressed the button to call her without texting back. "Sorry for the delay," she said. "I didn't want to call you until I gathered as much information as I could. I heard from my student Rafe, and he said the day of the assignment, he went to Laurelwood Park in San Mateo. Whenever he saw someone or something that looked interesting, he'd take a picture. He didn't chat with anyone beyond asking if he could photograph them. He didn't even ask anyone's name. But Talley was one of those people."

"So that's it," I said. If that was it, then what next? I pressed a hand to my face. I'd cry about this for sure, but I'd wait till I hung up with Nicole. "I really do appreciate that you tried to help," I said.

"Hang on," she said. "I have a little more information. Rafe told me he'd left his contact sheet and negatives in my darkroom, so I went searching for any other photos of your sister that he might have taken. I know if there were other photos of my dad out there, I'd want them."

"Yeah, anything you have with Talley in it, I definitely want it. Even if it's just her hands or whatever."

"Well, unfortunately, there weren't any additional photos of Talley. The photo of her hands was the second to last photo on the roll, and the last photo was of the guy she was with. Same hair, same chin, and you can actually see his face. I took the liberty of developing the photo. If you want it, I can text it over to you."

"Yeah, okay," I said. I could hear my dad's voice in my head: *I think you're missing a couple words.* "Thank you," I added.

"You're welcome," she said. "If there's anything else I can do, or if you do want to come to a meeting, just text or call, okay?"

"I will," I said.

Nicole sent the picture seconds after she hung up. It was a profile shot, but you could still see the guy's longish hair and the scruff on his face. There was a daisy chain of dandelions settled on his head like a crown, and I knew it was something Talley'd made for him. She'd made dozens for me over the years, maybe hundreds. But that was back when I was little. I hadn't worn a dandelion daisy chain in years. This guy looked about Talley's age, or maybe a little bit older, but not too much older. There were small lines at the corner of his eyes, but no major wrinkles. I'd say he was late-twenties, tops. He was sitting on a bench, and his body was facing the camera, so I could read the words on his T-shirt: *Must Love Dogs.*

I stared and stared at the picture. Who was he? Could he be Talley's large gentleman? Figuring out Talley's list was like climbing a mountain. I'd been totally exhausted and ready to give up and go home. Then I'd found the flyer, and it was like finally seeing the peak of the mountain—nearly there! I couldn't give up now! But it turned out all I'd seen was a vista point, and there was so much farther to climb.

I called Adam to update him on what I'd learned from Nicole, which was not much. Just a picture of the guy Talley'd been goofing off with, this one without her hands over his eyes. "I'm wracking my brain trying to think of ways to find him," I told Adam. "All I can think to do is make up our own flyers—like, have you seen this man? And then put his picture underneath."

"Just don't post them on trees," Adam said. "Bark is a protective layer, like skin."

"I know," I said.

"Sorry, I just said that to make you laugh. It wasn't funny."

"It was," I said. "I'm just trying to think of what Talley would want from me. When she gave me a game when I was little and I couldn't figure it out, she wouldn't tell me the answer straight out. She'd give me another clue, and another. But I don't have her to give more clues now, and I have no idea how to find a person I know next to nothing about—literally, all I know is what he looks like, that he hung out at Laurelwood Park at some point with Talley, and he had a T-shirt that said 'Must Love Dogs.'"

"Is it navy with a silhouette of a dog?"

"It's a black-and-white photo, so I can't tell the color of the shirt, but it could be navy, and there *is* a silhouette of a dog. Are you psychic or something?"

"Wouldn't it be your lucky day if I was?" Adam said. "But I might know where to find our mystery guy."

chapter twenty-eight

ADAM'S FAMILY HAD TWO DOGS, CHARLIE AND OTTO, and when the Hadlocks went on vacation, they left the dogs at a place called Must Love Dogs. The guy in the photo, whoever he was, was wearing an employee T-shirt.

Of course I was on Google faster than you can say "must love dogs." There wasn't any information about staff members on the website. But there was a lot of information about the company itself—it was the Bay Area's premiere place for vet care, pet training, day care, and boarding. (Or at least it was the premiere place according to the website.) Must Love Dogs had a handful of locations, and if I had to, I'd show up at every single one of them.

I figured I'd start with the one in San Mateo, because that's where Laurelwood Park was, which was where the picture was taken. If the guy in the photo didn't work at the San Mateo location,

I'd go to the next closest, and the next closest, and on and on until I found him.

I told Adam my plan—Must Love Dogs was already closed for the night. They had an emergency call line if your dog was boarded there. I doubted this would qualify as something they'd see as an emergency. But then I thought, it counted as an emergency to *me*, and if they got upset with me for calling, I'd just ask for forgiveness. I called—the guy who answered didn't seem upset, but he did say I couldn't show up outside their official business hours, which were from eight a.m. to eight p.m. So I planned to take the Caltrain to San Mateo in the morning and be on the doorstep of Must Love Dogs the minute it opened for business. Adam offered to drive me instead. I told him that he didn't need to, but he insisted, so long as I didn't mind getting there a little bit later, like around nine. He'd tell his mom he wasn't feeling well and couldn't possibly go to work, but then he wouldn't be able to leave the house till after she did.

"You don't have to miss work for me," I told him.

"You have no idea how much I want to miss work," he said. "I'll see you in the morning."

Adam pulled into Aunt Elise's driveway at eight thirty on Wednesday morning, as promised. "I can't thank you enough for everything you've done for me," I told him as we got on our way.

"I haven't done anything."

"You've done so much," I said. "You called me back two weeks ago, even though I was a perfect stranger."

"As anyone with any decency would've done."

"You helped me pinpoint places on the list; you took me to Grizzly Cove for lunch—"

"You wouldn't let me take you," Adam said. "And you paid for the ice cream."

"If you hadn't suggested ice cream, we never would've found the flyer, I never would've spoken to Nicole or gotten the picture of our mystery guy, and we wouldn't be headed to Must Love Dogs. Plus you're chauffeuring us right now," I said.

"Well, when you put it that way, I am pretty great," Adam said.

"Seriously, you are. These last few days have been really tough and you've keep me company—really good company. And I know you said you never met Talley—"

"I didn't."

"But if you *had* met her. I mean, if she had met you, she would've liked you. She would've told me you were the kind of person I should have as a friend."

"Aw, shucks, Weber," he said. "Thank you."

My phone buzzed and I looked down to see a text from Juno: U up? I'm hiding in the bathroom at the Hogans. It's an emergency.

Me: What happened? Is everyone ok?

Juno: An AUDREY emergency!

Me: But no one is hurt, right?

Juno: Not yet . . . but I might have to kill her

Me: Ugh. Sorry. In the middle of something with Adam right now. Will call later.

Adam pulled into the parking lot of a strip mall. The Must Love Dogs of San Mateo was in the corner of the building. Adrenaline was surging through my veins again. You'd think at this point I'd be used to the feeling; but if your body got used to the feeling of a surge of adrenaline, wouldn't that cancel out the adrenaline?

We crossed the parking lot. Adam pulled open the door and we entered a small-ish anteroom, at the end of which was a counter. Behind that, through a glass pane, I could see at least a dozen dogs yapping and running around, chasing each other, chasing tennis balls, chasing their tails, the way dogs do.

A man stood behind the counter—not the guy in the picture, though he was wearing the same T-shirt: navy, like Adam had said, with the words Must Love Dogs in a semicircle above the silhouette of a dog. The name tag pinned to his shirt said: *Derek* ♥ *Dogs*.

"Hi. Can I help you?" Derek asked.

"I really hope so," I said. "I'm looking for someone who I think might work here. I don't know his name, but I have his picture." I dug into my pocket for my phone and scrolled through my texts for the last one from Nicole, with the picture, which I held out toward Derek. My heart was thump-thumping away in anticipation, but Derek shook his head.

"Sorry, I don't know the guy. He told you he worked here?"

"Not exactly," I said. "It's a long story, but I think he knew my sister. Any chance you ever saw her?" I pressed the button to get back to the home screen, and Talley's face.

"No, don't know her, either," Derek said. "But I'm happy to answer any pet care questions you have."

"Thanks, man," Adam said. "We're good on that. We're just looking for this particular guy."

"We have a number of other locations," Derek said. "Burlingame and Foster City are probably closest."

"We're going to hit both," Adam said.

Back in the car, Adam told me he thought we should try Burlingame first, because it was the only location north of San Mateo, and if not Burlingame, we'd circle back to Foster City, and continue heading south. "You're the navigator," I told him. I was still hopeful, but after we struck out, first in Burlingame and again in Foster City, I felt the gloom settling in again.

I didn't say anything to Adam, but I guess he could tell anyway, because he reached over and patted my knee. "Belmont is next," he said, "and I have a good feeling about it. I think we'll get some answers there."

We got to the Belmont location, another outdoor mall, though a bit more picturesque than the one in San Mateo. It was nestled into the side of a hill, and the building had the same kind of Spanish-tiled roof as the townhouses in Aunt Elise's development. Must Love Dogs was in between a drugstore and a bagel shop. This time I got to the door first, so I held it open for Adam. I had the photo from Nicole already pulled up on my phone when I approached the woman behind the counter. Her name tag read: *Vera ♥ Dogs*.

"Hi," I said. "I'm looking for someone who I think maybe works here. Do you know this guy?"

"Oh yeah, that's Griff," Vera said.

Griff. His name was Griff!

"He doesn't work at this location," Vera went on. "But I can help you with whatever it is you need."

"Can you tell me what location he works at?" I asked.

Vera started to answer, but then changed her mind. "No, I can't tell you that," she said. "I don't know why you're looking for Griff, but I suppose you're not his friends, because if you were, you would've known his name without my having to say it. And I shouldn't have said it. You should probably go now."

"Please," I said. "We're not here to make trouble for you or Griff or anyone. I found a picture of him with my sister." I was scrolling through pictures on my phone to pull it up. "She died last month, and I'm just trying to talk to the people that knew her. That's all."

I held out my phone and Vera considered the picture of Talley and Griff.

"I know you can't see his face, but it's clearly the same guy from the other picture, and I know that's my sister with him, because those are her hands."

"We wouldn't make this up," Adam added.

"No, I suppose you wouldn't," Vera said. "I'm sorry about your sister. Griff works at our place in Redwood City. Let me give you the address." She recited it, and I typed it into my phone even though I already had the address of every Must Love Dogs location in the Bay Area. "I can call over there if you want and tell him to expect you."

"That'd be great," I said. "Thank you."

"Is there anything else I can do?"

"You already did a lot," I said.

"Hey," Adam said. "Out of curiosity, would you describe Griff as a particularly large guy?"

"Oh yeah," Vera said. "We call him the gentle giant."

Adam and I locked eyes. I sucked in my breath.

"Is everything okay?" Vera asked.

I never knew how to answer that question, ATD. No, everything wasn't okay. But I knew what Vera was getting at. "I think I'm finally figuring some things out," I said.

"That's good, right?" Vera said.

"Yeah, it's good."

"I won't tell Griff what happened," she said. "Unless you want me to. But I suppose he'd rather hear it from you."

"Probably. Thanks again."

"What was your sister's name?"

"Talley," I said.

chapter twenty-nine

ADAM PULLED INTO THE FIFTH PARKING LOT OF THE day, and we walked into the fifth Must Love Dogs location. My breath caught in my throat: there was Griff behind the counter. He was remarkably large, like a walking teddy bear, especially since his facial hair had grown in more. His hair was on the long side and was either wet or just greasy. His name tag said: *Griffin* ♥ *Dogs*.

"Picking up or dropping off?" he asked. "I don't see a dog, so I guess that's picking up."

"Neither," I told him. "I think Vera from Belmont may have called you?"

"Oh yeah, she just did." He knocked himself in the side of his head with the heel of his hand. "How'd I forget that already? She said someone was coming because I knew their sister."

"My sister," I said.

"Right, right . . . What's her name again?"

"Talley Weber."

Griff's eyes glazed over for a few seconds, and then he blinked and shook his head vigorously. His hair was greasy enough to not flop around. "Nope, there aren't any Talleys in the ole memory bank. Zip. Zilch. Zero. Don't think I knew her."

"But you did know her," I said. "I have a photo of you guys." I pulled up the photo of Griff's face covered by Talley's hands, and turned it toward him. He took my phone from me to look closer.

"You're right—I did meet this girl." His face had broken into a grin. "Oh, man, she's your sister?"

"Yes."

"Oh, man," he said again. "I totally remember her. She sent you here?"

"Sort of," I said. "When did you meet her?"

"That day," Griff said. "In the park. It was only for a few minutes, but sometimes there are minutes with a person that stick with you, you know?" I nodded; yes, I knew. Particularly minutes with Talley, I knew. "She had a different name, though," Griff said.

"Natalie?" I guessed.

"No, that's not it," he said. "But names don't matter. They don't make the man. Your parents pick 'em, and then you're saddled with someone else's idea of who you're supposed to be, but it's not you. I say parents should leave a blank space for their kids' name on the birth certificate, and let their kids fill it in when they're old enough to write. If you're old enough to write, you're probably old enough to know yourself, right?"

"Yeah, sure," I said. "So—"

"Then again, I probably would've named myself after Pikachu when I first started writing, so maybe you can have a placeholder name when you're like five or so, and then you can change it again when a better name strikes you. Maybe that's what your sister did."

"What?"

"Picked a better name when it struck her."

"Oh, sure," I said. "Can you tell me anything else about Talley, or whatever she called herself?"

"She was with another girl," Griff said.

"Do you remember *her* name?" Adam asked.

"Sure don't. But I can tell you that they were making these flower things."

"Daisy chains," I said.

"Right. Those. They had a dozen of them," Griff said. "I was watching them. They kept walking up to people, saying something, and then they'd put the flowers on their heads. I wondered what they were saying. I was trying to read their lips—some people can do that, you know."

I did know. Juno was pretty good at it. Whenever she was talking to someone, she liked to face them, because then she could read their lips and fill in the blanks of whatever she couldn't hear.

"But I couldn't tell," Griff went on. "Then your sister came over to me. She told me she was always on the lookout for people she could help, and she could help me by adding a daisy chain to my life. I bent down and she put it on my head. This other guy was walking around with a camera, and asked if he could capture the moment."

"His name is Rafe," I supplied.

"Okay, cool, he didn't tell us at the time," Griff said. "He just said he had some kind of assignment—NHL photo revolution."

"You mean revelations?" I asked.

"I don't know. Maybe. He asked if he could take a picture, and I said sure, why the hell not? I think he sensed it was one of those moments that you want to preserve. Though I don't really believe in photos. Make a memory, they last longer, as the saying goes."

Actually, it was the opposite of what the saying was: take a picture, it lasts longer. But I didn't correct him. "Did you—" I started.

The phone behind the counter started ringing. Griff said, "Hold that thought," and answered. "Must Love Dogs. How may I help you?" There was silence and then, "Uh-huh. Uh-huh. You can bring Diamond in, no problem." He hung up and turned back to Adam and me. "Sorry 'bout that," he said.

"Did you and my sister talk about anything else?" I asked.

"No," he said. "But there was something there. A moment of shared energy. You ask her. I bet she'll tell you the same thing."

I nodded as if I were able to ask her, and she'd be able to tell me, and I swallowed back the lump in my throat because the last thing I wanted to do was start crying here at Must Love Dogs in front of Griff.

"And the girl who was with her," Adam said. "Did she say anything?"

"Hang on," Griff said. He'd closed his eyes and had placed a hand against his forehead. "I'm feeling something." He drummed his fingers on the counter and mumbled, "Diamond. Diamond,

Diamond. Da da in the sky with diamonds . . ." His eyes popped open. "I've got it. The caller just now has a French bulldog named Diamond. Names don't matter to me, but songs sure do. There's a Beatles song called 'Lucy in the Sky with Diamonds.' Your sister said her name was Lucy."

"Oh, wow. Lucy and Ethel," I said.

"Ethel was her friend!" Griff said.

"Griff!" came a call from the back. "Did you give Mr. Shivers his worm medication?"

"Negative," Griff called back. "So," he said to us. "That it?"

"Just a couple more questions," I said. "Did you guys watch a sunset together?"

"Nope, it was the middle of the day."

"What did Ethel look like?" Adam asked.

"She was taller than Lucy. Talley, whatever you want to call her. Ethel was taller. Like yea high." Griff held a hand up to just below his nose. I'd guess that meant Ethel was at least five foot eight, given how big Griff was.

"Anything else? Hair color?"

"I don't know. She was wearing a hat."

"Did you talk to her?"

"She told me to sit on the bench so Talley could reach my head to put the flowers," Griff said. "Mostly she talked to Talley, not me. She was cracking her up. They were cracking up each other. They seemed very close. I asked Talley for her number. I didn't tell you that before—but that was the end of our convo, and she declined to give it to me, so maybe that's why. But I'll tell you something." Now he was looking at me again. "I felt something between us, a spark of something. Tell your sister I'd love to take her out sometime. Even if it's just as friends, if that's more her bag. I like to surround myself with good people who have good energy. Your sister had the good energy of a dozen good people."

Now I was going to cry. "I can't give her the message. She died. Talley died."

"Aw, man," Griff said. "I am sorry. I can't tell you how sorry I am to hear that. That's just . . . you meet a person like that, and they're frozen in that moment. You never think anything bad could happen."

Adam rested a hand on the small of my back, and I was grateful for the square of heat, like a palm-shaped blanket.

"Would it be all right if I texted you my phone number?" I asked Griff. "I know you only spent a few minutes with Talley, but if you remember anything else—anything at all—I'd love to know it."

"Of course you can text me," he said.

He recited his digits, and I sent a text: This is Sloane Weber, Talley (Lucy's) sister.

"And if you wouldn't mind," he said, "could you text me that photo of your sister and me? I have the memory, but sometimes it's nice to have the picture, too."

chapter thirty

ADAM SUGGESTED WE GRAB A BITE TO EAT. HE COULD GO for a fried-egg sandwich, he said, unless there was something else I was craving. I didn't have any idea as to where we should go next, so I said getting something to eat was fine with me. We went to the El Camino Diner, because it was close by, because it was a diner and therefore definitely had fried-egg sandwiches on the menu, and because eating there was a way to stay on task—the task being Talley's list. We'd made progress today—we'd found Griff, and found out about a friend of Talley's named Ethel.

But when I texted Aunt Elise from the car to see if she'd met anyone named Ethel, or at least someone who matched the vague description that Griff had given, she said no, she hadn't. So now what?

Adam plugged his car into the charging port in the parking

lot. There was still plenty of juice left—at least half a charge, but he said he might as well since there was an empty spot right there. Anna was there when we walked into the diner. She recognized me and even remembered my name. "Sloane!" she said. "Did you connect with Elise from Down Dog?"

"Yes," I said. "She's my aunt."

"Well, what do you know?" she said. "No wonder you look so much like her."

"I only found her because of you," I said. "I really owe you an enormous thank-you."

"You don't at all," Anna said. "I didn't even know what I was doing, but I am happy to have helped. Go on—take a seat." She raised the pot of coffee she was holding and gestured in the direction of the tables. "Anywhere you'd like."

The corner booth was empty again. Talley might have said it took sixty-six days to form a habit, but apparently after only four days, on my second visit to the El Camino Diner, I already felt like there was a table at the diner that was *my* table. I pointed it out to Adam. Anna came over within seconds of us sitting down to fill our water glasses. She also had a Coke with no ice for me—"On the house, dear," she told me. I thanked her profusely, and she gave me a wink and said it was her pleasure. She'd be back in a couple minutes, after my friend and I had a chance to look at our menus. "I think my friend knows what he wants already," I said.

"But do you know what you want?" Adam asked.

"Nah, I'm not really hungry."

"Are you sure?"

"Yes."

"Well, we didn't have to stop, then."

"It's fine," I said. "You're hungry, and I don't mind sitting and thinking for a little while."

"Okay, if you're sure," Adam said. I nodded, and he gave his order to Anna: "Two fried eggs on a roll please, and fries."

After Anna left, I flipped over the place mat. When I was little, I used to flip over the paper place mats at the Good Day Café in Golden Valley and draw on the other side. But the other side of this place mat was a map instead of a blank page, and there weren't any crayons on the table anyway. I flipped it over again.

"How are you feeling about everything?" Adam asked me. "Besides not being hungry."

"I don't know," I said. "Telling Griff about Talley was hard, but I'm glad we found him. Even if he isn't the large gentleman. This whole time I thought Talley'd put Lucy and Ethel on her list because she liked the TV show, which was weird, since I'd never seen her watch it. But now I know Ethel was a person in her life. And who knows—maybe Griff *was* the large gentleman. Maybe Talley and Ethel saw a sunset afterward or something, and it meant enough to them for Talley to put it on her list."

Adam stirred the ice around in his water. "That's entirely possible."

My phone buzzed with a text from Juno: U free yet?

I pressed the button to darken the screen, then turned the phone over in my lap. Whatever was going on with Audrey, I didn't have time for it right then.

"Do you think Talley called herself Lucy because Ethel was actually her friend's name, or that it was a fake name for her, too?" I asked Adam.

"I don't know," he said.

"You don't meet too many twentysomethings named Ethel these days, so it feels like they were both fake names. An ode to another pair of best friends."

"You think they were best friends and not, like, *together*?"

"I guess they could've been. I don't know what's harder to wrap my brain around—the idea that Talley would have a best friend she didn't tell me about, or that she'd have a girlfriend she didn't tell me about."

"Maybe it was both and she thought it would upset you," Adam said.

"No way," I said. "She knew me better than that."

"Sorry, I didn't mean you were the kind of person who'd be upset."

Anna arrived with the food. Adam and I had both been sitting forward, but we sat back, like retreating into our corners, as Anna put the plates down—one plate with Adam's fried-egg sandwich, and the plate of fries, big enough to feed half a dozen people. "Need anything else?" she asked.

I shook my head. "I think we're good," Adam told her. He picked up a small fry, crisped to perfection, and leaned forward again, holding it out to me. I nodded thanks and took it from him, not because I really wanted it, but because it felt like the fry was a peace offering, and I needed to take it to let him know that I wasn't mad.

"The truth is," I said, "I've been really struggling to understand why she did what she did. Maybe part of it was that she felt she couldn't tell me the truth about herself—about her sexuality. But that doesn't ring true for me. She knew what we did for Soraya. She's my closest friend, other than Juno. She came out to Juno and me and a few of our other friends at the beginning of ninth grade, and she was so nervous. Juno and I wanted to do something to assure her that we didn't think of her any differently. We were just so happy to know, because we love her and we want to know and celebrate the truth about her. So we told her to meet us at Golden Oaks Park just before sundown. There was a crew of us, and we gave her a big bouquet of flowers and half a dozen helium balloons."

"That's so sweet," Adam said. "I'm sure it meant a lot to her."

"That's not even the half of it," I said. "Juno had a whole elaborate plan. The flowers were for Soraya to keep, and the balloons were for her to share. One for each of us. We'd gotten biodegradable ones, because Talley insisted, and of course she was right that they're the best kind to use. I'd brought along Sharpies, per Juno's instructions, and we each wrote a personal truth on the balloon." I made air quotes around the words *personal truth*—those were the words Juno had used that day. "Then we released the balloons into the sky."

"You should write that up somewhere," Adam said. "I bet it would go viral. It's the exact perfect thing to do for a friend."

"Well, it was Juno's idea, really. I just brought the Sharpies."

"Those Sharpies were essential," he said. "How could you send personal-truth balloons out into the world without Sharpies? You couldn't do it."

"Fair point," I said.

"What did you write?" he asked.

I shook my head. "It doesn't matter."

I'd written that I wanted to be a writer when I grew up. It just wasn't my personal truth anymore. I didn't want to write anything since I'd written Talley's eulogy.

"My point is," I told Adam, "Talley knew all about that. She even supplied the champagne that we toasted Soraya with."

"What about your dad?" Adam asked.

"What about him?"

"Would one of his daughters having a girlfriend be the kind of thing he'd be upset about?"

"I don't think so. Once I had a study group at my house and this guy Tanner said 'that's so gay,' about something. My dad was passing through the kitchen and he interrupted our study session to say that kind of homophobic talk wasn't acceptable in his house. I was totally mortified."

"Sounds like Tanner was the one who should've been mortified," Adam said.

"Oh, I think he was. It was a bad moment for everyone. My friends don't talk like that. I noticed when he said it, and I'd like to think I would've corrected him, or that someone else at the table would have. But we didn't have a chance, because my dad jumped in immediately. It's a thousand times worse when someone else's parent reprimands you, so in retrospect, maybe it's a good thing that my dad did it before the rest of us could get a word in. Tanner was really contrite: 'I'm sorry, Mr. Weber. I didn't mean it. I won't do it again.' I bet he hasn't. Or if he ever does, I bet he'll hear my dad's voice in his head, reprimanding him again."

"Every time I hear someone else say something like that from now on, I'm going to think of your dad," Adam said. "But just because he wouldn't let someone use the word 'gay' in a derogatory way doesn't mean he didn't expect his kids to be straight. Most parents expect that. My parents pat themselves on the back all the time for how evolved they are, and yet they've been making the same joke my whole life that I'll marry my mom's college roommate's daughter Eloise. And it's not that they actually think I'll marry Eloise, but I know they do assume I'll marry someone of the female persuasion. Though I don't anticipate testing their preconceived notions on this one."

"I don't anticipate testing my dad on it, either," I said, and I felt my cheeks pink up. I hadn't meant to talk about my dating habits with Adam—even in the abtract. "Talley told me that it's a form of privilege to fit into the boxes of other people's default assumptions."

"She was right," Adam said.

"I know," I said. "And maybe you're right about her. She could've been in love with Dean, and then she could've met Ethel, whoever she is, and fallen in love with her, too. Talley just didn't seem scared of challenging my dad's assumptions. Like he had this *deeply* held assumption that Talley and I would go to college—especially Talley because she had this genius IQ. She didn't care about breaking the rules he set. Unlike me."

"What do you mean?" Adam said. "You're the quintessential rebel. In fact, look up the word 'rebel' in the dictionary, and your picture is there. It's a really good picture, by the way. I bet you've never taken a bad one."

"There are plenty of bad pictures of me," I said, blushing some more. I looked down at my place mat and flipped it over again, staring intently at the map like it was the most interesting thing in the world. There was the airport in San Francisco. I traced a finger south through Burlingame, San Mateo, Belmont, San Carlos, Redwood City, Palo Alto, and then toward the coast: Half Moon Bay, Santa Cruz, Monterey. "Oh, I found Big Sur," I told Adam. "It's right by the ocean on the map. I thought it was a forest."

"The mountains are on the left, and the ocean on the right," Adam explained. "Unless you're looking at it from the south, in which case flip that, and put the mountains on the right."

"When you said Big Sur, I thought you meant 'sir'—s-i-r."

"Like, hello, big sir," Adam said. "You look awfully large today."

"Yeah . . . oh my God."

"What?"

"Big *sir*. Large *gentleman*. A large gentleman's sunset. Talley's list."

"Big Sur has famously beautiful sunsets," Adam said. "There are cliffs that drop down to the Pacific."

"You said it's like a three-hour drive?"

"About that. Maybe not even."

"Can we—"

I didn't even finish my sentence before Adam had motioned for the check. "Absolutely," he said. "Let's go."

chapter thirty-one

ACCORDING TO GOOGLE MAPS, IT WAS JUST OVER A hundred and twenty miles from the parking lot of the El Camino Diner to Big Sur. Adam said his car's charge typically lasted up to a hundred and twenty-five miles, so we were cutting it *really* close. But he assured me that there'd be charging stations along the way if we needed one, and we'd charge up again in Big Sur before heading back.

Heading back. I couldn't think that far ahead. I could only think of getting there.

No one knew where we were going. Adam didn't tell his parents, and I didn't tell Aunt Elise, either. I just texted her to say I'd be with Adam for a few more hours, and she shouldn't worry.

I didn't tell Juno, either. There wasn't an explicit reason for me to hold anything back. I knew she'd want to know about the progress I was making, and maybe I even owed it to her to tell her; after all, I wouldn't have gotten to California without her. But I hadn't responded to her Audrey-emergency texts yet. Besides, Adam felt like my partner now. If you woke me up in the middle of the night and asked me who my best friend was, like a reflex, I would've said Juno. But in this moment, it wasn't true. Adam was the only friend who mattered.

I pulled Google up on my phone, and even though Adam already knew a good amount about Big Sur, I read aloud: "Big Sur is not a town; it's a region that stretches along eighty-five miles of undeveloped coastline, where the Saint Lucia mountains rise dramatically above the Pacific Ocean. Known for its scenic views, Big Sur is the longest undeveloped coastline in the contiguous United States, and some say it's the most beautiful in the world."

"It's definitely the most beautiful place I've ever been," Adam said. "Though when you're a kid, you're not really impressed by beauty like that. I was impressed by the jade, though—but only because I thought I could make a lot of money."

I'd read about the jade online—Big Sur had an underwater concentration of jade, and sometimes the stones washed up on the shore.

"We had a whole business plan," Adam went on. "Which basically consisted of finding as much jade as we could, selling it, and becoming super rich."

"Who had the plan? You and your friends from school?"

"Yep," he said.

"How'd that work out for you?"

"We found a few pebbles on one trip," Adam said. "My mom bought them off me for five bucks. So I'm not retiring just yet."

"You don't even have a job to retire from," I reminded him.

"Maybe today will be my lucky day. We'll hit the jade jackpot and I'll never have to have one."

"Maybe."

"Do you have any idea where in Big Sur you want to go?" he asked.

"The only clue I have to go by is what was on Talley's list—a large gentleman's sunset."

"I know," Adam said. "I just meant—did anything online pop out at you as the place we should go?"

The online pictures of Big Sur were as stunning as anything I'd ever seen—deep-blue water, vibrant green trees, and sunsets in every color of the rainbow. They'd all popped out at me, but I couldn't tell if there was any spot in particular that Talley had had in mind.

"I think we just need to go there," I said. "And we'll see what we see."

It took us three and a half hours, including a pit stop to charge the car, to reach the northernmost point of Big Sur. At some point along the way I lost my cell phone signal, but I'd expected that. A couple of the online articles had mentioned that the cell service in Big Sur was exceptionally spotty. The signal bars on my phone had been going down as we got closer, and now there was the X of no service. I couldn't write to Juno even if I wanted to.

The highway we were on was at the top of a cliff, and below

it was the ocean—the friggin' Pacific Ocean! It was so blue, like a mirror of the sky. Long ago, Talley had told me the reason the sky was blue: the sun looks white, but it actually contains many colors, and all the different colors collide with particles of air as the light from the sun travels to earth. Each color has a different wavelength, so it collides in different amounts. Blue has the shortest wavelength, so it scatters the most.

When the road twisted left, Adam and I headed toward the mountains. He pointed out various places we could turn off the road, park, and explore. "You tell me where," he said.

"Here," I said, the fourth time he pointed out a turnoff. Four had been Talley's lucky number. I didn't know why; I'd never asked her. I hadn't even remembered till Adam started pointing to turnoffs, and I decided to count to four.

Adam parked in a lot by the Big Sur Lodge, and we walked into Pfeiffer Big Sur State Park. I knew from the internet that the park was named for a man who'd lived in a cabin on the property in the 1800s. His parents were among the first settlers in the area, and there were a number of Big Sur features named for other members of his family.

"This way?" I asked Adam, pointing to a sign that marked a path toward Pfeiffer Falls.

"I'm following you," he said.

"This way," I said.

The path was paved for a little bit, but then the pavement gave way to dirt, and soon we were walking through a grove of redwoods. These were the redwoods Adam had told me about—older than the one on University Avenue by a thousand years or so. They stretched up hundreds of feet. How tall did something have to be to qualify as a skyscraper? I bet they made the standard.

There were a few other people on the pathway, but not many. Adam and I barely spoke. I had a feeling he was being quiet because I was being quiet, and it was another way he was following my lead. The redwoods smelled deep and earthy, and there wasn't a whiff of anything man-made to interrupt that smell. Sunlight was streaming in through the branches. The bark of the redwoods had a deep-orange glow, and the beams of light looked like something coming down from another dimension. I moved to stand directly under one of the beams.

Talley. Talley. Talley, I thought. *Where are you? Are you here? Can you see me?*

My face warmed, and it was not unlike the feeling of being loved by my sister. Sometimes I'd find her looking at me with a mix of love and amazement, like I was the center of the universe, which was exactly how I felt about her.

Adam and I crossed over a wooden footbridge for the view of Pfeiffer Falls, a waterfall cascading down about sixty feet of rock and moss. The breeze had picked up and I shivered a little. I hadn't dressed for this kind of adventure, and back at the booth at the El Camino Diner, it hadn't occurred to me that we should each stop back at our respective homes and change into jeans and sweatshirts. Adam put his hands on my shoulders. I crossed my arms and put my hands on his hands. He held me closer, warming me. Warming us both.

"You okay, Weber?"

"Mm-hmm," I said.

I closed my eyes and breathed in deeply. The water made the redwoods smell even earthier, the way seasoning food can bring out the hidden flavors. With my eyes closed, I could practically hear the water bubbling over each individual rock, and I remembered something I hadn't thought of in years: When Juno and I first became good friends, Talley asked her if her other senses were heightened. She'd read that when you cut off one sense, your other senses got better and picked up some of the slack. My face flushed when Talley asked Juno about it. I worried that Talley was reminding Juno of a disability that she might have momentarily forgotten she had.

Now I thought maybe Juno didn't ever forget. I certainly never forgot how much I was missing Talley. I opened my eyes and watched the water going down, down, down. "There are bigger, more impressive waterfalls in Big Sur," Adam told me. "If you want to check them out."

I shook my head. "The sunset is the thing on Talley's list. I think we should find a place to watch it over the ocean."

"We used to go to Sand Dollar Beach to watch the sunset," Adam said. "It's a bit of a drive, but if we hike back to the car now, we'll definitely get there in time."

chapter thirty-two

WE HIT UP THE BIG SUR LODGE GIFT SHOP FOR SUPPLIES, since it'd be even colder on the beach. We each got a sweatshirt, plus a blanket and a few snacks to share. My cash supply was seriously dwindling, and I briefly considered using Juno's credit card. But I didn't want her to trace me through the charges till I was ready to tell her what I was up to. Plus it really wasn't her responsibility to pay for me, no matter how much she was willing to do so. So cash it was. It was amazing how a year of babysitting wages could disappear so quickly.

We got back on the road, and pulled into the parking lot of Sand Dollar Beach just about an hour before sundown. The sun was still bright, but it was hanging lower in the sky, and the ocean was a mix of gold and turquoise. Adam and I navigated the steep but sturdy wooden staircase down to the beach. I didn't feel scared. I did, however, feel cold, even with my new sweatshirt, and I wished I'd bought a hat or a scarf as well—or both.

The beach itself was smaller than I'd imagined, with the water's edge just a few yards away. The sand part curved like a horseshoe. It was mostly the color you'd expect of sand save for a few purplish streaks. There were jagged rocks at each of the far ends of the beach, and the waves slapped against them, sending spray into the air.

I kicked off my Converse at the bottom of the stairs. The sand was cold beneath my feet, but I wanted to feel the water anyhow, since I'd never before had the chance to dip a toe into the Pacific Ocean, and didn't know when I'd get to again.

I knew the water would be cold, but it was shockingly freezing, as if someone was moving a block of ice over my foot, and I raced back to Adam, where he'd spread the blanket not far from the bottom of the stairs. Sand was speckling my feet like a thousand freckles. I curled my toes into the corner of the blanket to warm them. My doubts were settling in again. Maybe I'd found Talley's "large gentleman," but this spot in Big Sur, this beach—it didn't feel quite right. I just didn't know where else I was supposed to be, and by now we'd traveled so far and the sun was so low in the sky. If I told Adam I wanted to try another spot, we'd miss the sunset.

I was looking out at the ocean, thinking all this, when I noticed a gray ripple, far in the distance. Was that what I thought it was? No, it couldn't be.

Then something leaped from the water in an arc. It was a dolphin! A real-life dolphin! Even at a distance, it was beautiful and majestic. And it had friends, leaping in and out of the water alongside each other.

"Are you seeing them?" I asked Adam.

"I'm seeing them," he said.

"Talley loved dolphins," I said, as my eyes began to well.

Adam reached a hand out toward me. Those times when he'd touched my back or my shoulder—he'd made the choice to connect us. Now the choice was mine. I reached my hand out to his. Together we squeezed.

We sat that way until the dolphins stopped leaping. Or perhaps they still were, somewhere out there, too far away to see. Lately I'd been fascinated by the exact distance between being able to see a thing and having it disappear completely. Talley would know the answer. I knew I could go online and find out, but it was different from having her tell me. I scooted closer to Adam. The air was so cold, and the breeze coming off the water made it even colder. But his body just there, right beside me, was so warm. He was a human heater.

The sun dipped lower and lower down, as if the ocean was a magnet. The sky turned shades of pink and purple and red. "There's a saying they teach you at the Grizzly Cove sailing camp," Adam said. "Red sky at night, sailor's delight. Red sky in morning, sailors take warning. The way the sky is now, you know there isn't a storm coming in. It's safe to sail."

Safe to sail.

Safe.

Safe.

Safe.

The word knocked around my head, and I could hear it in Talley's voice, over and over again, the last time I ever heard her voice live, when she was talking about how those refugee kids in Sweden had known the world wasn't safe, and so they'd given up.

I hadn't looked at the article when Talley'd held her phone out for me to see, but I'd googled it after Talley herself had given up and was gone. There were pictures of the kids in hospital beds, looking as small as my sister had looked when Dad and I went in to say goodbye. I thought about where her small body was now—underground—and wondered again about where all her thoughts went, her infinity of thoughts. I hated thinking about the awful truth—they didn't go anywhere. They just disappeared.

But now it seemed like all Talley's thoughts—her love, her anger, her sadness, her hopes, her fears—it was all in this sky that was turning every imaginable color, stretching out forever and ever, or at least as far as I could see.

I blinked back tears so they wouldn't blur my vision, and kept watching. The sun dropped lower. There was a band of yellow just above the horizon, and then a thin line of pink, and above that, an endless deep-blue sky, darker and darker, the higher you looked. Things can be so beautiful, and they can be so sad, all at once.

"If I'd been here in my old life, my life before Talley died, I'd be taking notes right now," I told Adam. "I always took notes when I saw extraordinary things, and sometimes even when I saw ordinary things. Any time there was ever anything I thought I could put into a story, I'd write it down."

"Do you need some paper? I might have a receipt in my pocket. I don't have a pen, though. I could run back to the car."

"It's okay," I said. "I'm not going to turn this into a story."

"If you were going to write a story, what would you say?"

"Oh, I don't know. Maybe that being here feels like we went back in time. We're all alone on this beach, and our phones don't work. The sun has been setting like this for a few billion years. So, really, we could be in any year. There's no way to tell we're in the modern world anymore."

"We're definitely not in the modern world anymore," Adam said. "Did you see the *Gorgosaurus* that just ducked behind the cove?"

"A *Gorgosaurus*?" I said. "Is that the creature that killed Terrance J. Tenterhook?"

"It was a real dinosaur. Look it up."

"I can't look it up. These are prehistoric times. There's no such thing as looking it up."

"Right," Adam said. "You'll just have to take my word for it."

"I don't want to go that far back," I said. "I just want to go a little bit back . . . three weeks, six days, and a few hours back. Enough time to catch her before "

My voice caught. Adam pulled me even closer. I let myself fall against him.

"Talley had hundreds of books in her room. After she died, I was pulling them off the shelf, looking at things she'd underlined, like I'd be able to figure out . . . I don't know, like, why she did what she did. I picked up a quantum physics textbook, because if you're looking for answers, that'd be the book they'd be in, right?"

"I don't know if I'd understand the answers if I read them in a quantum physics textbook," Adam said.

"Yeah, I might as well have been reading Latin, for all I understood. But there was a part about how parallel worlds might exist and they could even interact with our world. So I was thinking— what if one of those parallel worlds is a past world? Like if time is a place you can travel to, then all I need to do is figure out how to go back in time and stop Talley."

"That's *all* you have to do?"

"I know I can't," I said. "But I owe it to her."

"I'm sure you did everything you could for her."

"You didn't even know me back then," I said. I scooted back to face him. "You barely even know me now, and you don't know what I did."

"I know the way you flew across the country because of a vague list that Talley left in her pocket. I've seen everything you've done since you've been here. I know plenty of people who'd never do what you do, and I admire it."

I shivered and folded my arms across my chest. "I don't deserve anyone's admiration," I said. "I haven't told anyone the whole story. Having this kind of secret, it's like picking up a brick. It doesn't feel too heavy at first. But the longer you carry it around, the heavier it gets. At this point, the brick feels heavy enough to crush me."

"I don't want you to be crushed," Adam said. He reached a hand to my cheek and pressed it there. He felt so real. "Sloane, whatever it is, you can tell me."

I stared at him. I could see myself in his eyes. Was I going to do this—was I going to tell him?

Yes, I was.

"Talley had moved back home. She wasn't going anywhere or doing anything. She got like that sometimes, and I didn't think anything of it, even though it was going on for a long time—for a few weeks. That last morning, she asked me to stay home with her. I told her I couldn't. I had a quiz; I had orchestra practice. And besides that, Juno's boyfriend had just broken up with her, and I felt like I couldn't leave her alone, and so instead I left Talley alone."

"You didn't do anything wrong," Adam said. "You went to school, just like you were supposed to, because you thought it was a regular day. You said she'd been home for weeks. Were you supposed to stay home every day?"

"If that's what it took," I said.

"Sloane—"

"She was never awake when I left for school. I should've known."

"That's just what you're telling yourself in hindsight. It's not actually what you should've known. It's what you know *now*. There's nothing about that story that makes me feel like you should've done anything different."

"I haven't told you all of it," I said. "She called me. I was in the car with Juno. We were talking about whatever. Nothing important. Even if it was something important, it wasn't more important than my sister. But I pressed the button to mute the call, and I didn't even think about Talley for the rest of the day. I didn't even think about her! People always thought we were such good sisters—better than other sisters. We never fought. In my whole life, I don't have a single memory of a fight with Talley, and I know most siblings can't say that. There was this one time we were at a family picnic for my dad's firm, and at the end of the day, all the kids were bickering with each other, but not Talley and me. In the car on the way home, we were talking about how weird it was to see siblings fighting. I thought it made us superior. But I bet all those fighting kids are alive right now. Talley's not and it's my fault."

"It's not your fault," Adam said. "She was sick. You couldn't have done anything about it."

"Sure I could've," I said. "She was my sister. I know you mean well, but you don't have a sibling. You couldn't possibly know what it's like when you let them down—right when they need you most."

"Oh, Sloane," Adam said. "There's something I have to tell you."

chapter thirty-three

NIGHT HAD FALLEN ON THE BEACH, AND IT WAS EVEN colder than before. Adam said we should go back to the car. I didn't ask him anything as we climbed up the staircase. I didn't speak at all. It was dark, and I concentrated on my steps.

When we got into the car, I tucked the blanket around my bare legs. Adam turned the key in the ignition and cranked up the heat. "There," he said. "Better?"

"Yeah," I said, though my teeth were chattering.

"I have a sibling," he said. "I understand if you're pissed."

"I'm surprised, not pissed," I said. "I know as well as anyone that there are reasons people need to keep secrets sometimes."

Adam nodded.

"Did she die?" I asked. "Or, is it he?"

"She," he said. "No, she didn't. That's not why . . . listen, this is hard for me. So let me get this out, okay?"

"Okay," I said.

"And I just want to say for the record, when you asked me back at Grizzly Cove whether I had any siblings, I said it was just my parents and me at home, that wasn't a lie—CJ hasn't lived at home for years."

"Her name is CJ?"

"Yeah," he said. "We're five years apart, like you and Talley. We didn't get along as well as you guys when we were kids, but I thought we had a pretty normal family. Actually, when I was a little kid, I took it for granted, and didn't think about whether we were normal or not, which just goes to show that we *were* normal. My parents worked too much, and CJ was a pain, but those were my only complaints. Everything changed the summer I was six and CJ turned eleven, because she got leukemia."

"Oh no," I said.

"It was the good kind," Adam said. "Like, all leukemia is bad, but if you *have* to get it, this is the kind you want, because the cure rate is ninety percent. When CJ was diagnosed, my dad kept repeating that to my mom, 'ninety percent, ninety percent.' And my mom would say that means ten percent don't survive. She'd run the numbers—one out of ten die, two out of twenty die, and on. I literally taught myself what percentages mean because of all the conversations they had about CJ's chances. They had these whisper-fights, trying to be quiet so CJ and I wouldn't overhear. But sometimes they got loud, and the air vent in my bedroom goes down to the kitchen, where their late-night talks tended to take place. My mom was mad at my dad because when CJ had first gotten sick, he said she just needed more iron in her diet. Since he's a doctor, my mom trusted him, and it was a few weeks before she finally brought CJ to the doctor and the real diagnosis was made. So there was our formerly normal family—now CJ was fighting a potentially deadly illness, and my mom was so mad at my dad for the delay. He said CJ getting diagnosed a few weeks earlier wouldn't have made a difference, but that just further enraged my mom. My dad had been wrong about CJ being sick; what if he was wrong about the delay not being a big deal? My mom kicked him out of the house. It felt like all the worst things that could happen had happened to us."

"But . . . she was in the ninety percent, right?"

"Yeah, she was," he said. "And my parents got back together, too—though not till after CJ was done with the intense part of the treatment, which lasted almost a year. She was basically absent for all of sixth grade. I was a total jerk about it, acting like CJ had gotten sick on purpose. As if she wanted that kind of attention."

"You were a little kid."

"Yeah, and a dense one at that."

"Not so dense. You figured out percentages."

"My one shining moment, but the rest of the time, I was just pissed. My dad bought the boat with CJ's name on it. That really pissed me off."

"CJ stands for Cara Joy?"

"Yeah," he said. "Sorry I wasn't honest with you about it—but it did come with the name, like I said. CJ was sick, and my dad saw an ad for the boat, and he thought it was a sign that she'd get well, as long as he bought it. We weren't a boating family, but that hardly mattered to him when it came to his daughter's life. I wouldn't categorize my dad as a superstitious person, but I guess despite what he told my mom, the ninety-percent statistic wasn't making him entirely secure, either. He brought us all out to see it, and I threw a fit because he said he wouldn't add my name to the boat. He said it was bad luck to change a boat's name, and the whole point of buying the boat was to bring good luck to our family, and to CJ especially. I'd never gotten a present that was anything close to that big, and I was pissed at CJ for getting everything, and pissed at my dad for giving it to her, and pissed at my mom for kicking my dad out. And I was pissed at everyone for missing every single baseball practice I had for two years straight. Not that my parents ever came to my practices. They didn't even always make it to my games because they were usually working. They used to be fairly hands-off parents, if you can believe it. When CJ got sick, they changed their style—my mom especially. But back then it was only directed at CJ, and I was insanely jealous. My mom said she couldn't come to baseball because it conflicted with when she had to take CJ to her support group at the hospital for kids who had cancer." He paused. "It was called Sunshine Crew," he added. "And I'm—"

"Wait," I said. "Stop talking. You told me you didn't know anything else on the list."

"I know. I should've told you. I'm sorry."

"You lied to me."

"I tried not to."

"Oh, just because you didn't *technically* tell me you didn't have a sibling, and the boat really did come with that name, you think you're off the hook? You knew what you were doing. You knew you were hiding something about Talley from me. And why— because the Sunshine Crew conflicted with your baseball games a dozen years ago?"

"No, of course not," he said. "And it may not have anything to do with Talley. This all happened a long time ago—for all I know, the Sunshine Crew doesn't even exist anymore, and even if it does, Talley could've been writing about something else with the same name."

"That's beside the point."

"It's actually not," Adam said. "The Sunshine Crew was a support group for kids with cancer. If Talley wasn't a kid with cancer, why would she know about it? When you think about it, it's much more likely that it's two different things with coincidentally the same name, and then it'd be a waste of time for you to pursue it."

"Did you even bother to ask CJ if she knew Talley?"

"No."

"Call her," I said. "Right now."

"I don't think we have service yet."

"Fine. As soon as we're in range, call her."

"I will," Adam said. "But she's not going to answer. This is why I really didn't tell you about CJ—she's been MIA for months now. She's checked in a few times so we know she's alive, but she won't answer if we call or text her. She said she's tired of my mom trying to micromanage her life, and she needs to be free from all the attachments for a while. Who does that?"

He paused, waiting for me to say something. But I was too mad to take his side about anything.

"Yeah, so, my mom's a control freak," he went on. "She's obsessed with things like what we're eating, and whether we're drinking or smoking, or doing anything that can cause cancer. It makes me nuts, too. But I think that's a really shitty excuse to just up and disappear. My parents are a wreck about it, and fighting all the time. I've left messages for CJ to clue her in—you think she wouldn't want to be the reason my parents split up for a *second* time. Maybe the cancer wasn't her fault. But this sure is. She was so abrupt about it, too. It's not like she had a big blowup with my mom—or my dad for that matter. She was talking to them all the time, and then all of a sudden she just decided she'd had enough. It didn't make any sense. But now I've been wondering . . . maybe she met Talley, and Talley told her how she didn't follow the life plan your dad had for her."

"Oh my God. You did NOT just try to pin this on *Talley*."

"I'm not trying to pin it on anyone. I'm just trying to understand what's going on with my sister, the same as you're trying to understand yours."

"We're not the same. I wouldn't have kept this from you for so long."

That was it for a while. We lapsed into silence. I had my cell phone in my hands, and I was checking the bars every minute or so to see if we were in range. It turned out I didn't have to check, because the instant we were back on the grid, both my phone and

Adam's starting pinging with notifications of messages. Adam's parents were looking for him, and both Aunt Elise and Juno were worried about me.

I made Adam call CJ first. As he'd predicted, she didn't answer. He left a message: "Please call back, or send a text, or a carrier pigeon—whatever. It's really important that you get in touch. It has nothing to do with Mom and Dad this time. You don't have to worry about them—not that you ever do. But still, I need to tell you something, so get in touch, okay?"

He hung up and glanced over at me, like he was expecting a nod or a smile or a thumbs-up sign. I looked down at my own phone, typing "Sunshine Crew Stanford Hospital" into an internet search box. There was a brief explanation about the program—they offered support groups to kids aged three to eighteen who were going through treatment, and there was a phone number to call if you had a child in need. I didn't have a child in need. I tried calling anyway, and after three rings, the call went to voice mail. It was after hours. I texted Aunt Elise to say I was sorry to have worried her, and that she didn't need to wait up. I'd see her in the morning.

I also texted Juno. The messages from her had stacked up all day, first all Audrey-related. But then she got increasingly worried that I was mad at her for some reason, and that's why I wasn't responding, and then she was worried that something terrible had happened to me. The last few texts, in all caps, were all the same: I NEED TO KNOW THAT UR OK

I wasn't okay, but I did want to assure her I wasn't, like, in a ditch somewhere or anything like that.

I'm safe, I wrote.

She was probably sleeping anyway. But a few seconds later, my phone rang with a call from her. I pressed the button to reject the call, just like I'd done to Talley.

She texted again: Glad ur safe but are you ok??????

Me: Not really. More later.

Adam and I hardly talked the whole way home. When he pulled into a rest stop to charge up the car, we just sat in silence. I made myself look busy pretending to scroll through things on my phone. Adam did the same. Back home, Dad occasionally got worked up about how cell phones contributed to the breakdown of social etiquette. But sometimes you really don't want to have to talk to someone, and in those cases, having a cell phone at your fingertips is a saving grace.

Finally, close to midnight, Adam pulled into Aunt Elise's driveway. I had my hand on the door handle even before he'd fully slowed to a stop.

"Sloane," he said. "Wait. I just want to tell you—look, things have been hard with CJ, but I still should've been honest with you, and I know that. I really am very sorry."

"Is that all?" I asked.

"I don't know what else to say."

My hand was still on the door handle. "You know," I said, "when I left Talley that last morning of her life, I didn't know it'd be the last time I'd see her. I didn't tell her all the things I should've, and now for the rest of my life, I have to live with all that was left unsaid. But in this case, I know it's going to be the last time I see you."

"I hope that's not true. Even if we've only known each other a few days, you're my friend. A really good friend."

I shook my head. "I'm not your friend," I said. "And you're not mine. My friends would never do what you did. Goodbye, Adam. That's all that's left to say—goodbye."

I opened the door and headed up the walkway to Aunt Elise's front door. I would've heard if he backed up out of the driveway, but the car stayed idle. I knew Adam was watching me, but I didn't turn around. I just let myself into the house.

chapter thirty-four

I MADE IT TO STANFORD AFTER ALL. NOT IN THE WAY that I'd told my Dad, but still: there I was, on Thursday morning, exactly four weeks to the day that Talley had died.

I took the Caltrain back to University Avenue in Palo Alto, which was the Stanford University stop. It was just over a mile walk from the train station to Stanford Hospital, and from there I followed the directions that Alba Castall had given me.

Alba was the person who'd answered the phone on Thursday morning, when I'd called the number listed online for the Sunshine Crew. Unlike every other person I'd contacted based on an entry from Talley's list, when I said who I was and gave Talley's name, Alba said, "Oh yes. I do know Talley. How may I help you?"

You'd think after having to talk about Talley's death every day for four weeks, the words would come more easily, but they didn't.

They still took the spit from my mouth, and simultaneously I felt my eyes filling, as if there was only so much liquid in my body, and at that moment, the liquid was allocated to tears. "I don't know how to say this, so I'm just going to say it," I said. "Talley died."

On the other end of the phone, I heard Alba suck in her breath. "Oh, dear," she said. "I'm so sorry for your loss. I wasn't aware that she was ill."

"She wasn't ill," I said. "She died by suicide."

"Ah," Alba said. She went quiet for a couple beats, and I didn't rush to fill the silence. "Unfortunately, we do see increased rates of depression among cancer survivors. The suicide rate is markedly higher, too, even years after remission is achieved."

"What was that?" I asked.

"We see—" she started, but then she cut herself off. "Sloane, I'm sorry. I hate to do this, but I'm getting another call. Would you mind holding? I'll be back with you in just a second."

"Okay," I said.

I heard the line click, and then hold music started softly playing. Alba's voice was running through my head: *The suicide rate is markedly higher, too, even years after remission is achieved.*

Remission is the term used when someone's cancer has been successfully treated. But Talley never had cancer.

Had she?

She couldn't have hidden a *cancer* diagnosis from me.

But what if she had?

She'd always been so clued in to people who were going through a particularly hard time. "Imagine if you'd had childhood cancer," she might have said. I didn't remember her ever saying those words in particular, but I did remember how she'd tried to get me to read the memoirs about sick kids. Was it a test to see if I could handle the news of her own diagnosis—a test I failed?

And then there was the time she got all her friends and me to donate our hair to make wigs for kids with cancer. Was that to give back to an organization that helped her in her time of need?

Was Talley wearing a wig at some point during our childhood? How could I have missed that? Presumably she would've been absent from school a bunch, but I wouldn't have necessarily known, since the only year we were ever in the same school at the same time was when I was in kindergarten and she was in fifth grade. After that, we were never together again. If she missed days, I wouldn't have noticed her missing. If she had to stay overnight at the hospital, she could've told me she was staying over at a friend's house. It wouldn't have been easy, but she could've pulled it off.

As for her connection to the Sunshine Crew—could she have commuted back and forth to Stanford? Dad would've had to be in on it. Was it his idea to hide it all from me, or was it Talley's? I imagined the conversation she would have had with him: *Sloane couldn't even make it a chapter or two through a memoir about a stranger. She can't handle my illness.*

Whoever said what, they would've been partners in the decision. I always thought of our family as Talley and me, and Dad. Talley and I were partners, we were one unit, and Dad was his own entity. We loved him, but he was separate from us. But maybe I'd been the one who'd been separate from the two of them.

It all could've happened before I was even born. The Sunshine Crew was open to kids as young as three, and I didn't come onto the scene until Talley was five. Maybe that was why Dad was adamantly opposed to me pursuing Talley's list; it wasn't the "moving on" crap so much as his worry that I'd find out about a secret from the past they'd held together.

But now that Talley had died, what was the point of him keeping that a secret? Even if it happened before I was born, she was still my sister. I was entitled to know what had happened to her, and I would absolutely confront Dad about it.

But before that, I wanted to get as much information that I could from Alba Castall.

"Sloane?" she said. "Are you still there?"

"I'm still here. Ms. Castall—"

"Call me Alba."

"Alba," I said. "Talley had . . . What kind of cancer did she have?"

"Acute lymphoblastic leukemia."

So there it was. Leukemia. My sister had had *leukemia*. And whether it was the good kind or not, it had killed her. There are increased levels of depression and suicide in cancer survivors, and it had killed her.

"I can only imagine how difficult things are right now," Alba said. "Is there anything I can do?"

"Yes," I said. "I know you're probably very busy, but I'm just here in California for a couple more days. I came out here to connect with people Talley knew, and I'd really love to talk to you in person, if you have time."

"I'll make time," Alba said. "Let me give you directions."

Her office was on the second floor of the Lucile Packard Children's Hospital. I hadn't been to a hospital since Talley died, and this time around, I was focused on getting to the hospital; I didn't stop to think about how it would *feel* to get there.

But when I walked through the front door, the floor and the walls were exactly the same colors as the floor and the walls of Golden Valley General Hospital, as if there was one company that all the hospital decorators went to for such things. The smell was the same, too. That was the hardest part. Talley'd once told me that memory and smell are linked. The part of your brain that processes smell is connected to the parts of your brain that store emotions and memories. There was even a phrase for it, she said: the Proust phenomenon. It was named for the French writer who'd once written about the memories evoked from the particular smell of a madeleine biscuit soaking in tea.

I felt like my legs were going to collapse under the weight of the rest of my body, and I cupped my hands over my nose and mouth to try to filter the smell as I breathed.

Talley had been in this building. She'd been *here*. And upstairs there was a woman who'd known her, who was waiting to meet me.

Somehow I got my legs working and walked to the elevator bank. I rode up a flight, and walked down a long hallway, following the signs for the Child Life Program. There was a woman sitting at the end of a bench, and next to her was a young girl in a wheelchair, a knit beanie cap on the girl's head. Our eyes met in the couple seconds it took to walk past, and I wondered if it was cancer, if it was leukemia, if it was the *good* kind of leukemia. I hoped she'd be one of the 90 percent who got cured, and I hoped what had happened in the end to Talley wouldn't happen to her.

I pushed through double doors at the end of the corridor and entered a waiting room. There was a reception desk at the back, and I gave my name to the guy manning the phones. "What time is your appointment?" he said.

"I spoke to Alba Castall on the phone, and she said I could come in," I said.

"All right," he said. "Take a seat. I'll give her a call."

The waiting-room chairs were the same as the ones in the waiting room back at Golden Valley General, though the fabric was gray and not blue. I sat right on the edge of one. My heart was pounding in my chest like a jackhammer. I tried the yoga breathing exercises that Aunt Elise had taught me, lengthening my inhale by counting to three, and then exhaling to the count of three. In for three, out for three. Rinse and repeat.

This part of the hospital, I realized, didn't smell like hospital. Or maybe I'd just gotten used to the smell.

"Sloane Weber?" a voice called.

I looked up. A woman was standing by the reception desk. She had a small face, dark-rimmed glasses, and remarkably long and thick hair. Like hair in a shampoo commercial. How weird to have hair like that and to work with kids who'd lost theirs.

I stood up and walked toward her, expecting to exchange a handshake, but she opened her arms in a hug. "I'm Alba," she said. "Come on back. Let's talk."

I followed her back to her office, a box-sized windowless room that was nevertheless quite cheerful looking, with posters on the walls, and a bright-red beanbag chair in the far corner. I sat in one of the regular chairs, and Alba sat in her desk chair. "Can I ask— was Talley ever in here?"

"A couple times," she said. "Does that make it too difficult for you?"

"No," I said. "It makes me feel like I'm where I'm supposed to be. I want to know as much about my sister as possible—about the things that were important to her. I know the Sunshine Crew meant a lot to her, but I don't know how she got involved with them. Did she come when she was a kid?"

"I met Talley in January," Alba said. "She came in to be a volunteer in our Sunshine Crew program. I don't know how much you know about it."

"Not much," I said. "Just what's up on the website."

"Well, let me tell you a little more. Many of the kids who come into this hospital for cancer care, they're going through physical changes—losing their hair, gaining or losing weight from treatment—and those physical changes are not only uncomfortable, but they also have psychological effects, especially because when these kids go back to school, they are usually the only ones they know experiencing things like that. It can be very lonely. Even if you have a well-meaning group of friends, it's easy to feel self-conscious and isolated because of your differences. We started our program two decades ago, and we strive to have a safe community for these kids to be themselves, to feel like they're not alone, and to have whatever conversations they need to have—and sometimes those are really tough conversations. Kids don't always like to talk to their parents about what they're feeling, because they don't want to worry them."

"Or to their siblings," I said.

"Or to their siblings," Alba repeated. "In a lot of families, the refrain is, 'You're going to be fine.' And while I certainly believe in the power of positive thinking, the truth is that cancer is a serious illness and you can die from it. Kids with cancer need to be able to talk about the possibility of death. And they need to talk about what their lives are like, too. The particular challenges of a life spent with a serious illness—which your sister knew all too well. She was very helpful."

"Can you put me in touch with any of the kids Talley helped?" I asked. My mind flashed to the little girl in a wheelchair. "Maybe they're here and I can talk to them today."

"I'm afraid not," Alba said. "We're very careful about who we bring into the kids' lives. They're minors—the most vulnerable of minors. This is in no way a judgment of you or your character, and I'm certainly empathetic to your plight. I've lost people close to me, too, and in their absence, I wanted to learn as much about them as possible, in order to keep them close. So if there's any more information that I can give you personally, as long as it doesn't violate anyone's privacy, I'm happy to give it to you."

"There are things Talley told you that would violate her privacy?" I asked.

"We make an agreement with the kids that what happens in the room stays in the room. That's all."

"Okay," I said. "I understand that. How did Talley know about your program?"

"A lot of our volunteers are former members of the Sunshine Crew, and Talley came in with one of our alumni, who happened to be a friend of hers."

"Was it CJ Hadlock?" I guessed.

"Oh, yes. You know CJ?"

I shook my head. "I'd really love to talk to her, though. Is there any way you could put us in touch? It wouldn't be like meeting one of the kids. She's not a minor."

"Oh, I know that. But if you're not in touch with CJ, then is she aware of what happened to your sister?"

"I don't think so," I said.

"CJ has a lot on her plate right now," Alba said. "I don't want to pile more on."

"Please—" I started.

"Hang on. I don't want to give her more to deal with. But at the same time, in my experience, when you try to keep a secret, even if you convinced yourself that it's for someone else's own good, it often backfires."

"That's my experience, too."

"Why don't you step outside for a moment. I'll give her a call and let her know what happened, and tell her that you're here."

"Okay," I said. "Thank you. Thanks so much."

I went back to the waiting room and sat down in the same gray chair I'd been in before, a chair that Talley herself might have once sat in, or maybe CJ had, and Talley was in the chair next to her.

What would I do if CJ told Alba that she wouldn't speak to me?

I guess I'd continue trying to get in touch with CJ for the rest of my life. I'd call Ada and make him give me her number. I'd call and I'd text. I'd search for her on every social media site, and I'd send messages in every way that I could.

And while I waited for her to get back to me, I'd go back home to Minnesota and confront Dad about hiding Talley's illness from me.

When you try to keep a secret, even if you convinced yourself that it's for someone else's own good, it often backfires, like Alba said.

I knew from the clock on my phone that it'd only been four minutes, but I felt like I'd been in that room all day, waiting for Alba to finish up the call to CJ. The clock ticked up another minute. Five minutes. Then six.

Actually, I decided, it was a good sign that the minutes were ticking by. If Alba had come out too quickly, it would've meant that CJ hadn't answered the call, just like she wouldn't answer her parents' calls, or Adam's.

But the waiting was getting to be excruciating. An eternity passed, aka fifteen minutes, then twenty. I guess it takes time to deliver the news to someone that a friend has died.

Unless Alba hadn't been able to get CJ on the phone, then she'd gotten another call right away, or started another little task, and been distracted, and forgot about me sitting in the waiting room. I wondered if I should ask the guy behind the reception desk to call her and remind her I was there.

I'd give it another minute or two. Five, tops. Then I'd have him call her.

But Alba came back out before five more minutes had gone by. There was a piece of paper in her hand.

Please, please, I thought to myself. *Let that be a paper with CJ's phone number on it for me to call.*

"Okay, Sloane," Alba said. "CJ said she'd speak to you."

"Oh, thank you. Thank you."

"I don't think it's going to be easy," Alba said. "Not on either of you. But it'll be important, so—" She handed over the paper. "This is where you can find her."

I looked at the numbers Alba had written. Not a phone number. A room number.

"We only see children in this building," Alba explained. "CJ is across the street."

"She works at the hospital?"

"She's a patient," Alba said.

chapter thirty-five

CJ HADLOCK WAS SITTING IN A HOSPITAL BED, EYES closed. She had a purple scarf twisted around her head. A tube ran up from a needle in her arm to a plastic bag filled with clear liquid, hanging from an IV pole.

I stood in the doorway looking at her, taking it all in. It'd barely been twelve hours since Adam had first told me that he had a sister, and that he didn't know how to get in touch with her. Now here she was, in a hospital bed, and her family didn't know.

Before I'd left the children's building, Alba explained that CJ had been diagnosed with a secondary cancer, which can happen even years after being treated for childhood cancer. It may be that a body is genetically more prone to cancer, or it could be a delayed side effect from the original treatments themselves.

CJ had a good prognosis. But first she had to go through a round of chemotherapy, which was hard and debilitating. She'd been hospitalized for dehydration a couple days ago. She'd probably get released tomorrow. Saturday at the latest. She'd have a week off before it was time for her next treatment. "It's a long, winding road," Alba said.

It was hard to tell if CJ looked like Adam. There was the headscarf, and her eyebrows were missing, too. I'd never thought about how essential eyebrows are to how a person looks, till I saw CJ without hers. She was paler than her brother. Except around her eyes, where she was red and puffy—maybe from the treatment, or from crying about the news. I felt so bad hitting her with what happened to Talley at a time like this. My heart ached for her.

And my heart ached for Talley, for all the things she'd gone through and didn't tell me about.

And for myself, for missing her, and the pain of not knowing.

And for Adam, because now his sister was sick—again, and he didn't know it. And for his parents, for the same reason.

And the tiniest sliver of me ached for Dad, too.

Someone was pushing a cart down the hall. As it clanked closer, CJ's eyes fluttered open and she spotted me. "Oh," she said. "You're Sloane."

"Yes," I said, stepping into the room.

"God, I would've known you anywhere. Talley showed me about a thousand photos."

"Really?"

CJ nodded. There was a box of tissues on the tray next to her bed. She pulled one out and pressed it to her face. "Sorry," she said. "It's a shock—the news about Talley, and the fact that you're here."

I didn't even realize that I'd started crying, too, until CJ held the tissue box out to me. "Thank you," I managed.

"Come in," she said. "Sit. I understand we have some things to talk about."

I sat down on the visitor's chair beside her bed. "Thank you," I said again.

"You know, when Alba told me, I told her it couldn't be true and I needed proof. She found a death notice online. I guess whoever wrote it could be in on the story, but that seems a bit far-fetched—even for Talley."

"Half of me feels like any minute she'll burst through the door and say, 'Just kidding!'"

"Did she do that a lot? Make things up?"

"When she made up stories for me, I believed them," I said. "She made puzzles, too. She used to leave clues for me to find things. I'd hunt around the house, and there'd be fuzzy socks or a headband she'd bought me. When she died, she had a list of random things in her pocket. I figured out that some of those things were out here, in California, so that's what I'm doing here—I came to find them."

I didn't say anything to CJ about Adam, just as I hadn't called or texted him on my way from Alba's office over here. I was too mad at him, and besides that, clearly CJ didn't want him or his parents to know where she was. It wasn't my place to tell them.

"The last time I saw Talley, we had a big fight," CJ said. "Did she tell you that?"

"To be honest, she never told me anything about you."

"She had a lot of secrets."

"Yeah. I'm learning that," I said.

"I thought we were so close," CJ said. "I'd never felt as close to another friend as I felt to Talley. But looking back now, I didn't even know her that long. Just a few weeks."

"How'd you meet?"

"At a support group for cancer survivors. I'd been having a hard time for a little while, and I knew it had to do with everything I'd been through when I was a kid." She paused and shifted in bed. "Ow."

"Are you okay? Should I get someone?"

"No. It'll pass." She breathed in deeply, and exhaled just as deeply. "Cancer's a real shit-slammer."

Talley's voice echoed in my head: *It's already a shit-slammer of a day.* My eyes went hot, but I blinked the tears away.

"When you're first diagnosed and you're in it," CJ said, "all you can do is keep your eye on the prize—on being done with this part. And don't get me wrong, I can't wait to be done with treatment. But afterward, you think you'll have a greater appreciation of life. And you do, but you also know there are no guarantees. It can happen again, just like that." CJ snapped her fingers. "There's so much guilt, too. Not everyone gets to live, so why did I? When I was young, I made friends with the other kids in the hospital. A few of them didn't make it. Sometimes I lie awake thinking about them, remembering them, reciting their names because when someone dies, people don't say their names as much."

Talley, Talley, Talley, I said it my head. *Natalie Belle Weber. Talley.*

"I felt like I was letting everyone down for not getting my second chance at life exactly right," CJ said. "So when I found that survivor support group, I decided to go. They met in a room at the library in Redwood City, which was good because it wasn't at a hospital, and I have PTSD about setting foot in a hospital. But given my current situation, it's clear that cancer doesn't give a shit about my PTSD."

"I'm so sorry."

"Talley was the only person at the meeting in the library who was my age," CJ said. "Everyone else was so much older. We went around the circle sharing: name, age, type of cancer. Talley went before I did, and it turned out she was my exact age, and she said she'd had acute lymphoblastic leukemia, which was the same thing that I'd had." CJ paused for a beat.

"Are you in pain again?" I asked.

"It's not as bad as before."

"Good," I said. "I mean—not good for the pain, but good it's not as bad."

"I knew what you meant," she said. "Anyway, that's how we met. When the group broke up, I made a beeline for her. We went for coffee and swapped stories for another hour or so. It was like meeting my twin. Or like, a better version of myself. We started calling ourselves Lucy and Ethel, from *I Love Lucy*. I'd watched a lot of Nick at Nite when I was sick, and there was so much in the show about being best friends and having madcap adventures together. Talley was my new best friend, and we were on the adventure of being survivors. She said that she thought since we were so lucky to recover, and so lucky to find each other, we should give back to people who weren't as lucky and volunteer somewhere together."

"She was always doing things like that," I said. "Looking for ways to help people who weren't as lucky as she was."

"Yeah, so," CJ said, " I called over to Alba to see if they needed anyone at the Sunshine Crew. I was really nervous about stepping back in that hospital, but I knew I could do it if Talley was with me. Alba expedited our applications, and we started meeting with the Sunshine Crew twice a week. Being back there as a volunteer and not a patient helped me process the things I'd gone through as a kid. One day Talley made up this thing that she called the Survival List. There was a nine-year-old named Louie who was having a really hard time. He kept saying, 'If everyone dies in the end, what's the point of going through so much pain?'"

"He was *nine*?"

"I know," CJ said. "Nine-year-olds don't usually say things like that. But most nine-year-olds aren't on their third round of chemo. Talley told him that she knew how he was feeling, and when she felt that way, she'd make a list in her head of the really good things."

"She never told me she did that," I said. I thought of my sister, sitting alone on her bed after I'd left for school. Was she making a mental list that day? Trying to remember the really good things? Oh, poor Talley.

"She told Louie we should each make a list of things to survive for, and we'd write them down," CJ went on. "That way we could go back and read them and remember that the point of the treatment was to be able to keep living and adding to our lists.

"The whole time, I was feeling comfortable in my skin in a way I hadn't felt in a really long time. But I went in for my regular checkup. When you're a cancer survivor, every time you go to the doctor, you have this pit of dread inside you, because you know you can't count on everything being A-OK. I guess it's some kind of irony that for the first time in my life I wasn't feeling a sense of impending dread, and that's when I got the call that there was a malignancy."

"I'm sorry," I said. "I can't imagine how awful that must've been."

"I called Talley, and she came right away. I didn't know how I was going to tell my family. It nearly destroyed my parents the first time around. How could I do that to them again? I just couldn't. Talley said she'd get me through it. We hadn't met each other's families. That was Talley's doing. She didn't want to introduce me to her aunt. I didn't know why, but suddenly it worked in my favor, because our friendship was a secret, and I put the cancer in that place between us. We both got wigs because I needed one and she didn't want me to feel alone in it. She brought out the best and the bravest in me because she was the best and the bravest. But she wasn't scared of the worst of me, either. She never left my side. Even when I was sleeping, she'd stay right there in the room. Sometimes I'd have to close my eyes because my eyelids were too heavy. I was too tired to talk, and too scared to really fall asleep. I could feel Talley next to me, and that made it a little bit easier. She'd say, 'You're going to be okay, Ethel. You're going to be okay.' I think she was saying that for herself, not for me. Or maybe for us both.

Anyway, one day when she thought I was sleeping, she finally told me the truth about herself."

"What?" I asked.

"I've been waiting for you to interject this whole time, because you must know it."

"I don't know anything," I said. "That's why I'm here."

"Talley never had cancer!" CJ said. "She lied to *me*! Our whole friendship—this friendship that meant more than anything in the world to me—it was based on a lie! How could she do that to me? I told her I hated her and I never wanted to see her again. And now you're telling me she *died* because of it?"

I felt like someone had punched me in the gut and knocked the wind out of me. I couldn't move or even make a sound. CJ had started to cry out loud, and a nurse flew into the room. "What's going on in here?"

CJ grabbed at the tissues so violently she ended up knocking the box onto the floor. The nurse picked it up and set it right on the tray. She rubbed CJ's back as CJ swiped a tissue across her face and blew her nose.

"I think it's time for your guest to leave," the nurse said. She was looking at CJ, but she was talking to me.

"Yes, okay," I said. I clutched the arms of the chair and shakily pushed myself up to stand.

"Wait," said CJ. "Stay."

"You need your rest," the nurse told her. "You can't have a guest come in and agitate you to the point that it interferes with your health."

"Just a few more minutes. Brenna, please."

"I'm coming back in ten minutes. Capiche?"

"Capiche."

Brenna left and I sat back down. Then CJ asked if I needed a tissue, and I stood again to reach for one. My body felt like it had that first night without Talley, when it seemed like it wasn't really my body. I held the tissue in my hand, and I almost didn't know what to do next. I lifted it to my face, moving as if in slow motion, and wiped my eyes and nose.

I felt CJ's eyes on me the whole time.

"I didn't know," I told CJ. "When Alba told me, it was unbelievable to me, but then I started thinking that maybe Talley'd had cancer when she was a kid, and she'd tried to hide it from me." I shook my head.

"She'd been so convincing the whole time," CJ said. "She knew so much, down to the drugs you'd have to take. It was like she studied up to be able to lie. She told me she didn't plan it out like that. She was just in the library when she saw the sign for the support group, and she decided to go. She said the trauma felt familiar to her, even if she hadn't had cancer. When it was her turn to share, she borrowed the details from a book she'd read. Then we became friends, and then we became best friends, and I got sick again, and it got out of hand. I was so mad at her. How could she have done that? How could she have thought that what I went through—what any cancer patient went through—was familiar to her in any way?"

"I don't know," I said.

"It's the most offensive thing anyone ever told me," CJ said.

"I can't believe she said that."

"I'm not the liar in this story."

"Oh, I know you're not," I said. "It's just . . . Talley used to make me play this game. She'd say 'imagine if' about all these terrible things. She was trying to get me to understand that I was lucky, and that other people had it so much worse."

"So this time she was playing a real-life version of her game," CJ said. "Like playing dress-up. I'll put on this outfit and pretend that I'm a cancer survivor. It was . . . it was *humiliating*. I brought her into the Sunshine Crew—this sacred space. I let everyone down."

"No, you didn't," I said softly.

"I couldn't even tell Alba the truth about it. She knows all the secrets I'm keeping from my parents, but I was too ashamed to tell her about this."

"I'm sorry," I said. "I wish I knew why Talley did what she did. With her gone, everything is just so hard to understand. I've been playing the Imagine If game a lot—I've been imagining being Talley and being in so much pain. All those memoirs she read, and the volunteer work—I think it was at least partly because she was hurting and she wanted to remind *herself* other people had it worse, and to try to feel better about her own life. I didn't get that. Not till right now, this second." I started crying again. "Talley wasn't just carrying the burden of other people's stories. She was carrying hers, too. And I'm sorry she hurt you. Really, I am. But mostly, I'm sorry that I didn't know how bad it was for her. I had no idea. She knew me the best out of anyone else in the world. When someone knows you that well, you think that means you know them right back. But I didn't. When I walked out the door that last day, it didn't occur to me that she wouldn't be there when I got home."

CJ and I shared the box of tissues again. "I thought I knew her so well, too," CJ said. "But she keeps surprising me. She keeps breaking my heart. She was the one telling the rest of us how much we had to live for. She made those lists with the kids."

"You said she made one, too?"

"Yeah."

"Do you have it?" I asked, but as the words came out of my mouth, I realized of course she didn't. I did.

TSL.

The Survival List.

I reached into my bag. "This was in Talley's pocket on the day she died," I said. CJ took it from me. She ran her fingers over the page. "Do you know why she picked those things?" I asked.

"Yeah," she said. And she began to fill me in: *Grease* at Mr. G's was because they went there one night and a woman was singing the theme song, and she sounded as good as any professional singer they'd ever heard. They went to the Bel Air Arcade at midnight because a guy CJ had known in high school worked there now, and he'd let them in. More pie was something CJ herself had said when she'd gotten the diagnosis: "We're all going to die, so let's eat more pie." For whatever reason, it really cracked them both up. "Total gallows humor," CJ told me. "But at that moment I really needed it."

Ulysses wasn't a nod to the James Joyce novel. It was a species of butterfly, and they'd both gotten the tattoo. CJ pulled down the sheet and hiked her hospital gown to show me her hip, the twin of Talley's hip. "I needed something to mark what I was going through. Butterflies are symbols of so many things—fragility, change, hope. I wanted us both to get one, and once that thought was in my head, I worried it'd be bad luck if we didn't. I told Talley, and she was so anti-tattoo, but then she was worried about me, so she got one."

"She never showed me, but I saw it in the hospital."

"It's been weird to have this thing that connected us still marking my body. I want to get it lasered off, but my doctor said not until I finish the treatments. Eight down, two more to go."

"So you're in the homestretch," I said.

"It doesn't feel like that when you're in it," CJ said. "You just feel in it. Each treatment is a hurdle unto itself."

"I can only imagine," I said.

"Imagine if," she said.

"Imagine if," I echoed. "Any idea why she wrote down the scientific name for California grizzly bears?"

"I don't know. Once when I was having a particularly hard day, I told her that I wasn't fierce like she was. So maybe she put it there because she knew that fierce things can also be fragile. But really, I don't know."

"What about eggs at the diner—I figured out she meant the El Camino Diner. My aunt's yoga studio is next door. But they don't have anything called Sunny's eggs."

CJ shook her head. "I don't know that, either. Sorry."

"I guess those are mummy stories."

"What do you mean?"

"Someone I know was driving the other day, and the people in the car next to him were dressed as mummies. They drove off before he could roll down the window and ask, so now he'll never know."

"Ah. That's super weird."

"Yeah, I know." I paused. "CJ. It was Adam."

"Adam—as in, my brother? But how—"

"Turn over the paper," I said. "She wrote down his number."

"You called him?"

"I did everything I could to figure out Talley's list."

"I only gave her the number in case something happened to me and she needed to get in touch. But I didn't tell him or anyone about her. Adam wouldn't have even known her name."

"I know," I said. "He didn't. But he was still helpful—he recognized some of the Bay Area things. That's how I knew to come out here. He drove me around to different places—to Mr. G's, to Bel Air, to Big Sur."

"Wait a second, you've been taking road trips with my brother? You didn't tell him anything about me, did you?"

I shook my head. "He didn't tell me about the Sunshine Crew till last night. I don't think he has any clue that anything bad is happening to you now."

"Good. I'm trusting you to keep it that way. He'll tell my parents."

"He said they're a wreck with worry about you."

"It'd be worse for them if they knew."

"It's worse not knowing," I said. "Finding out after the fact that someone you loved was in pain and hiding it from you—it's so much worse."

"Oh, Sloane," CJ said. "I'm sorry about Talley. I don't think I've said that yet, but I am. These past few months, I've had a million conversations with her in my head. In person, that last day, I told her I never wanted to see her again. But I guess if I keep coming up with things to say, then I didn't really mean it. Even though she did this unspeakably terrible thing, she gave me a lot of support, too. All I did was yell at her, and now . . . "

"It's not your fault," I said, echoing what Adam had said to me. "She was sick. She gave you support because you can do that for a friend who has cancer. But that doesn't mean you can cure their cancer. And you can offer support to a friend with a mental illness, but you can't cure that, either."

"Still, I could've been kinder."

"You didn't even know Talley was sick. Maybe because it made her too ashamed. I don't know; she didn't tell me. She was a really good poker player. She didn't have any obvious tells. She did everything she could to hide how she was suffering, and that sounds like shame to me."

"It does to me, too," CJ said. "I never thought I'd feel sorry for her, but I do."

"I do, too."

"Do you think it had anything to do with your mom and . . . you know, the way you guys lost her?"

"I don't know," I said. "Talley always seemed okay to me. And even when she didn't, she never talked about our mom."

CJ shook her head. "You're too young to have gone through all the things you've gone through."

"You, too," I said. "You're not much older than I am."

"And yet here we both are," CJ said. "I guess we're not too young after all."

"If you were my sister, I'd want to know what you're going through. And Talley—God, I really hate it when people say, oh, your sister would've said this, or thought this, or wanted that. It's impossible to know what she would've done about anything. But I think she'd want you to tell your family. I don't think she would've wanted you to be alone. She knew too well how awful that felt. She wouldn't have wanted that for anyone she loved."

Brenna came back into the room and tapped an imaginary watch on her wrist. "I gave you twenty minutes, ladies," she said.

"I better go," I said.

"Sloane, wait," CJ said. "Just one more thing. I'm not going to laser off the tattoo, okay? I'm going to keep it."

I swallowed hard and nodded, thinking maybe I'd get a blue butterfly tattoo one day, too.

"And I'll call my parents," she said. "I promise. You check in with my brother tonight if you want. He'll know."

"You're going to be okay, Ethel," I told her.

CJ reached her arms up in bed and I crossed the room and hugged her goodbye.

chapter thirty-six

ON THE TRAIN TO REDWOOD CITY, I HAD ANOTHER conversation with Talley in my head:

Hey, Tal. Can you hear me, wherever you are? I wanted to tell you that I forgive you. I've been afraid to say that word, because I didn't want to admit that I was mad at you in the first place. I know your depression was an illness, and what happened wasn't simply a choice you made. You were sick and it's not your fault. That's why they say "died by suicide" and not the other way. But it's one thing to say those words. It's another to actually feel them. I do now and I forgive you. I forgive us both; at least, I'm trying to. I'll still always wish you were here. The same way I wish Mom hadn't gone out to pick up the dry cleaning on such a freezing cold night.

CJ's voice popped into my head: *Do you think it had anything to do with your mom and . . . you know, the way you guys lost her?*

It probably did. Talley was five years older than I was when

Mom died. She had more memories, and more memories mean more reasons to miss someone. Maybe that set off the sadness inside her, or exacerbated it. Maybe she'd needed a mom to talk to.

Oh, Tal. I didn't realize how much that loss hurt you—and the reason I didn't realize was because you always did such a good job filling in the empty spots for me. But you needed someone to fill in your empty spots, too.

The train rolled into the station. I crossed El Camino and made a left on Poplar Avenue. For some reason, CJ's words were still rolling around in my head: *Do you think it had anything to do with your mom and . . . you know, the way you guys lost her?*

Why had she said it like that? Especially the words *the way*—maybe she'd meant that Mom had died so suddenly. But she'd paused awkwardly, like there was something she wasn't saying.

I was still a couple blocks from Aunt Elise's, and I started jogging. Soon I was all-out running. It wasn't a conscious decision, but my feet pounded the pavement the rest of the way to 124 Crescent Street. It took me three tries to get the key to go in the keyhole. My breaths were coming short and fast. I pushed the door open without bothering to close it behind me.

"Sloane?" Aunt Elise called from upstairs. "Honey, I'm upstairs."

I raced into the living room, grabbed at the photo album on the coffee table, and I flipped the pages to Talley and me in our coordinated red outfits. There I was on my mother's lap, in my birthday dress with the white trim on the collar, and capped sleeves.

My mother had died two days later, when her car skidded on black ice.

"Sloane?"

I could hear Aunt Elise crutching her way down the stairs. I tore the photo from the album and ran to her.

"Why did she dress us in short sleeves if it was cold out?" I asked. My whole body was shaking.

"What are you talking about?"

"This."

I held the photo out. Aunt Elise dropped her crutches, lowered herself to a sitting position on the steps, and took it from me. "Oh shit," she said.

"Talley said there was ice on the road. Mom went to pick up the dry cleaning, and she lost control of her car."

I'd heard the story so often it got to the point that I was able to picture it in my head, as if I'd been there—as if I'd been the driver—and it was my own memory. I could feel my hands on the steering wheel. I could feel my heart thumping. I was pumping the brake so hard, but it didn't matter. The tree was coming at me, closer, closer, *closer*. I squeezed my eyes shut and braced for impact.

"Don't tell me," I said. I sank down to the floor at the base of the stairs. "I've already learned too much today."

Aunt Elise reached down to me. "Sloane, Sloane, Sloane," she said.

I wished I could close my ears the way I'd closed my eyes. I didn't want to hear what I knew was coming next. But my aunt didn't say anything else. She moved down a couple more steps and wrapped her arms around me. Her touch was so warm and it made me shiver. I was too cold. I was too hot. What was I? I'd lost all sense of myself. I cried and cried.

"All right, sweetheart," Aunt Elise said. "Let it all out. It's okay. It's all right."

When I opened my eyes and twisted around to look at her, her face looked blurry. She hadn't said it, so I said it myself: "It wasn't an accident."

"No, it wasn't an accident."

"Mom hit the tree on purpose?"

"There wasn't a tree," Aunt Elise said. Her voice was steady and even, like she'd been practicing these words in front of a mirror so that when the time came, she'd be able to deliver them, just like this. "She was sick, like Talley. She pulled into the garage and shut the door and left the engine running. She didn't see another way."

"My whole life," I said. "I'm looking back on everything, and I can't even tell what parts were real, or if anything has been real at all."

"The love has been real, Sloane. You're so deeply loved. You always have been. Talley loved you beyond measure, and so does your dad. He wanted to protect you. And even though I haven't been physically present, I've been loving you, too."

I pushed myself away. "But what good is love if you're not there? I couldn't feel it. You might as well have been dead, too."

"Oh," she said softly, and I knew I'd wounded her.

"I'm sorry," I said. "I didn't mean that."

"Yes, you did," she said. "And you're right to feel that way. Your dad and I did it all wrong. When Dana died, we were sick with grief, and so scared. The night after the funeral, we were sitting at the kitchen table in utter shock. What our lives had just become . . . we couldn't believe it. You girls were asleep in your rooms. You were so little, Sloane. Barely two years old. I don't know what was harder—talking to Talley, who understood she was now motherless, or you, who kept looking for your mom around every corner, like she was playing an extended game of hide-and-seek. Your dad told me that he never wanted you girls to know *how* it happened. He said . . . he said some hard things about Dana, things I don't think he even meant. He was just heartbroken. You can save the people you love from a lot of things, but you can't save them from themselves. But oh, how we wanted to—your dad and I. I think that's why he didn't want to tell you and Talley. He said he thought if you knew what really happened, it'd be worse. Losing someone to suicide, you can start to blame yourself."

"He thought we'd think it was our fault?"

"That's what he said. But looking back now, I think he thought it was *his* fault. I think he was afraid you'd blame him, and he'd lose you, too."

"I wouldn't have," I said. "I don't think I would have."

"Maybe you would have," she said. "Either way, he was the parent, the only one you and Talley had left, and he decided he wanted to tell you it was an accident. I told him if either you or Talley ever asked, I'd tell you the truth. We had a terrible fight. He said he'd keep you two from me."

"So Talley grew up, and came out here, and you told her?"

"No, sweetie," Aunt Elise said. "She already knew. It turned out that she'd known all along. That night we were sitting in the kitchen after we'd put you both to sleep, Talley had apparently gotten out of bed, and she stood right outside the doorway. She heard every word—the things your dad said, in the midst of his deepest grief, about Dana's selfishness, and all the rest of it. Talley carried that secret around. She never told anyone, until she called me to ask if she could come out here."

"So that's why she went to you and not me," I said. "Because you'd already heard what Dad had said, and she didn't want me to know he thought all those things about our mother?"

"Partly," Aunt Elise said. "But she was more worried that if you knew, you'd feel the way she did."

"I don't understand."

"Your father'd said he thought that knowing the truth would make it worse, and Talley wondered if he'd been right—if that's what made things worse for her. If that was the root of all her sadness. She didn't want to take that risk with you."

"Do you think Talley would be here now, if she didn't know?"

"I suspect that kind of sadness was in her all along," Aunt Elise said. "Maybe she inherited it from your mother. Probably she did. You know how we were talking about the Holocaust the other day? I've read studies that experiencing that level of trauma can affect people on a cellular level. It can change your DNA. It's not just things like eye color or athleticism; it's also environmental factors and experiences that can alter things inside you and get passed down through the generations. There's a word for it: 'epigenetics'."

"That's exactly the kind of thing Talley would've been interested in learning about," I said. "She would've told me all about it."

"Maybe it would've helped her to understand herself," Aunt Elise said. "She and your mom—they didn't endure the concentration camps firsthand; thank goodness for that. But the trauma of it may still have been written into the genes they inherited from your great-grandma Nellie."

"I always thought Nellie's genes were bravery genes."

"People aren't just one thing. It'd be easier if they were, because then we'd know what to expect all the time. But it doesn't work that way. Each of us comes to the table with a unique and sometimes contradictory combination of genes and experience. Talley might've been the boldest person that either of us ever knew, but she still needed to hide under the covers sometimes."

"Fierce and fragile," I said.

"Exactly," Aunt Elise said.

"Was that true for Mom, too?"

"Oh, yes. Absolutely."

"What about me?" I asked.

"From what I've seen, your moods don't go as dark as theirs did."

"Do you think what happened to Talley will happen to me, now that I know the truth about Mom and everything else?"

"Do *you* think it will?"

I took a moment to consider it. I *had* thought about dying in the last month. One night when I'd been roaming the halls in my endless insomnia, I'd gone into the bathroom we used to share. I'd lain down on the floor and pressed my cheek to the tile, trying to feel what it had been like to be Talley, in her very last conscious moments. It was so hard to live without her. I'd never done it before. When I was born, she was already there, and it felt like she was the thing in the world that everything else hinged on. Like the way gravity keeps us rooted to the earth, and keeps the planets orbiting in perfect alignment. That was Talley; she was my gravity. Now she was gone and I was lost in space.

"No," I told Aunt Elise. "I don't. But when Talley first died, I wasn't sure. Missing her hurt me so badly, I thought maybe it might kill me. Even if I wasn't helping death along, I just thought it might happen on its own, and if it did . . . well, if it did, I would've been okay with that. And now, I know the pain isn't going to kill me. It's kind of strange."

"Why is it strange?"

"Because the most important people in our lives aren't essential *to* our lives. Food, water, air, sunlight—those are the things we need. We don't necessarily feel any kind of emotional attachment to them, but take them away, and we're goners. Whereas you can get really attached to people. You can love them with every ounce of yourself. Then take them away, and you're still breathing. Your heart is still beating. You still get hungry, you still have to go to the bathroom. I remember really having to pee the night Talley died and feeling so angry at my bladder, going about its everyday business like always. But the people we love are expendable. Our bodies keep on working. It's strange. It's offensive."

"The way I look at it," Aunt Elise said, "after someone that important to us dies, we rebuild our lives in a different direction. So, in a way, the old version of us doesn't survive. But a new one does. You're never going to be the same person again."

"No, I'm not."

"But you *are* going to be okay, Sloane. You really are. I promise you."

"I don't want to have any more secrets between us," I said.

"I don't, either."

"So I have to tell you . . . I lied to you. On the very first day I walked in the door, and you told me I could stay here as long as I okayed it with Dad."

"Your dad still thinks you're staying at a hotel?"

"No. He thinks I'm in a dorm room at Stanford. He thinks I came out here for a writing program, because I lied to him, too. I knew he never would've let me come otherwise, and I really needed to. I needed to figure out Talley's list, and it turned out that I needed to meet you. I don't regret lying to him, but I wanted to set things straight with you. Are you mad at me now?"

"God, no," she said. "Of course not. I understand why you did what you did. But I think it's time to set the record straight with your dad, too."

"Why? He hasn't exactly been honest with anyone else. And besides that, he was so cruel to you. You lost your sister, and then he took away your nieces. That's . . . that's *unconscionable*."

"I agree," Aunt Elise said. "I've spent a fortune on therapy talking about it. But we've all lost so much, and I can't stay mad forever. In the spirit of no secrets, I have something to tell you, too. When Talley left California so abruptly, she assured me that she was fine, but I was so worried about her. I didn't know what to do. I thought about it for days, going back and forth, picking up the phone and putting it down. Picking it up, and putting it down again. Finally I picked up the phone one last time and called your father."

"Wait, you spoke to him *before* Talley died?"

"It was a very short call," she said. "I told him that she and I had briefly been in touch, and I was worried about her. He wasn't interested in talking about it."

"That doesn't surprise me," I said. "He's terrible at hard conversations—especially the ones he needs to have."

"But when we spoke again," Aunt Elise continued, "the day he called to tell me that she'd died, he told me that after the last call, he'd tried to get her some help."

"He tried to get her to go to college," I said.

"And he tried to get her to go to therapy, too. Not for the first time. He said he'd tried off and on for years."

"He had?"

"That's what he said. But Talley didn't want to."

"I'll bet," I said, shaking my head. "That last month, she didn't want to do anything."

"Your dad made a lot of mistakes," Aunt Elise said. "But we all did. I really think he did the best he could."

I took a deep breath, inhaling to the count of three. Then I exhaled to three. In to three, out to three. Finally, I heaved myself up and offered Aunt Elise a hand to help her stand.

"Thank you."

"I need to go wash my face," I said. "And then . . . and then I'm going to call my dad and tell him where I am and what I learned."

chapter thirty-seven

TWO DAYS LATER, I TOOK THE CALTRAIN INTO PALO ALTO
one last time, to say a proper goodbye to Adam.

He'd offered to come to Redwood City and pick me up at Aunt
Elise's. But I didn't want to make him spend that much time in the
car. He and his parents were catching up on time with CJ, and helping her recuperate.

Me: We don't need to meet at all, if it's too much of an
inconvenience

Adam: Gotta eat anyway. And CJ's resting. She'd be
creeped out if I sat there and watched her sleep.

He said we should meet at Round Table Pizza, which was the
pizza place he'd mentioned a week earlier, when we were deciding
where to go to lunch that first day. Apparently there were Round
Table locations all over the Bay Area, and one of them was right

on University Avenue. I got there a half hour early and picked up a present for Juno at Retro Planet before heading to the pizza place. Adam was already there. He stood up from a booth in the back and waved his arms to signal me. We hugged hello in the stiff kind of way you do when you're hugging someone who's not quite a stranger.

"Thanks for coming all the way down here," he said.

"It's no problem at all," I said. "Thanks for meeting me."

"What'd you get?" he asked, nodding toward the brown paper bag I was holding.

"It's a present for Juno. An old-fashioned-looking map of the Bay Area."

"She'll love it," he said.

"I hope so," I said. "I have some things to make up to her."

"I have some things to make up to you," Adam said. "I'll start with pizza. The way this place works, you go up to the counter to place the order and pay, then they bring the pizza to your table."

"Oh, it's not just slices?"

"You worried we can't house a whole pizza?"

"We're only two people."

"Trust me, when you taste this, you're going to eat more pizza than you heretofore thought you were capable of eating."

"Heretofore," I repeated. "You sound so serious."

"I'm always serious about pizza. Now: toppings. I usually get peppers and mushrooms, but we can get whatever you like."

"I like plain," I said. "But I can just pick things off."

"Plain works for me."

"But I want you to get what you want."

"I want you to get what you want, too."

"How about half and half?" I said.

"The perfect compromise," he said. "Hold my place. I'll be right back."

"Hang on," I said. I dug into my pocket. "I want to pay for my half."

Adam held up his hand. "No, Sloane," he said. "I'm treating. And don't worry; I'm not being benevolently sexist. My mom gave me money as I was walking out the door. She was pissed I'm taking you here and not somewhere nicer."

"Oh, pizza's fine," I said.

"Good, because it'd be a shame for you to go back to Minnesota without having Round Table. It's a staple out here. But you should know how grateful my parents are to be back in touch with CJ, and I'm grateful, too. You can't imagine."

"I think I can."

"Yeah, you probably can. Let me order and I'll be right back."

A few minutes later, a large pizza was delivered to our table. Adam was right about how much we were able to eat. Granted the slices were cut quite thin. But still, I barely took a breath before I polished off my third, and then I reached for a fourth. "You were so right about this pizza. I'm eating so much more than I heretofore thought was possible."

"I was going to bring you here last Sunday, but you said you'd had pizza the night before."

"I remember."

"Still, I should've taken you sooner. I should've done a lot of things sooner."

"Listen, I'm officially letting you off the hook on all of that, okay? We did things the way we did them, and I ended up learning what I needed to know anyway."

"That's really generous of you," Adam said. "And probably more than I deserve, but I'm glad it all worked out. It's amazing the way one thing led to another. How did all those coincidences happen?"

"Talley said what we think of as coincidence is just about math," I said. "Like how you're more likely to meet someone with your same birthday than you think you are."

"There were two other kids in my kindergarten class with my same birthday," Adam said.

"Case in point," I said. "If Talley were here, she'd explain all about the probabilities that made that happen. I always thought Talley was right about everything—and she usually was. But on the coincidence thing, sometimes I think it's more than just math. After everything that happened, it feels like more than just math that I'm sitting across from you right now."

"It definitely feels like more than just math to me, too," he said.

"I don't know if Talley left that list for me to find on purpose," I said, "but if she did, I'm pretty sure I solved the puzzle in ways she never could have anticipated."

A few minutes later, we'd finished up the pizza. I knew Adam had to get home to his family, and I had to get back to Aunt Elise. We had less than a day left of quality time to spend with each other.

"You feel okay about going home?" Adam asked.

"Oh yeah," I said. "I'm sort of looking forward to it. I understand things better now. When I left, I was grieving so hard. Grief is such a personal thing. My dad was grieving too, but he didn't know how it felt for me, and I didn't know how it felt for him. It's a little like how we've all agreed yellow is yellow and blue is blue, but who's to say what looks like yellow to me looks like yellow to you, and the same for blue?"

"You know, I've never thought about it like that," Adam said.

"We made a pact to try to talk to each other more," I said. "I used to always go to Talley when I needed to talk something out, and if she wasn't available, I had Juno. My dad was in the background. He took care of the kinds of things parents take care of, and I took care of what I thought I was supposed to take care of—I studied hard, I made my bed every day, I never broke curfew. It was like we'd negotiated conditions, but we never did it out loud, and I think those are the worst kinds of conditions. The ones no one says out loud. So now we're going to try to be more up front and honest about things. Talley's gone and it's the worst. It'll always be the worst. We don't get a happy ending. But things are already better between us. We agreed if they start to feel bad again, we'll do our best not to turn away from each other, and just keep talking."

"My family had a long talk about open communication going forward, too," Adam said. "CJ gave her doctor permission to talk to our parents if they have questions about the medical stuff."

"Oh, that's good," I said. "She deserves to have support from people who know what's going on."

"I think we should make open communication a goal, too," Adam said. "I mean, you and me."

"Okay," I said.

"Okay. Well . . . this week—it's been a year, hasn't it?"

"At least," I said.

Adam slung an arm around my shoulder and pulled me in for a hug, a real hug, close and comfy. I could smell his shirt, and I thought of Juno's attachment to Cooper's shirts, and the Proust phenomenon, and I knew I would always remember this moment. It would always mean something to me.

"You know, Sloane," he said. "I'm really going to miss you."

"Me, too."

"I hope we can keep in touch."

"We have to if we're going to have open communication."

"That's right. Good point," he said. "And if you ever find yourself back here, I expect some quality time on your dance card."

"I'll definitely be back here," I said. "My aunt lives here, after all. And if you ever find yourself in Golden Valley, Minnesota, I'll expect time on *your* dance card. Not that that's a place you're likely to visit."

"Oh, I'd say it's a distinct possibility," he said. "Because you're there, and I'd love to visit you."

chapter thirty-eight

JUNO WAS SUPPOSED TO PICK ME UP FROM THE AIRPORT. But when I stepped off the escalator into the baggage claim area, it was Dad standing there waiting for me. He was holding up a sign with my name on it, just like the taxi drivers do for their customers.

"Dad!" I called.

"Sloane!" He raised his arm and waved. "I'm here!"

I jogged the rest of the way to him and we hugged hello. "Did something happen to Juno?" I asked, as we broke apart.

"Don't worry, she's fine," Dad said. "I was just anxious to see you."

"Me, too," I said. "So what's with the sign?"

"I didn't want you to walk past your old man," he said. "I wanted to make sure we found each other."

His eyes were shiny. I reached to hug him again, longer and

harder this time. I was crying, and I could tell he was, too. His body shook a little. My whole life, I'd never seen my dad cry. Then Talley died, and he did cry in front of me—that awful night at the hospital, and again at her funeral. But this was different; he was crying for me.

We finally pulled away from each other. Around us, other passengers were greeting people, pulling luggage from the baggage claim, rushing to wherever they needed to go.

Everyone was busy in their own story, but a couple of people paused to look at Dad and me. Given our teary reunion, I bet they thought I'd been away for way more than a week. They'd never know our real story.

"It feels like I haven't seen you in a long time," I told Dad. "I'm so glad you're not mad at me for lying to you about Stanford and all the rest of it."

"Oh, Sloane, you did me a favor," he said. "I knew that I needed to tell you about your mother. But it had been so many years, and after what happened with Talley . . . I didn't know how to start the conversation. I thought I might lose you if I did, so I stayed quiet. You did the right thing by lying to me. That's not an easy thing for a father to admit to his child, but it's true. Just don't ever do it again."

"I won't," I said.

"I promise that you won't ever need to. And for the record, I'm glad you're not mad at me, too."

"I was. I'm not anymore."

"That's good. Shall we get going?"

"Yeah."

He picked up my bag and I let him. I don't think it counts as benevolent sexism when it's your own father.

"Hey, Dad," I said. "I was wondering—you have the car here, right?"

"Of course I do. How else do you expect us to get home?"

"Can I drive?"

"*You* want to drive?"

"I should practice if I'm going to take my driver's test."

He raised his eyebrows.

"I mean, if I'm brave enough to go to California by myself, and learn everything I did, then I'm probably brave enough to drive, too."

"You've been brave all along," Dad said. "But perhaps your first session shouldn't be on the highway."

"Fair point."

"How's this for a driving plan—I'll do the first part, and the minute I'm off the exit ramp, I'll pull over. We'll switch seats, and you can take us the rest of the way home."

"You're on," I said.

But as time wore on, I got more and more nervous. My palms were sweating hard, and I wiped them against my jeans a half dozen times. Dad noticed, despite my attempts to be subtle about it. "You know," he said, "you don't have to drive today if you don't want to. The car is here for you whenever you're ready, and whenever that day is, I'll be your copilot."

"Thanks," I said. "But it's not like anyone ever feels 'ready' for the things that scare them. You just do them. I have to just do this."

"That's my girl." We were approaching the highway exit. Dad clicked on his turn signal. That *tick-tick-tick* sounded like a clock on countdown mode. My heart was racing. He pulled over to the side of the road and turned off the car. The countdown was over. Dad undid his seat belt, and I undid mine.

He put a hand on his door handle. I put a hand on mine. It was like a game of monkey see, monkey do. I waited for him to open the car door. When he did, I opened mine and stepped out. We switched car seats and rebuckled seat belts. "How are you doing?" Dad said.

"The seat doesn't feel right."

"You have to adjust it. There's a button right on the side. It's shaped like an oval. Push it to move the seat up."

I slipped a hand down and found the button. "How far do I go?"

"Until you feel like your feet can comfortably reach the pedals."

Duh, as Eddy would say. "Sorry I'm being a total moron about this," I said.

"You're being someone who doesn't have much driving experience," Dad said, "which is, incidentally, exactly what you are. But we're setting out to change that. How's the seat now?"

"I think it's good," I said. "Don't I have to do something with the mirrors, too?"

"The side mirrors and the rearview. Adjust them so you can see whatever is beside and behind you."

"Okay . . . done."

"Okay. Now put your foot on the brake and start the car."

"Gotcha." I pressed down all the way on the brake pedal and moved my hand toward the ignition switch. "Wait. The brake is the one on the left side?"

"Right."

"Do you mean, right it's left, or right it's actually on the right?"

"Left side," he said. "Correct."

"I bet you're having second thoughts about giving me the driver's seat."

"Not at all. Start the car when you're ready."

"Ready as I'll ever be," I said, and turned on the engine.

"Now foot off the brake," Dad said, "and foot on the gas, gently at first. There's no one behind you, so you can go as slow as you want to."

I went really slowly, though my heart was pounding as if I were driving on the autobahn in Germany, where (I knew from Talley) there wasn't a speed limit. I was doing this for her, because she'd always wanted to teach me how to drive, and for the women in Saudi Arabia who she'd told me all about, who'd waited a very long time for the right to drive. But mostly, I was driving for myself. I made sure to stay in the middle of the lane. A car was coming from the opposite direction. It whipped past me and I gasped.

"It's okay," Dad said. "You're all good. But you may want to inch a little closer to the right, so you don't drift to the other side." He put a hand on the wheel, and turned it just slightly. It brought me closer to the tree line on the edge of the road, which I'd been trying to avoid.

Mom didn't hit a tree, I reminded myself. *Trees didn't have anything*

to do with it. Neither did black ice. And anyway, it's the middle of summer.
There isn't any ice of any color on the road at all.

I kept going. "A car is creeping up on me in the rearview mirror," I told Dad.

"You're below the speed limit. Speed up if you want."

"Oh, I don't want to."

"Then don't worry about him."

It was hard not to worry with him so close behind, especially when he honked at me. Finally he pulled around me, pausing long enough to give me a hard look and a last honk. "He hates me," I said.

"People who have been driving for a while tend to forget they were once new at this, too," Dad said. "Asshole."

"What was that?"

"I'm not going to say it again."

"Talley and I used to love to hear you curse," I said.

"All those arts and crafts projects, and trips to the beach, and family game nights, and it's a curse that made my children happy?"

"The other stuff was good, too. But a Dad-curse was exciting because hearing it was so rare. Like finding a four-leaf clover."

"Ah," he said. "Well, I save the curses for those occasions on which it's truly called for. That way you know I really mean it."

"Thanks."

"You just missed the turn," he said. "I know you've been gone for a week, but we live back there."

"I missed it on purpose," I said. "I want to stop by Juno's house, if you don't mind."

"I don't mind at all," Dad said. "I think she was a little disappointed when I told her I'd pick you up. You know you're special when people are fighting to be the one to get to pick you up from the airport."

"If you want to spend more time, we don't have to go to Juno's."

"No, let's go," Dad said. "Stay as long as you like, and I'll come back and pick you up whenever you're ready."

"Or Juno can take me home so you don't have to worry about it."

"Or I can come get you, and then you'll drive us both home," Dad said. "Whatever works for you."

I twisted through our neighborhood, and the houses got bigger and bigger. A few streets later, I turned onto Cheshire Court, where Juno lived, and where the stone houses were the largest of all the houses in Golden Valley. They all had enormous lawns with grass so green, it was like the coloring-book version of what grass is like—you take the greenest crayon in the box, and shade it in all over. Back at our house, the yard was much smaller, and our grass was patchier. No one in my family had the kind of green thumb required to make sure the grass was always evenly watered and growing in the perfect way. Not that Juno, her parents, or her brother did, either, but they could hire someone who specialized in that kind of thing.

I pulled up to the curb, bumping it a little. "Sorry," I told Dad.

"That's all right. It won't leave a mark."

"You're being awfully cool about all this. Like, more than I expected."

"How did you expect me to be?"

"I don't know. I never wanted to learn to drive till now, so I didn't really think about it."

"I think I was pretty cool when I was teaching Talley," he said.

"I wish I could ask her."

"I know you do." Dad paused. "But since you can't, trust me: I was very cool. I was as cool as they come."

"Did Talley bump into the curbs, too?"

"She got the hang of it pretty quickly. You will, too."

"It may take me a little bit longer. Don't forget—she was the genius."

"Your sister certainly was a smart cookie," Dad said. "The other day I remembered something she said—something I hadn't thought about in a long time. When Talley was three years old, we spent a week at a beach house on Lake Superior. I had this ritual of taking her to watch the sunset every night. We'd been at it for a few days, and when we went back to the beach on the third or fourth day, Talley said, 'It shouldn't be called the sunset, Daddy. The earth moves, not the sun. They should call it the earth-set.' That was the moment I knew—this kid was different. She was something special. Every parent thinks that about their kids, but she really was."

"She was *three* when she said that? Really?"

"Yes," he said. "Except Talley didn't say it. You did."

"But that's just . . . it couldn't have been me. That sounds so much like Talley."

"I think it sounds like you," Dad said. "You've paid attention to the details since you were a little girl. You've always been interested in language, and why things are called what they're called. You notice things I never would. I love that about you. But I'd love you no matter what."

"I love you, too."

"Now," he said. "Before I let you escape to Juno, there's the matter of the money you owe her. She wouldn't tell me how much she laid out for the plane ticket."

"She gave me her credit card to use, too," I said.

"Did her parents approve that ahead of time?"

"She used her own money."

"She's a minor," Dad said. "That makes it the kind of thing Amy and Randall should approve."

"Talley said don't ask for permission, ask for forgiveness," I reminded him. "And besides, Juno is allowed to decide for herself what's important enough to spend her money on. She thought this was."

"That Juno," Dad said. I expected his next words to be something about how spoiled and irresponsible she was, but he said, "She's been a really good friend to you."

"Not just good. She's the best."

"I'm not surprised," Dad said. "You are who you hang out with, and she hangs out with you."

"Thanks, Dad."

He shifted in his seat and pulled out his wallet. "All right. I have a check with me. Whatever you put on her card, add that in so I can pay her back for everything."

"I didn't use her card at all," I said. "Except for the plane tickets—which were three hundred and nine dollars. Just so you know, I'm babysitting for the Hogans for the rest of the month, and I'll give you everything I earn till it's paid back."

"I don't want you to worry about it," Dad said. "I'm not worried about it."

"Really?"

"I'm careful with money, but I'm not worried about it," Dad said. "I understand what it's like to be worried about money, and I'm grateful that at this point in my life, I'm in a different place. I can pay Juno back for your trip. I should've been the one to pay for it in the first place."

"I didn't think you'd let me go, if I asked."

"I probably wouldn't have," Dad said. "Scratch that. I definitely wouldn't have. But give Juno the check. Tell her I want to make things right, with both of you."

"I will," I said. "Thanks, Dad. Can you pop the trunk? I have a present for Juno in my bag."

"You pop it," Dad said. "You're in the driver's seat."

"Oh, right. I am."

We hugged again when we got out. I grabbed the bag from Retro Planet. Dad got back into the driver's seat.

chapter thirty-nine

AS I STARTED UP THE DRIVEWAY, THE FRONT DOOR banged open. Juno came sprinting toward me, a blue ponytail swinging in the breeze. "Sloane! Oh my God!"

She grabbed me in a hug so fierce that we both nearly fell over.

"How'd you know I was here?" I asked.

"Eddy was by the window and he said he saw a gray car parked out front," she said. "I know your dad's car is gray, and obviously I knew he was picking you up today. I didn't want to get my hopes up about him bringing you by to say hello, but they were up anyway. You can tell yourself not to hope for something, but if you're telling yourself not to get your hopes up, that means they're already up. And now, here you are. I missed you so much."

"I missed you, too, Ju."

"I even have a new metaphor for you," she said. "You know

that feeling when you have to pee so badly that you're about to burst, but you can't burst because then you'd just pee all over yourself? So you're holding it in, and *finally*, you get to a bathroom, and it's the sweetest relief you've ever felt. That's what it's like to see you—it's the sweetest relief."

"Oh, Ju," I said. "Not only is that the best metaphor I've ever heard, but it's also the best compliment of my whole entire life. Thank you."

"You're welcome."

"It feels that way to see you, too," I said. "I have so much to tell you. First off, this is for you." I handed her the Retro Planet bag. "There's something in there for Eddy, too. Yours is the thing that's not a stuffed grizzly bear."

"Ah. *Ursus arctos californicus.*"

"I saw it at the airport, and I had to get it for him."

"That's sweet," she said. "But obviously I care more about what's for me." She pulled out the poster tube and popped it open. "Oh my God, Sloane. This is the best thing you could've brought back . . . besides yourself, of course. I didn't want to tell you this when you were still in California, because I knew you'd probably hit your limit on information you could process at one time. But now that you're here, I can't keep this to myself anymore."

"What happened?"

"Well, you know how the kids and I ran into Audrey on the street that day, and they just went nuts for her?"

"Oh no," I said. "Don't tell me. She stole your job?"

"Worse," Juno said. "So much worse. Infinity times worse. Mr.

and Mrs. Hogan decided I needed a co-babysitter till you returned, so it was Audrey and me all day every day for three days straight."

"Oh my God," I said. "I'm so sorry."

"Audrey was delighted when they asked her. Apparently her summer job had fallen through, and I had to go along and pretend I was fine having her help for a few days, even though she kept rubbing it in my face that she got Cooper and I didn't. I'd say something that seemed totally harmless like, 'Melanie wants green grapes cut in half,' and Audrey would say, 'Speaking of green, I just thought of the funniest thing. Oh, ha ha ha.' And I'd ask her what was so funny, and she'd be all, 'Nothing. Just a private joke between Cooper and me.' But the good news is, Cooper broke up with her."

"What? When?"

"Friday afternoon, about an hour before Mr. Hogan came home. He did it over text, and I had to deal with the kids on my own again, because she was totally losing it. I almost felt sorry for her."

"That's kind of you."

"I said *almost*," Juno said. "But anyway, it doesn't matter anymore. You're back, and she's back where she belongs, which is out of my life. Phew. This past week was so much harder than I expected, on so many levels."

"Oh, I know," I said.

"You had it much harder than I did," Juno said. "I didn't mean to complain."

"And I didn't mean to compare," I told her. "My aunt says

hardship isn't a contest, and she's right. Besides, I want to know when people I love are having a hard time. I want to show up for them. That includes being a better friend to you. When Cooper broke up with you, I didn't take it as seriously as I should have. It was a really big deal."

"You were a little distracted. Understandably."

"But even before Talley died, that night at Trepiccione's. I wasn't as supportive as I could've been—as I *should've* been."

"Well, you thought Cooper was a loser."

"He's not with you, so he must be," I said. "But you were still grieving him. Because you really loved him. It's like what Talley's friend Tess read at the funeral."

"Yeah . . . what'd she read again?"

"From *The Prophet*—'The deeper that sorrow carves into your being, the more joy you can contain.' Love is like that, too. The more love you feel for someone, the more space there is for grief when they're gone. I didn't understand that you were grieving back then. And to be honest, I was even jealous."

"Jealous that he broke up with me?"

"Jealous that you had him in the first place," I said. "You'd loved someone, and someone had loved you back."

"Whether he ever loved me back is up for debate."

"Regardless, it was more than I'd ever had."

"You'll have it one day, Sloane," Juno said. "I thought maybe you'd even have it with Adam."

"There was a moment on the beach when I thought we were about to get together. But then we fought, and I despised him for a couple days, and now we're friends again. It was a whirlwind non-romance. There's nothing romantic between us."

"You've only known he existed for a little over a month," Juno said. "And you only met him in person a week ago. Look what happened in one single week of friendship. Anything is possible."

"Yeah, but the sheer geography of it probably makes it unlikely."

"So there's a few thousand miles between you . . . for now," Juno said. "Maybe you'll end up at the same college next year."

"Maybe," I said. "I wouldn't mind that at all. But back to you and me, I don't want to let myself off the hook on this. I wasn't the best friend to you. Meanwhile, you did everything for me—you sent me to California; you checked in constantly. When you texted me that you had an Audrey emergency, it took me so long to call back. When I finally did, I was so wrapped up in my own stuff that I didn't even find out what it was, till just now. I mean, I'm assuming that's what it was—the co-babysitting thing."

"Yep. Luckily that was the only Audrey emergency—though every second of it felt like a fresh emergency."

"I'm going to make it up to you," I said. "If Audrey is free, and you want the rest of the summer off, then I can suck it up and co-babysit at the Hogans' with her."

"You don't have to do that," Juno said. "I'd rather be with you and the triplets than doing anything else. So that's what I pick . . . unless you'd pick babysitting with Audrey over me."

"Are you kidding?"

"Just checking. She's a pretty good babysitter. She was great at

playing the whisper challenge with the kids, and I'm not so great—
for obvious reasons."

"I don't even know what the whisper challenge is, so that's how
good *I* am at it."

"It's when you put on headphones and play music really loud.
The person next to you whispers something, and you try to hear
it through the headphones, and then you whisper it to the person
next to you, who's also wearing headphones, and on and on, until
you get back to the first person, and see how everyone mangled
their original phrase."

"Like a game of telephone, but with hearing damage."

"Yeah. Except my hearing is already damaged, so it's hard for
me to play, which I'm sure is why Audrey taught them the game in
the first place."

"Which makes her a pretty shitty babysitter. She was modeling
insensitivity on top of hurting their ears."

"They loved it."

"Kids love things that are bad for them all the time."

"Seriously, when we showed up in the morning, they were
happy enough to see me, but with Audrey, it was like Taylor freak-
ing Swift had just shown up. If they had to choose between the two
of us, they totally would've picked her over me. It made me feel so
bad."

"I'm sure it did. But anyone would be lucky to have you as the
babysitter. Anyone would be lucky to have you as a best friend.
You're so extraordinary. You could basically be best friends with
anyone, and you picked me. Lucky me."

"Lucky me, too," she said.

"And as long as I've already triggered the cheese-whiz alarm, just one more thing. Talley's friend CJ said that Talley brought out the best in her, and she wasn't afraid of the worst in her. I think it's the best definition of best-friendship I've ever heard, and I want to make sure that you know it's how I feel about you—you bring out the best in me, and every time I've given you my worst, you've been there. You haven't been afraid of any of it. Just so we're clear, I'm here for you, too, for all of that."

"I know," Juno said. "Thank you. Ditto. And you're off the cheese-whiz charts. The alarm is broken beyond repair."

"I did it on purpose," I said. "I never liked that alarm."

"Hey!" came a shout, and Eddy was flying out the front door. "You didn't tell me Sloane was here!" He flung himself at me.

"Wow," I said. "Is it possible that you grew in just a week? Because I'm pretty sure you're a few inches taller than the last time I saw you."

"It's probably a growth spurt," Eddy said. He moved his hand between the top of his forehead and my chin. "Yep. I think I'm chin height."

"Oh no," Juno said. "That hand is going vertical instead of horizontal."

"It's not! I swear!"

"You too big for a present?"

"Definitely not."

"Good," I said. "I brought you something back from California."

"Really?"

"Uh-huh. Your sister has the bag."

Juno handed it over and Eddy pulled the stuffed bear out. "Neato bandito!" he said.

"Neato bandito," Juno echoed. She grabbed my hand and squeezed really hard, and the three of us walked into the house.

Epilogue

*I'm freewriting in Dr. Lee's class at Hamline. This is what
she makes us do every morning, just to get our creative
juices flowing. We can write about whatever we want. The
only rule is we can't lift our pen from the page for the whole
15-min period. My hand gets pretty cramped up by minute
10, but I power through.*

*The reason I'm writing out the rules right now is because I
don't have anything else to say. I'm totally blocked.*

*I know, I know, Dr. Lee, you don't believe in writer's
block.*

*(Not that you'll ever see this. Another rule of freewrite is
that we never have to share it.)*

*I always agreed with the no-writer's-block thing. Dr. Lee
said it, so I agreed with it: there's always SOMETHING to*

*say. You might not know exactly how to say it, but you can
certainly start by saying it badly.*

*But now . . . I don't know. It's pretty early in the
morning, and it's August, which is generally the laziest of the
months, and so much has happened in my life that I barely
recognize it anymore. So right now, writer's block feels like a
distinct possibility.*

*And I'm all out of freewrite rules to write down, but I
know Dr. Lee is watching to make sure none of us lift our
pens.*

Blah.

Blah.

Blah!

Dr. Lee just said, "Five minutes down."

She always updates us in five-minute increments.

*You may be watching, Dr. Lee, but you can't see what
nonsense I'm writing. Thank goodness, or you'd probably
regret asking Hamline to let in this high schooler.*

*I didn't get a scholarship, à la the fake Stanford writing
class. But Dad agreed to let me spend a chunk of my
babysitting money on tuition. We're getting better with each
other. We're not at 100% total agreement on everything. Just
last night, he flipped out because I was texting Juno during
dinner. But it no longer feels like we're strangers sharing the
same house. I found a suicide survivors' group that meets at
the rec center on Sunday evenings. The kind of group Nicole
told me about. Dad and I have been going together.*

Last Sunday, we stopped by Talley's grave on the way home. I'd been scared to do it, because I didn't want to see her name etched into a stone on the ground. Turns out, her gravestone isn't even there yet. According to Jewish tradition, sometime before the 1st anniversary of her death, there will be an unveiling, and the gravestone will be put into place. It gives family members some time to get used to the absence before they see the name like that, the death so official. Not that I ever think I'll be used to this. It's been more than sixty-six days. I'm not even counting days anymore. But I'm still not in the habit of not having a sister. Part of me still thinks I'll wake up tomorrow, and Talley will be calling to me, "Hey, Sloaners, I just had the best idea." I'll run down the hall toward her, and the memory of this horrible nightmare will fade to nothingness, the way dreams do. Maybe I'll vaguely remember that I had a bad dream, but I won't be able to recall what it was.

Dad and I didn't stay long at the cemetery. We cleaned the dirt from the crevices of Mom's stone, and left little rocks on top of it. Another Jewish tradition is to leave rocks, not flowers, on graves. Flowers die, but rocks don't. Leaving them on someone's grave symbolizes the enduring legacy of love. We left rocks for Mom, and we left rocks on the empty space beside her, where Talley's stone will go someday—someday soon, I know. But not today.

By the time we walked back to the car, it was nearly eight o'clock. The sun had set. (The earth had set.) When Talley died back in May, it was the time of year when days were getting longer. Now three months and five days have passed. The days are shortening again. I let Dad drive home. I've been practicing a bit, but I'm not quite comfortable with night driving just yet. I'd just been to a suicide support group, and then to my sister's grave. I know Talley was right—I can do hard things; but there are only so many hard things you can fit into one day.

"Five minutes left."

My hand is really cramping. But, in general, I'm writing more, again. Which isn't to say that I'm not totally overwhelmed by sadness, because I am. I miss my sister so much that sometimes it's like I can feel her absence even more than I ever felt her presence. And that's saying a lot, since Talley had a more palpable presence than anyone I've ever known.

But Dad was right about life going on. I'm working on my short story again, the one I started last spring, that I thought I'd hand in at the end of the semester, but it never got out of the vomitous first-draft phase, so I handed in an old story that Dr. Lee had never seen. Now I'm mining for the diamonds in this one, and making it better. (I hope I'm making it better.) It's realistic fiction, like I usually write. The characters are completely made up. It's not about Talley.

But, of course, things are about her even when they're not. Having her as my sister will affect everything, always. It's like the butterfly effect. She flapped her wings in my life.

Everything I do from now on will be different, because of her.

I always said that I loved to write because I loved making new things—things that wouldn't exist if I didn't exist. Well, everything I write is only because Talley existed, too. Maybe one day it won't just be Dr. Lee and my workshop classmates reading my stuff. Maybe I'll get published, and strangers will read books with my name on the cover. And it'll be the exact right thing they need to read at the exact right moment, and it'll help them, somehow. Talley will be a part of all of it, and she'd love it, because she loved making a difference.

That's my dream.

In the meantime, I'm trying to make a difference in other ways, too. This fall, when I turn eighteen, I'll be able to volunteer at the crisis hotline. I'm already signed up for training. It's run by the mental health department at Golden Valley General, the hospital where Talley died. I haven't been there since that night, and I'm scared, but Talley will be with me in her way. I wouldn't be doing it if she hadn't been my sister. She'll always be part of my story.

"Thirty seconds," Dr. Lee just called. "Write your last sentence."

Here it is: our stories never really end, because the love goes on forever.

Author's Note

DEAR READER,

The book you are holding in your hands is a work of fiction. Sloane and Talley Weber are products of my imagination. But Talley's experience with mental illness and the shame she felt about it are real-life struggles for too many people. Depression is one of the most common mental illnesses in the United States, but it is often undiagnosed, untreated, or ineffectively treated. It is the number one cause of suicide, and suicide is the third leading cause of death for people ages fifteen to twenty-four.

Those statistics are overwhelming. I think we tend to underestimate the prevalence and power of depression because it can be so hard to see; people who are depressed often look exactly like those who aren't, and that can also make it more difficult for those who are experiencing it to seek help. But just because others can't tell by looking at you that you're suffering doesn't mean you deserve to suffer, and it certainly doesn't mean you should suffer alone. There is no shame in being sick. There is no shame in asking for help.

The National Suicide Prevention Lifeline is free, confidential, and available twenty-four hours a day, seven days a week. If you need support, or if you think someone you know does, you can call them at (800) 273-8255, or chat online at suicidepreventionlifeline.org.

With love,
Courtney Sheinmel
September 2019

Acknowledgments

MY HEARTFELT THANKS:

To my agent, Laura Dail—thank you for being a fierce advocate, a loyal friend, an enthusiastic supporter, an opportunity-finder, a follow-upper, a fashion-inspirer, and for connecting me to my editor, Claudia Gabel.

To the aforementioned Claudia Gabel—what can I say? It's hard to admit when a book gets the better of you, but this book *did* get the better of me . . . at least for a little while. Thank you, Claudia, for your kindness, your patience, and your steadfast belief in this story and my ability to tell it.

To the team at HarperCollins, especially Stephanie Guerdan, for entertaining and productive brainstorm sessions; Judy Goldschmidt, for her thoughtful notes; Becca Clason and Aurora Parlagreco, for designing a cover that I can't stop staring at; Shona

McCarthy and Kathryn Silsand, for their careful reads of the manuscript; Maya Myers, for going over every single sentence with a fine-toothed comb; Shannon Cox, Haley George, Ebony LaDelle, and Kaitlin Loss, for helping to get this book into readers' hands; and Katherine Tegen, for giving this book the very best home.

To Lia, Rachael, and Daniel Carson—my boots-on-the-ground-in-Minnesota friends, who answered all my pressing questions (is it a highway or a freeway? Seltzer or bubbly water?); to my Bay Area pals, especially Lisa, Peter, Marachel, and Lily Leib, who have traveled down Memory Lane with me approximately a million times, usually while sharing Round Table Pizza; to Alex Coler Warren (and Lucy!), who answered all my questions about cochlear implants; and to a few friends who let me ask some very personal questions, and helped me get Talley's story just right.

To my extraordinary writing community. Shouts-out to three in particular who helped with this book: Adele Griffin, who mined for diamonds in my (vomitous) first draft, and went line by line, page by page, chapter by chapter, on the phone into the wee hours, talking me through every one of her excellent notes; Sarah Mlynowski, whose eyes beam sunshine and optimism, and who often gets to the heart of what I'm trying to say faster than I do; and Meg Wolitzer, who was one of my very favorite writers long before we met in person. Thank you, Meg, for taking me seriously as a writer, for challenging me to go deeper, for making me laugh, and for sharing boatloads of guacamole.

To my Writopia Lab family, especially Yael Schick, Danielle Sheeler, and Rebecca Wallace-Segall; and to my beloved Tuesday workshop alums who still hang out on our group text-chat, and remain endlessly inspiring: Drew Arnum, Lily Davis, Altana Elings-Haynie, Katie Hartman, Pilot Irwin, Georgia Silverman, Carly Sorenson, and Kai Williams.

To Amy Bressler, Jennifer Daly, and Arielle Warshall Katz, who are the kind of friends who bring out the best in me, and aren't afraid of the worst in me.

To Regan Hofmann, my daily sounding board and the Queen of Metaphors. Speaking of metaphors: sometimes when writing gets tough, I remember the time she taught me to chop firewood. I swung the ax, it got stuck, I wanted to give up, and she made me keep going. Boom! Firewood. Thanks, Regs.

To all my friends, who show up, whether to celebrate or to commiserate: Lindsay Aaronson, Andrew Baum, Jen Calonita, Maria Crocitto, Erin Cummings, Gitty Daneshvari, Julia DeVillers, Melissa Eisenberg, Gayle Forman, Jackie Friedland, Jake Glaser, Mary Gordon, Corey Ann Haydu, Mary Beth Keane, Logan Levkoff, Melissa Losquadro, Geralyn Lucas, Samantha Moss, Richard Panek, Laura Schechter Parker, Stacia Robitaille, Jess Rothenberg, Jill Santopolo, Katie Stein, J. Courtney Sullivan, Bianca Turetsky, Susan Verde, and Christine Whelan.

To my parents . . . most people only get two parents, but I have *three*, and they are constant sources of love and support: my father, Joel Sheinmel; my mother, Elaine Sheinmel Getter; and my stepfather, Philip Getter.

To my sister, Alyssa Sheinmel, and my brother-in-law, JP Gravitt; to my stepsiblings and siblings-in-law, Laura and Rob Liss,

Doug and Sunčica Getter, and IanMichael Getter.

To the five best nieces and nephews on the planet: Nicki, Andrew, and Zach Liss, who have aged out of being my test readers; and Sara and Tesa Getter, who have aged into it, and whose excitement and encouragement are the most meaningful.

To the ones I miss, especially my aunt Jean V. Odesky; and my grandparents Diane and William Buda, and Doris and Archie Sheinmel.

And to my grandma Diane's sisters, who were killed in the Holocaust: Minka, Esther, and Yedith Liebson—oh, how I wish I'd met you. This book is for your older sister, and for you.